Sharon couldn't tear her eyes away from Steve's

He looked so grief-stricken. Why had the homicide detective insisted Steve sit in on this interview?

"Miss McClure . . . ?" Sharon forced herself to focus on what the detective was saying. "When you were an army nurse in Vietnam, you had to treat many dying soldiers who were in a great deal of pain. Is that right?"

Sharon nodded, feeling the knot in her stomach tighten. She knew beyond doubt what was coming next.

"I have a report, Miss McClure, that you *deliberately* gave a certain young soldier a fatal overdose of morphine. Is that correct?"

"Yes," she admitted in a tortured whisper. What did Steve think of her now? She wished she could risk a glance at him, but didn't dare.

"And did you, Miss McClure, also deliberately kill Mr. Nordstrom's brother?"

At last, she risked a glance at Steve. She wished she hadn't. The look on his face told her that in his heart he'd already convicted her.

ABOUT THE AUTHOR

"I wrote this story as a tribute to the heroism and compassion of the tens of thousands of women who served in Vietnam," says former air force cryptographer Kelly Walsh. "Women served as doctors and nurses, intelligence officers and air-traffic controllers.

"Some were killed or injured. Others—like Sharon McClure, the heroine of *Nightshades and Orchids*—suffered psychological wounds, returning from the war unable to trust in life. This book is for them. May they all find the happy ending that Sharon finds."

Kelly Walsh lives in Florida and, when she's not busy writing, raises orchids for a living.

Books by Kelly Walsh

HARLEQUIN SUPERROMANCE

Nightshades and Orchids

KELLY WALSH

Harlequin Books

TORONTO • NEW YORK • LONDON
AMSTERDAM • PARIS • SYDNEY • HAMBURG
STOCKHOLM • ATHENS • TOKYO • MILAN

Published November 1991

ISBN 0-373-70475-5

NIGHTSHADES AND ORCHIDS

CHAPTER ONE

MURPHY'S LAW IS in full swing, Sharon McClure thought as she massaged the tense muscles at the back of her neck. The head nurse on ICU, she'd been on duty since midnight, and anything that could have possibly gone wrong seemed to have done exactly that.

Her alert eyes swept across the patient-monitoring equipment. Then she glanced at the wall clock: almost 5:00 a.m. Quickly she unlocked the drug cabinet and removed several small bottles and ampoules, carefully rechecking each doctor's order as she prepared medications for the seven patients on the ward and the young man in the isolation room, Richard Nordstrom. A hit-and-run victim, he had sustained severe abdominal trauma and was running a high fever. Until Pathology determined the cause of the fever, Dr. Wilson, the ICU chief resident, had decided to isolate him.

Automatically Sharon lined up prepackaged disposable sterile syringes on the cart under the cabinet. It was a procedure she'd done uncountable times. She'd given eighteen years to nursing, her entire adult life, except for the five years when she left the profession soon after spending two years as an army surgical nurse in Vietnam. Twenty-one then, nothing in her training had prepared her for what she had experienced during her two tours of duty in combat areas. Nor had she foreseen the traumatic readjustment that would lie ahead of her upon her return to civilian life: the sleepless nights, the flashbacks and periodic bouts with depression. Dealing with the painful wartime memories had cost her her marriage and almost cost her career in nursing. But, she'd told herself repeatedly, she was a survivor.

Reaching into the drug cabinet again, Sharon jerked her head around when she heard the dreaded beep coming from the patient-monitoring equipment. The signal light indicated trouble in the isolation room.

She flew into the ward, told Dave Schaeffer, one of the other nurses on duty, to call the code, and in seconds she was at Richard Nordstrom's bedside.

Dave struck the emergency call button and was close on her heels. Seeing she had initiated CPR, giving the patient mouth-to-mouth ventilations, he began the chest compressions, counting, "One one-thousand, two one-thousand..." At the count of five Sharon gave the patient another ventilation.

A flurry of activity followed when the cardiac arrest team scurried into the room with a crash cart. Sharon's hands were a blur as she passed on the first round of medications and instruments from the cart to Dr. Wilson. Aided by a young intern and others on the team, he went to work with the defibrillator machine and the paddles. He called for the shock, used the ten-inch needle through the chest wall to the patient's heart, then called for another shock.

"Nothing, damn it!" Wilson wailed. "Go to four hundred. Stand clear!"

Sharon inched backward as the arrest team worked feverishly, her heart lurching each time the patient's body did. She wiped the perspiration from her upper lip, and her breath caught when the cardiac-monitor alarm squealed.

The line went flat.

Dr. Wilson tried again and again, then, the paddles still in his hands, he stood erect, looked over at Sharon and shook his head. "That's it," he mumbled, his forehead damp with sweat. He checked his watch. "Chart the time of death as 5:10."

She slumped back against the wall, trying to force down the lump in her throat. It didn't help at all when she reminded herself that the man lying in the bed, ashen and still, wasn't the first patient she had lost, nor would he be the last. But after so many years, losing a patient still felt like losing a part of herself.

The suddenness of Richard Nordstrom's death troubled her deeply. What had gone wrong? Had she missed some indication of problems? No, she decided instantly, reviewing her assessment of his condition when she last checked on him.

"It's been one of those nights, hasn't it?" Dr. Wilson said, placing a gentle hand on Sharon's shoulder.

"I don't understand what happened to him," she said, shaking her head slowly. "It was so sudden and unexpected."

"You know it can be like that. Don't dwell on it." He gave her shoulder a shake and offered her one of his easy smiles that made him look younger than his fifty years. "I prescribe a cafeteria break for you. It'll do you good to get away from here for a few minutes."

"I can't," she said appreciatively. "I've got to get the ward medications ready."

"Dr. Wilson," Estelle, another nurse, said from the doorway, "I think Mrs. Garcia is entering septic shock."

The chief resident rushed from the room, and once again Sharon thought of his dedication to their patients. She liked James Wilson. She had ever since he'd joined the hospital staff six months ago, leaving a lucrative private practice to his ex-partner, Dr. Franklin Shaw. Speculation as to why he'd left his practice had caused a lot of tongues to wag, but she'd found him to be an excellent physician, dedicated and caring. Unlike most doctors, he took the time to credit nurses when credit was due, and he wasn't above listening to their thoughts on patient care.

With effort she willed her thoughts back to the business at hand and returned to the nurses' station, where she found Louella Frawley, the night nursing supervisor waiting for her.

"What happened?" the Faye Dunaway look-alike asked crisply.

"Nordstrom arrested," Sharon answered in a monotone, pulling his chart from the rack by her desk.

Louella eyed her critically, then grabbed the chart from her and scanned it. "You gave him an injection of morphine?"

"He was in pain. The morphine was ordered."

"You could have checked with me first."

Wide-eyed, Sharon stared at her. "Why would I?"

"The patient was given morphine in ER. The injection you gave him could have induced the arrest."

"Ten milligrams certainly wouldn't have," she insisted, jerking the stethoscope from around her neck. "And you know it. Dr. Wilson ordered eight to sixteen intramuscular. I always start with the lower end of an ordered dosage, and when I monitored Nordstrom, he responded well to ten milligrams."

"You made a medical diagnosis and acted on it."

Baffled by the woman's verbal jabs, Sharon said, "Louella, you're losing it! I did no such thing. I followed Dr. Wilson's written order. Can't you read?"

The nursing supervisor's nervous eyes darted to the open cabinet door. "Apparently you left the drugs unattended. You know that's strictly against procedure."

Sharon glared at her. "What did you expect me to do, stay in here as the man died?"

"There were three other nurses on the unit and an arrest team to handle that."

"Those three nurses have seven patients who are just about hanging on. If you want to take out your hostility on someone, tell the chief nurse that our staffing here is as critical as the patients we have."

Smugly Louella tilted her head up. "I thought you ex-Vietnam nurses were used to doing the impossible and performing miracles. Apparently your military experience didn't help Nordstrom very much."

Sharon fought hard and bit back the angry words she wanted to toss at the woman. Louella had been a thorn in her side ever since Sharon had been appointed head nurse on ICU a year ago, after having been at the hospital only three years. Louella had worked for ten years before becoming a head nurse, and for six after that before being named night nursing supervisor. The woman's resentment had soared when she learned that Sharon had been considered for the job Louella now held.

"The last time I checked on Nordstrom," Sharon said as calmly as she could, "he was groggy but only slightly arrhythmic. His arrest came out of nowhere. If you're truly concerned about what happened, you should ask the chief nurse to request a medical inquiry."

"Don't be ridiculous. We have enough problems as it is. We don't have time to look for nonexistent ones."

"If you don't suggest it to her, I will."

"Sharon," Louella said, her voice a thinly disguised warning, "your independent actions are going to get you into serious trouble one of these days. Ever since you became a head nurse, you think you're more knowledgeable than anyone in this hospital. The only reason you are one is because of the nursing shortage."

Squaring her shoulders, Sharon aimed cool blue eyes at the woman. "You have to think that, don't you? Your pride won't—" The ringing of the phone interrupted her. "ICU, Sharon," she answered between clenched teeth. "Yes, she's here." Dropping the receiver onto the desk, she said, "It's for you, the agency," then she energetically rolled the medication cart out of the nurses' station.

She hadn't gotten very far into the ward when she heard a soft knock on the open door at the glass-enclosed station. Glancing back over her shoulder, she saw a tall man looking inside the office, a man she had noticed Dr. Wilson talking to earlier in the hallway. Now she made a closer inspection. His jaw was covered with stubble, his sun-streaked brown hair was disheveled. He wore jeans and a sport jacket over a white shirt that was open at the collar.

"I'm Steve Nordstrom," he said to Louella, who was now at the doorway. "I'd like to check on my brother."

"Miss McClure, the head nurse, will help you," Louella advised, nodding to her right. She stepped toward Sharon and said curtly, "The agency nurse will be here shortly. Her name's Anna Stein." Her shoulders drawn back, Louella strode off toward the isolation room.

The man's troubled eyes fixed on Sharon's, and he asked quietly, "How is Richie?"

"Just a second, please, Mr Nordstrom." She glanced toward Dr. Wilson, who was busy at Mrs. Garcia's bedside, then she called Rebecca, the third nurse on duty, and asked her to dispense meds. After gesturing Steve into the nurses' station, she said softly, "I'm sorry to have to tell you this, but your brother just had a heart attack."

"He'll recover, though." His words were more a plea than a statement.

"He didn't," she said gently. "Believe me, everything possible was done to save him."

Sharon glanced through the window toward the isolation room, thinking she'd take him to see his brother, but she decided against it, realizing that a nurse and an LPN had probably begun the postmortem care: the bathing, tagging and shrouding.

When she looked back at Steve Nordstrom, her heart went out to him as he slumped into a chair, his features a pained mask of disbelief. "Would you like some coffee?" she asked.

He glanced up, his blue-gray eyes dull, weary-looking. "Thank you, no," he replied, in a low, strained voice.

Squeezing his hands together, he swallowed hard, letting it sink in that Richie was dead, Richie, his vibrant younger brother who had so much to look forward to in life. What would he say to their parents? Steve wondered. Suddenly the acrid odor of disinfectant and medicinal aromas gagged him. He looked over at Sharon, dragged himself up from the chair and raked his fingers through his hair. "Maybe I will have that coffee."

A tapping on the window drew Sharon's attention, and Dave gestured for her to come into the ward.

"I don't want to keep you from your work," Steve said huskily. "I'll help myself... if that's all right."

"Please, go right ahead. We'll talk when I get back."

On the dimly lighted ward, over the hums, hisses and occasional beeps of life-supporting equipment, Sharon and Dave discussed the declining condition of an emaciated elderly man with multiple intubations. His skin was cold and clammy to her touch; his breathing was barely audible.

"Should I notify Dr. Shaw?" Dave asked.

Sharon shook her head, knowing that Dr. Shaw had seen his patient less than an hour ago and had discontinued his prior orders for increased medication or mechanical support. Quietly she said, "He's probably at home by now and asleep."

"I was surprised to see him here this time of the morning, considering he's not a staff member."

"Dedication, I guess," Sharon said absently as she scanned the activity on the ward.

While he checked his other patient's respirator, Dave asked, "Why was Louella climbing all over you before?"

A grimace curving her lips, Sharon said, "The woman's out of sync with reality."

"You'd better be nice to her. If Riley does leave, you know who our new chief nurse will be."

"If it's Louella, I'll reenlist in the army."

Sharon's eyes drifted over to the gurney that a nursing assistant was wheeling from the isolation room that was only a few feet away. When it reached the door to the nurses' station, she saw Steve Nordstrom lift the sheet from his brother's face. He smoothed back the hair on the prone man's head, then slowly replaced the sheet, standing rigid as he watched the man in white guide the gurney toward the elevator.

"Dave, keep an eye on things, would you? I've got a hurting man over there." Crossing the ward, she touched Steve's arm and said softly, "I'm sorry you had to wait."

For a moment he just stared at her as if he hadn't comprehended her words. Then he said quietly, "Uh . . . no problem."

Inside the station Sharon saw that he hadn't touched his coffee, so she poured it down the sink, refilled the cup with hot coffee and handed it to him.

"Thanks," he said, his voice having gained a modicum of energy. After a sip, he shook his head slowly and emitted a deep, pain-ridden sigh. "I still can't believe it. Everything's happened so fast. Richie was only thirty-three, in great physical shape. I guess the accident must have damaged his heart."

It didn't, Sharon noted silently, a resurgence of concern gripping her because his brother had gone into cardiac arrest so unexpectedly. "He was treated by Dr. Gomez in ER when he was brought in last evening. Dr. Gomez is still on duty if you'd like to speak with him."

"Yes, I would." Steve inclined his head and, as though talking to himself, added, "I guess it doesn't make any sense for our parents to fly down here now. I can take care of the arrangements to have Richie—" he hesitated, thinking how cold his next words would sound "—to have him flown to Wisconsin." After a long pause, he looked up at Sharon. "Did he suffer before he . . ." Steve couldn't get the word out.

"No," Sharon said to reassure him. "He was quite groggy from medication. Again, I'm sorry I couldn't have given you better news about your brother."

Tapping on the office door, Dave said, "Mr. Carbone's having respiratory distress."

"I'm sorry, Mr. Nordstrom," Sharon apologized, rushing from the room.

She was busy checking the patient's respirator when Flora, the floor ward clerk, said, "ER's sending up another one, says the girl's in a diabetic coma."

Half an hour later the agency nurse finally arrived. Sharon met her in the office, noticing Dr. Wilson talking with Steve down the corridor by the elevator. Inside the station she estimated the agency nurse in whites to be in her early fifties. Silver-gray hair waved to just above her shoulders. Her eyes were dark, her features striking.

As she drew her fingers through the side of her light brown hair, Sharon forced the semblance of a smile. "You're a sight for sore eyes. I'm Sharon McClure."

"Anna Stein," the woman said pleasantly.

After a glance through the window to check the ward, Sharon asked, "Are you a coffee drinker?"

"I'm a nurse, aren't I?" Anna responded with a smile.

"All of us probably have more caffeine than oxygen in our blood," Sharon quipped, then gestured toward the stainless-steel sink. "You can wash up there."

As Anna did so, Sharon poured coffee for them. "Have you worked ICU before?"

"Yes."

"Good. It's been a little crazy around here tonight. How long have you been in nursing?"

"Almost thirty years, most of it in pediatrics, but I haven't worked with children for the past two."

Sharon wondered why not, knowing that pediatric nurses usually had to be dragged away from caring for children. "Well," she said, handing the woman her cup of coffee, "we sure could use your experience on a permanent basis here on ICU. There's an opening if you're interested."

"I'm not really ready to work full-time yet. My husband died two years ago, and I'm still a little at sea as far as plans go."

"Maybe full-time work is what you need," Sharon suggested, thinking that two years of grieving was a little long.

"You're probably right, but I may go back home."

"Where's that?"

"London...Ontario," Anna clarified. "My husband's parents moved here from Buffalo. After Joshua died, I came down to be near them for a while. I just haven't left yet."

"So most of your nursing was in Canada."

"At first, then in Buffalo after I came back from Vietnam."

"Vietnam?" Sharon repeated. "How long were you there?"

After a sip of coffee, Anna said, "Five years."

"You did five tours?" Sharon exclaimed, wondering how the woman could have stood it.

"Josh and I were civilians," Anna explained. "I met him while he was a resident at a hospital in Buffalo. A year later we were married and went to Vietnam as part of IVS, International Voluntary Services. I taught nursing in a school in Nha Trang until Josh was assigned to Quang Ngai. I worked mostly with children there." She shook her head slowly. "Their suffering was so overwhelming, and the conditions were unbelievable—no running water on the wards, not even in the emergency room, and electricity was a sometimes thing."

She paused thoughtfully, then said, "I still dream about the sick kids back there, those sweet children with their unsmiling round faces and sad almond-shaped eyes. They had diseases that I thought had been eliminated from the face of the earth, things like typhoid, polio, cholera, leprosy. You name it, it was there, and so many children were maimed in the bombings."

"I know," Sharon said quietly. "I spent two years in Vietnam, one tour at the Twelfth Evacuation Hospital at Cu Chi, the other at the Seventy-first in Pleiku."

Anna chuckled dryly. "You got both the heat and the freezing weather."

"I don't know which was worse. In Pleiku the red dust was everywhere—in the drapes we made from parachutes, in our clothes, even in our hair."

"Did you ever work with children?" Anna asked.

Sharon nodded. "I thought the war would be men against men, not against children."

"The memories stay with you, don't they?"

"They do," Sharon agreed pensively. It was as if those two years would always be trapped inside her in a raging ball, waiting to burst. But she was fortunate. It had been a long struggle, but she had learned how to cope with what was now called PTSD, posttraumatic stress disorder, a disorder usually thought of as being a male soldier's problem.

After a swallow of coffee, Sharon said, "A few of my friends who were in Vietnam are coming over to my place Monday night. If you can clear your social calendar, stop by around eight o'clock. They'd love to meet you."

"I'd like that," Anna said appreciatively.

Sharon jotted down her address on a small pad lying on the desk, then pulled off the page and handed it to Anna. "I even supply the cold beer and coffee." Checking the ward again, she said, "Enough relaxation. We'd better get to work."

She guided Anna to each bedside, briefly describing the condition of and doctor's orders for the occupant. After she alerted her to the problems of the last patient, a man with a nasal-gastro tube that suctioned his stomach, Sharon said, "You're assigned to Gail and Mr. Gonzales here. Looks like his bottle needs changing."

By habit Sharon glanced around the ward, then watched closely as Anna carefully unscrewed the suction top and removed the plastic bottle from the heavy cylinder and replaced the disposable bottle with a new one. From the corner of her eye Sharon saw Louella speaking with Dr. Wilson near the door to the isolation room.

Nodding toward them, she said, "That's Dr. Wilson, the chief resident. The woman is Louella Frawley, our night nursing supervisor. She'll be looming up behind all of us every now and then, but you'll know in advance. The perfume she douses herself with could be used as shark repellent."

The phone in the nurses' station sounded, and Sharon went back to the office.

A little after 8:00 a.m., as she was charting before going off duty, her thoughts returned to Richard Nordstrom. It was true that the man had suffered severe abdominal trauma, but as his brother had confirmed, the patient had been in prime shape before the accident. Nothing in his condition forewarned of cardiac arrest.

She replaced the last chart in the rack, picked up her plaid tote bag and headed to the elevator, intent on expressing her concerns about Richard Nordstrom's death to Clara Riley, the chief nurse.

Minutes later she was in Clara's secretary's office, waiting for the morning meeting to end. The chief nurse exited the conference room, followed by Louella, who glared at Sharon, then passed through the room without a word.

"You had a busy night," Clara said, smiling and motioning for Sharon to follow her into her office. "Have a seat," she said, but before Sharon could open her mouth to speak, Clara did. "We went over Richard Nordstrom's chart. Louella questioned your having administered the second injection of morphine, but I don't. Everything you did was absolutely correct, exactly according to the book. In fact, I want to compliment you on your charting. It's exemplary."

"Mrs. Riley, the man sustained no injury to the heart in the accident. Doesn't what happened strike you as odd?"

"What strikes me as odd is your assumption that a medical inquiry is needed. Dr. Wilson signed the death certificate, stating cardiac arrest as the cause. Surely you're not questioning his judgment."

"Of course not, but it was the suddenness of the arrest that disturbs me. A medical inquiry board might recommend an autopsy."

"Sharon, the hospital picks up the bill for any autopsy performed. Aside from that, our requesting an autopsy would suggest doubt on our part about the quality of care the patient received.''

Mimicking Louella, Sharon thought, knowing the two women were close friends.

Clara held up the much-erased projected nursing schedule for the next month. "If you want to see real problems, look at this. I'm ready to go bananas trying to fill the slots. Never mind the funding problem, I can't even find qualified warm bodies. If the nursing shortage gets any worse, this hospital's going to have to shut down another wing. Now this is what I call a real problem, so let's not hear any more talk of unnecessary inquiries. Is there something else on your mind?''

Leaning forward, Sharon said, "Mrs. Riley, a patient of mine died last night, and I'm not sure he had to.''

Clara studied Sharon's troubled expression, then leaned back in her chair. "Like all of us, you're tired. If I could do without you, I'd tell you to take time off and kick up your heels, but we both know I can't. Go home, and have a hot bath and get some sleep. I may need you to do a double shift again this weekend.''

Sharon realized she wasn't going to get anywhere, so she held back her words of protest and left the office.

The rubber on her white shoes muffled her steps as she walked quickly to the elevator, deciding to speak to the chief of staff herself, even if Mrs. Riley became her enemy for life. She punched the down button harder than necessary, but as she waited she decided she'd most likely get the same response from the chief of staff. Don't look for trouble, and don't make waves. That seemed to be the order of the day at the hospital lately.

Inside the elevator she changed her mind and pressed the button for the second floor, where she went to the lab to find Tony Catalano.

"Hi," the attractive black-haired man said cheerfully, looking up from a microscope when she slipped onto the stool next to his. "Are you on overtime?"

"No, thank goodness." She laid her tote bag on the long, high table strewn with lab paraphernalia, then faced the white-jacketed man. "Tony, I've got a big favor to ask you."

"Put in a good word for me with Debbie, and I'll do anything you want . . . as long as it's legal," he added, grinning.

"How about if I fix the two of you a gourmet dinner?"

"Think she'd really find the time? With her working nights and my working days, the best we usually manage is having breakfast together. And look at me. I'm Mr. Wonderful and I've got a steady job."

"We'll quibble about your humility later. Right now I need your help. Last night a man died on ICU."

"Well, now," he said, swinging around on the stool and propping an arm on the table, "that is news."

"Tony, this is serious. He was a hit-and-run case who went into sudden cardiac arrest."

"So?"

"His name's Richard Nordstrom. He's in the morgue now, but I don't know how long he'll be there. I want you to get a blood sample from him, analyze it and check the results against the initial blood workup that was done last night when he was brought in."

His eyes narrowing, Tony asked, "What am I supposed to be looking for?"

"I don't know."

"Oh," he remarked, arching his dark eyebrows. "You're sure you don't want me to try to get a family history from him while I'm at it?"

"I said this is serious."

"You be serious. If the guy died of a heart attack, why are you so interested in his blood?"

"He was my patient, my responsibility. I want to know what went wrong, if anything. I'll just feel better if the blood results match."

"Why shouldn't they?"

"They should, and that's what I want you to tell me. Will you do it?"

"Sharon," he said, moaning her name, "look at the backup over there." He gestured toward a long double row of wire-mesh trays filled with patient specimens. "Those take priority. They're from live people." Frowning at her stony-faced expression, he acquiesced. "Okay, the first chance I get I'll go down to the morgue, but I can't promise I'll get to the analysis today."

"First thing tomorrow?"

"If I have to, I'll come in early." Wrinkling his brow, he shook his head. "You're sounding like you think the guy was murdered."

Murdered? No, that possibility seemed too farfetched even to consider. Recovering, she latched on to her tote bag and stood. "That's nonsense. I don't think any such thing. I just want to know if you find anything unusual, okay?"

"Will do."

"Thanks, Tony," she said sunnily, and headed for the hospital cafeteria.

CHAPTER TWO

ONE LOOK at the long line at the cafeteria food counter caused Sharon to reconsider. Deciding that joining it wasn't worth breakfast, she went to the urn of free coffee at an island stand, poured herself a cup and took a seat at a small table alongside the far wall, where the drone of voices wasn't so noticeable.

Maybe Tony was right, she thought as she mulled over the conversation she'd had with him. Maybe she was crazy. Maybe as Clara had said, she just needed some rest and some fun.

"Mind if I join you?"

Looking up, she saw Steve Nordstrom holding a tray. "Please," she said pleasantly, thinking his smile half-hearted, but even so it transformed the rather haggard look on his face that she'd seen earlier.

Steve placed his tray on the table and eased onto the chair across from her, eyeing her solitary cup of coffee. "You're not a big breakfast eater, are you?"

Her stomach grumbled as the aroma from his scrambled eggs and warm toast swirled up into her nostrils. "Usually I am," she admitted, "but this morning I just didn't have enough energy to wait in line. I'll fix something when I get home."

Casually he shifted his plate of toast to her side of the table. "This'll help keep you going till then."

"Thanks," she said, smiling her appreciation. "One slice will do the trick."

As she buttered the toast, Steve transferred the strips of bacon from his plate to the one he'd given her.

"You're generous to a fault," she remarked, judging him to be thoughtful, as well.

He glanced down at the scrambled eggs in front of him. "I'm not really hungry. Guess I'm just going through the motions out of habit."

Once more Sharon realized how dreadful the past hours had been for him. "You've had a difficult night, Mr. Nordstrom," she said sympathetically. "I wish I could say something that would help."

Manufacturing a reluctant smile, he said, "You could help by calling me Steve. Right now I need to feel less isolated than I do."

"Steve," she said. Then she added, "I'm Sharon."

His remark about feeling isolated caused her gaze to slip down to his ring finger, which was encircled by what appeared to be a college ring. She decided that if he weren't married, a man as attractive as he was would have someone close to him, someone who would help see him through this difficult period. After munching on some toast, she asked, "Did you speak with Dr. Gomez?"

"Just now. They're so busy in Emergency that he was late getting off duty. He was surprised that Richie succumbed to a heart attack, but he and Dr. Wilson said that even apparently healthy people could go into what they called sudden cardiac arrest."

"That's true," Sharon said reflectively.

"Nothing showed up in Richie's annual physical a month ago, and there's no history of heart problems in our family. Dr. Gomez told me Richie was in bad shape when he treated him in the emergency room, but he had expected him to recover after surgery.''

As Sharon listened to Steve, she was at odds with herself. Richard Nordstrom had been brought to ER a little after 10:00 p.m. last evening and then underwent surgery for a ruptured spleen and stomach trauma. He'd had no severe post-op difficulties, and although he'd begun running a fever after he was brought to ICU, she had expected him to be transferred to another ward this morning. Now she couldn't shake the nagging belief, an almost sinister suspicion, that something went wrong while he was on her unit.

Steve forked up some of the scrambled eggs, then set the fork down on the plate and moved it aside. "How long have you been in nursing, Sharon?"

"Eighteen years, counting school."

"That's a lot of experience. I'm guessing that you spent more time with my brother on ICU than Dr. Wilson did. Were you surprised by what happened?"

Sharon pondered how to respond to him. If she told him what she had asked Tony to do, she knew it would only upset Steve more and lead him to believe that something had definitely gone awry on ICU. But nothing had, nothing she could point to, anyway. Even Dr. Wilson and the chief nurse had told her that she had done everything by the book.

"Steve," she said, aware of the legal ramifications of anything she might tell him, "in hospitals there's a distinct chain of command, just like in the army. Nurses follow doctors' orders, and it's the doctors who decide cause of death and sign the certificates." Moving a finger slowly over the handle of her coffee cup, she lowered her eyes. "Like Dr. Gomez, though, I wasn't expecting what happened." She heard Steve sigh and looked up at him.

"Excuse my sounding like an interrogator," he apologized, "but right now I'm questioning everything, mainly Richie's being gone." His gaze lowered to his clenched fist that rested on the edge of the table. "I still can't accept that he is."

"That's understandable," she said, compassion in her words. "You're going through a period of denial and anger."

His eyes met hers, and in them he saw a world of sympathy and concern. "Denial and anger," he repeated quietly. "You're right there. It's all I can do to keep from picking up this tray and hurling it against the wall. Not very adult of me, is it?"

Sharon placed a comforting hand over his tightened fist and said softly, "It only proves that you loved your brother very much."

Steve's lips pursed and he lowered his eyes again. "I just wish I could be sure he knew that." A silent moment passed before he became aware that Sharon's hand was covering his. As though embarrassed, he looked up at her, and his lips curved into a faint smile. "Your listening to me carry on is far beyond the call of duty. I want you to know that I appreciate it."

Withdrawing her hand, she picked up a strip of bacon and returned his smile, but hers was more open. "I'm willing to share your breakfast, why not your feelings also?" After sampling the crisp bacon, she said, "It's good. You should try some."

He shook his head, took a swallow of coffee, then asked, "Do you have brothers or sisters?"

"Uh-uh. Just my parents."

"Same here now. They don't even know Richie was run down by a car yet. I wanted to wait until I could assure them he'd be okay. God, I'd rather take a beating than tell them that he's dead. He was still their little boy."

"They're in Wisconsin, you said?"

"In Madison." Rather perfunctorily, he added, "I've been here in Florida seven years now. Richie just moved down four months ago."

Seeing him becoming pensive again, Sharon attempted to get his mind off his sorrow. Lightly she remarked, "From the looks of your tan, I'm guessing you're a lifeguard."

Her supposition brought an instant smile to his face and brightened his eyes. "Uh-uh," he said, searching her amused expression. "I doubt if there are many forty-four-year-old lifeguards."

"A beachcomber, then?"

"Wrong again. I import and ship orchid plants."

"Sounds exotic," she allowed, pleased that the taut muscles in his jaw had relaxed some. But once again he became lost in private thoughts, and she almost felt as if she were sharing the sadness that robbed him of his fleeting smile.

She guessed that under normal circumstances Steve would be a man in total control of his life. Strength was obvious in his commanding physical appearance. He was the picture of health, broad-shouldered and trim. His baritone voice suggested authority, and she detected a sensitivity in him that was quite compelling.

"I've taken up too much of your time already," he said apologetically, then pushed himself up from the table. As he gazed down at her, his voice took on a warm, sincere quality. "My heartfelt thanks again for everything you did for Richie," he said, extending a hand.

Sharon perused his attractive face as she felt the strength of his hand encase hers. She had always taken time to be supportive to grieving relatives, not because it was her job, but because she was genuinely sympathetic to their sorrow. And she did feel sympathy for Steve Nordstrom, but as he held her hand, she felt something else, something that seemed out of place at the moment. The feeling was soothing but also intimate, and moments later, as she watched him carry his tray toward the exit, she found herself wishing they could have met under different circumstances.

When he disappeared from view, Sharon shook her head and smiled at her reflections, deciding she needed a vacation desperately.

She had just polished off the last of the bacon when Dave joined her. Eyeing the ample stack of pancakes and sausages on the breakfast tray he placed on the table, she tilted her head sideways. "Dining out, huh? Is your wife on strike?"

"No. Louella blabbed to Riley that Betty took the kids to Disney World, and our chief nurse hit me for an extra four hours. Want one of my sausages?"

Frowning, Sharon asked, "Why is everyone trying to feed me this morning? Do I look undernourished or something?"

"You look pretty good to me," he said as he squeezed the plastic packet of syrup over his pancakes. "Wife's out of town. Wanna fool around later?"

Sharon chuckled at his feigned wolfish grin. "Betty would kill you if I didn't first."

"True. The sweet lady's hopelessly in love with me."

"I'd say the feeling between you two is mutual. She showed me her anniversary present, the gold chain with the heart on it."

"Did she also show you the French underwear she bought me? They look like eye patches." After a swallow of pancakes, he asked, "So, why are you just having toast and coffee this morning? That's tantamount to a fast for you."

"I'm too tired to eat. In fact, I'm too tired even to drag myself up and head for home."

"Being exhausted goes with the glamorous job we have. Still off Monday night?"

"So far."

"Betty wants you to come for dinner."

"Can't. It's my turn to host the henhouse club."

"How's the women's auxiliary getting on?"

"We were *not* auxiliary," Sharon informed him, smirking good-naturedly. "We are legitimate veterans."

"It's a shame I was too young to be involved in Vietnam. I would have loved to have seen First Lieutenant McClure in action."

"Believe me, you didn't miss much."

"Got any medals?"

"A few...none for good behavior."

"You oughta wear them in tonight. That'd really shake Louella up."

Sharon diverted her eyes, thinking that the army didn't give medals for what she'd lost in Vietnam. It had been so many years ago, yet the memories lingered: nurses and doctors running and shouting over the deafening sound of landing choppers, the groans of bloodied young soldiers being rushed to OR, her assisting at operations while trying to ignore the incoming rockets, mortars and artillery.

"Have you heard the latest about Louella and Wilson?" Dave asked, drawing Sharon's attention.

"And they say women love gossip."

"Okay, I won't tell you."

"Yes, you will. You're dying to."

"Well," he said, lowering his voice, "they're flying off to the Bahamas for the weekend."

"You're kidding."

"Nope. Rita's furious because she has to take Louella's shift Saturday night."

"Humph! For the life of me I can't understand what Dr. Wilson sees in her."

"My guess is he's tired of cooking and doing his own laundry, or maybe it's mutual troubles that brought them together—his divorce and her husband walking out on her." Dave pierced a piece of sausage with his fork and waved it. "Could be she's a different person outside the hospital."

"If you're going to keep talking about Louella, I'm leaving." Sharon stood and collected her cup and plate.

"What night can I tell the wife you'll deign to have dinner with us? She's got a successful lawyer she wants you to marry."

"Ha! Tell Betty I'll plot my own disasters."

AFTER EXITING the administrator's office, Steve went to the water fountain and took a quick swallow, then drew his fingers through his hair before pressing the elevator button with a thumb. As he waited, he tried to formulate his plans. There was so much to do: phone his parents, contact a funeral home in Clearwater and one in Madison, then arrange for air transportation. He also had to check with the post office to see if his shipment of orchids had arrived from Thailand. Somewhere in between he just had to get some shut-eye or he was going to crumple.

The elevator doors parted, and he joined the medical personnel inside, the hum of their voices diminishing as his thoughts drifted back to the shocking phone call he'd received from the emergency room last evening. The race to the hospital. Richie, unconscious, black-and-blue. The argument he'd had with his brother yesterday.

"Excuse me."

He felt someone nudge him and realized the elevator doors were open. Quickly he exited into the lobby and stepped aside to let the flow of passengers go by. Slumping back against the wall, he took a long, deep breath. *Some year,* he thought. *First Laura and now Richie.* He sagged under the heavy weight in his chest, but after a moment he cleared his throat and headed for the parking lot.

As he inserted the key in his car door, he glanced over at the automobile pulling out several cars away and saw that it was Sharon McClure. He waved, but she didn't notice him. For a moment he watched her drive off. Then he opened his car door and slipped onto the seat.

Like a drugged man, he sat motionless, his thoughts replaying the past hours. They seemed more like a nightmare than waking life. Sharon's sympathetic concern, however, had been like a soothing balm, and he wondered if she was aware of how much her caring attitude had helped. He was happy, or relieved, anyway, that she'd been his brother's nurse, that she'd been with him in those final hours. He remembered her saying that Richie hadn't suffered greatly, that he had been groggy. Probably from medication she had given him, Steve guessed. An overwhelming gratitude eased some of the heaviness of heart he felt, and he decided to do something to demonstrate his appreciation to Richie's nurse.

SHARON MOANED, then twisted her body and thrust out a hand to silence the buzzing of the alarm clock that seemed to rattle inside her head. She slapped the snooze button with a finger once and then again, harder, but the irritating noise continued.

Opening her eyes to mere slits, she realized the sound was coming from her apartment door and not the clock. She pushed away the strands of hair that streamed over her face and peered at the digital clock: 4:05 p.m.

"No rest for the weary," she muttered, not having gotten to bed until shortly before noon. She dragged herself up, grabbed her plaid bathrobe and slipped into it as she trudged barefoot over the carpet to the door. Squinting through the peephole, she was surprised to see Steve Nordstrom on the landing.

Not removing the chain, she opened the door a crack. "Yes?" she asked, her voice raspy from lingering drowsiness.

"Hi," he said with a hesitant smile. "Do you have a minute?"

Coping with cobwebs of slumber, she unhooked the chain, opened the door and saw that he was holding the most stunning orchid plant she had ever seen. He had shaved and was wearing a beige suit, looking as if he had just stepped out of *Gentlemen's Quarterly*. And she felt like a worn-out dishrag!

"I've come at a bad time, huh?" he said, his eyes sweeping over the robe she wore.

"No problem," she lied as she drew her fingers through her tangled mass of hair. "I'm usually up by now, but I was a little off schedule today."

When her eyes lowered to the plant he was holding, he said, "I'd like you to have this with my sincere thanks for everything you did for Richie."

"It's gorgeous," she remarked, her surprised gaze examining the plant's four striking blossoms, each a ruby red lip backed by brilliant yellow petals.

"It's a cross I developed from Brazilian laelio and cattleya orchids." He handed her the gift, saying, "I call it Fascination."

Looking up at Steve, she smiled warmly. "Please, come on in." After closing the door behind him, she admitted, "I'm not exactly known for having a green thumb. Are you sure you want to leave this beautiful plant with me?"

With a boyish grin, he said, "I can't think of anyone who would give it better care."

After placing the orchid plant and its clay saucer on the coffee table, she gestured Steve to an easy chair across from the sofa. "Please, have a seat." She was about to sit herself when she caught a glimpse of her bare feet. "Excuse me," she said quickly. "I need a minute to get myself together." She headed to the bedroom, but at the door she glanced back at him. "How did you find out where I live?"

"You're the only S. McClure in the phone book. I chanced it."

"Oh, right," she said, then closed the door behind her. In the bathroom she braced her hands on the sink, peered into the mirror and groaned. Her hair looked as if she'd arranged it with an eggbeater, and without her makeup she imagined Steve must have guessed she was a decade older than her forty-one years.

"This is going to be a three-cups-of-coffee wake-up session," she mumbled, then palmed some cold water and doused her face.

Ten minutes later, in green slacks and a yellow pullover, she returned to the living room. "Would you like some coffee, Steve?"

His eyes raked over her fresh appearance, taking in the graceful contours of her slender body. "You look different in clothes. Uh...I mean not wearing a nurse's uniform."

"I know exactly what you mean," she said, smiling at his discomfort. "In white we nurses do look like part of the hospital equipment." She glanced at her watch. "Coffee is a wake-up necessity for me. Would you rather have a drink?"

"To be honest," he admitted, "I'd love one."

You should smile more often, she thought on the way to the kitchen. "Only have bourbon," she said, bending down and taking a near-full bottle from a lower cabinet.

"Perfect," he said standing at the archway, watching her intently.

After handing him a glass, she placed some cubes from the freezer into a leather ice bucket. "Wish I could join you, but I'm on duty tonight."

As she started the automatic coffee maker and he readied his drink, Steve glanced at the amethyst on her ring finger. He had planned to drop off the plant and leave, but suddenly he was seeing Sharon McClure in a different light. She wasn't just a woman who happened to be a nurse. She was a woman who happened to be exceptionally attractive. Casually he asked, "Do you work nights all the time?"

"For the past year I have. It has its advantages and its disadvantages."

She handed him a napkin, and he followed her into the living room, where she sat on the sofa in front of the gift he had brought her. "The orchids are exquisite," she commented sincerely. Leaning forward, she sniffed one of the sweet-smelling blooms. "And the aroma is heavenly!"

"They'll give it off about this time each day."

Relaxing on the easy chair opposite her, Steve began to feel half human for the first time since the hospital had phoned him last night. He took a moment to study the way her silky brown hair fell in soft waves, framing a flawless complexion, compelling blue eyes, a pert nose and sensual lips. He particularly liked the sound of his warm voice. Maybe it was seeing her in ordinary clothes, he pondered, or maybe it was the different setting, but whatever it was, he felt as though he were really seeing her for the first time. Unobtrusively his gaze wandered over the apartment that was tastefully appointed and every bit as comfortable as she was to be with. Then he looked back at her and found himself fighting an incipient smile.

Aware that Steve was scrutinizing her, Sharon lowered her eyes, feeling a pleasurable sensation curl within her; it was one of comfort and contentment more than raw excitement. She chided herself, rationalizing that his presence and his gift were only his way of showing his appreciation, just as relatives of other patients she had nursed had done.

When she did look back at him, she watched him take another sip of his drink and realized that the only mutual experience they could talk about would be his brother. She didn't want to bring that up, so she turned her attention to the orchids again and smiled. "You must have been born with a green thumb."

"I was raised working in greenhouses," he said, settling back in the chair, feeling the tension in his neck and shoulder muscles ebbing away. "My parents have a floral import business in Madison, and my father's always been partial to orchids."

"It's easy to see why," Sharon remarked, glancing at the plant briefly, then again noticing Steve's engrossed gaze. "So now you import them."

"The majority of them I do." The lovely sheen in her blue eyes brought something to mind. "But last year I found a rare blue cattleya orchid in the Sarapiqui Canyon—" his expression darkened suddenly "—in Costa Rica."

Sharon wondered at his sudden change of mood, but she wasn't going to ask why. Instead, she placed her coffee mug next to the plant, asking, "You actually go hunting for orchids yourself?"

"I deal with collectors in South America and the Far East, but I used to hit the jungles of Central America twice a year."

"Jungles?" Sharon grimaced. "As in snakes and creepy crawly things?"

Steve chuckled at her description, but at the same time he found himself charmed by her lighthearted playfulness. "It's not all that bad if you watch where you walk and wear insect repellent. The main problem was that there were no roads in the places I explored."

Her imagination taking over, she pictured him in a khaki suit, complete with pith helmet and machete, hacking his way through a tropical rain forest. Dressed as he was now, though, he presented the image of a highly successful businessman. Yes, she decided, Steve Nordstrom was an interesting man. Earlier she'd wished they'd met under different circumstances. Now her wish became more of a yearning.

Leaning forward, Steve clasped his hands. "If you're interested in orchids, you're invited to tour my greenhouses whenever you have time." He reached into his inside jacket pocket, withdrew a business card and handed it to her. "Here's the address. You don't have to phone, just stop by. If I'm not in one of the greenhouses, I'll be in the office in the house on the property. That's where I live." After a quick swallow of his drink, he stood. "I'd better be on my way. You must have things to do."

"No," she said quickly. "I did all my shopping on the way home from the hospital this morning." Wanting to prolong his visit, she asked, "Would you like another drink? I could fix something to snack on."

"You're sure I'm not interfering with your schedule?"

"Positive. The only thing between me and going on duty tonight is having dinner."

"Would you consider having dinner with me?" he asked.

Genuinely surprised by his invitation and struck by the intensity she saw in his shining eyes, her breath caught momentarily and she felt her heart begin a little dance. "Well, yes, I would, but the lovely orchids are enough of a thank-you. You don't have to—"

"I'm not asking because I have to," he said warmly. "I want to."

CHAPTER THREE

SHARON HAD DINED at Jesse's Landing several times. A sprawling gray-and-white wooden mansion, it was built on a curve of Lake Seminole. The table Steve had requested was by a window in the Victorian Room, which overlooked the calm water dappled by lavender hyacinths and white water lilies.

Smiling over at Steve, she said, "From the way you were greeted you must be a regular customer."

"It's convenient. I live just on the other side of the lake," he explained, absorbed by the way the overhead Tiffany stained glass lamp cast an amber hue over her lovely face.

"Not much of a cook, I take it," she suggested, running her fingers over the stem of her wineglass.

"I'm no stranger to the kitchen . . . but it's not much fun eating alone." He paused for a disquieting moment, then asked, "What does a night owl do with her days?"

Arching her eyebrows, she said, "This one sleeps them away."

"And the evenings?"

She felt it again—that tantalizing ripple of pleasure that wove its way through her whenever Steve showed more than casual interest in their newfound friendship. To answer his question she said, "I'm not exactly a gadabout, but I'm not antisocial, by any means. With my hours, though, I can only party when I have a night off." Wondering if that sounded too much like an open invitation, she added quickly, "I have a friend, Debbie Weston, who works nights also. She's a pianist at a lounge on Clearwater Beach. We do a lot of things together."

Steve rested back in his chair, content to listen to Sharon's soft, soothing voice and to bask in the inner glow she exuded. It had been a long time, so very long, since he'd been able to enjoy the carefree, relaxing warmth of feminine companionship.

Yes, there were friends who'd tried to get him to socialize after his wife's death, and there were women he knew in the course of business, but barriers of his own making had kept him from sharing his personal self with them. Somehow with Sharon it was different. Because he had known her for such a short time, however, he didn't understand why she already affected him so deeply or why he felt so at ease with her, so at peace, so nourished by her nearness.

"What about you, Steve?" she asked. "When you're not trekking off to exotic jungles, do you explore Florida?"

"Not really," he said quietly. "My wife was a semi-invalid during the last years of our marriage. Laura died six months ago."

"I'm sorry," Sharon said sincerely, realizing that his brother's death had only added to a fairly recent loss. She did wonder what his wife's medical problem had been, but she wasn't about to pry.

"And you?" Steve asked, changing the subject. "Have you seen all there is to see?"

"The highlights, I suppose. Earlier this year Debbie and I spent a week in Key West, and I've been to St. Augustine and toured the Everglades."

"With Debbie, or is there someone special?"

Wondering if Steve could hear her heartbeat, she smiled at his blunt inquiry. "No one special at the moment," she replied softly.

He had done it again, she thought, deciding that with just a simple remark, he could give her the feeling that he was searching for an opening, a means through which he might become a part of her life. But how big a part, she wondered, and for how long?

Her silent question took on an import she couldn't dismiss. She was attracted to Steve and he seemed to be attracted to her, but she had the uncomfortable feeling he might be reaching out to her from a sense of gratitude or perhaps necessity. She wasn't sure. But maybe, she speculated, they were just two unattached people who happened to meet at the right time. Or maybe she was just making too much of his having asked her to dinner.

After their waitress served them, they started in on their prime rib dinners and Steve remarked offhandedly, "You could have been a model. What made you settle on nursing?"

Sharon smiled, bemused that he had a way of making her do that when she least expected it. "I haven't quite figured you out yet, Steve," she said with a teasing lilt in her tone. "Nordstrom sounds Scandinavian, but I have a feeling you've kissed the Blarney Stone."

"If I give that impression, the company is responsible."

Flustered by his elusive half smile, she immediately redirected her thoughts to his question. "As for nursing, I really started when I was about ten. My cousin David came to live with us...for family reasons, and when he was eight he was in a carnival accident. The ride he was on fell apart and left him crippled. His recuperation and physical therapy took several years. He walks with a slight limp now, but he's fine. He has a great wife and two healthy kids in Virginia."

"Good. I like happy endings." Steve paused to chew on a piece of prime rib, then asked, "How did Uncle Sam get hold of you—the snappy posters?"

"Necessity," she said, taking hold of her napkin and wiping her lips. "My family lived from paycheck to paycheck. One day a lovely lady army recruiter offered us nursing students a monthly check while we were still in school. I grabbed at it because it meant I wouldn't have to take out loans or get a night job to cover tuition and expenses. That captain was one smooth cookie. She had several of us thinking we were going to Hollywood, not the U.S. Army. She stated flatly that only volunteers were sent to Nam."

"Shafted you, huh?"

"Well, I did volunteer to go. At the time I thought I should back my country, right or wrong, but some nurses I worked with in Nam had no intention of being there."

Sharon's thoughts began to drift to that time long ago, but quickly she forced her attention back to the present. Smiling at Steve, she asked, "Do you miss the change of seasons you had in Wisconsin? Down here summer seems to last all year long."

"Originally Laura and I relocated here for just that reason, but I'm not moving back north," he said, hoping Sharon cared one way or the other. Then he decided his reasoning was ridiculous. Why would she care? They barely knew each other. Yet he did want her to be glad he hadn't packed up and returned to Madison now that his wife was gone.

Out of the blue, memories of Laura suddenly tumbled into his mind, charging his brain with sudden pricks of guilt for wanting to be happy again, for wanting to reach out to the desirable woman sitting across from him, for wanting her to want him.

"Florida's a lot like California," Sharon said matter-of-factly, putting her fork down on her plate, "better in some ways, though. The West Coast can be cold and damp."

Pulled from his preoccupation, Steve looked up and smiled. "Are your parents still in California?"

"Yes, but Debbie settled here, so I decided to, as well. I like palm trees and beaches. Coming here I could still enjoy both."

"Then I can assume you're not planning to leave Florida anytime soon, either."

"At least not until I've had dessert," she said, matching his smile.

"I recommend the baklava."

"Calorie city," she said, frowning, "but you're tempting me."

"Let's be wicked. After dinner we can walk off the calories in the park across the road."

While Steve ordered coffee and the rich flaky pastry smothered with nuts and honey, Sharon could almost feel the invisible strands of friendship that his presence was weaving around her, drawing her closer to him. He was so comfortable to be with and so easy to talk to. Perhaps too much so, she warned herself, wondering if she would ever see him again once the evening was over.

After they left the restaurant, Steve drove out of the parking lot and headed east a short ways, then crossed Park Boulevard and pulled into Seminole Park, a recreational area that skirted the south side of a lake.

As they strolled under a canopy of oaks toward the palm-lined water, he said, "This was one of my brother's favorite places. He used to bike through here several times a week."

"I've driven by hundreds of times," Sharon admitted, her eyes wandering over the idyllic setting, "but I've never stopped. It is peaceful here."

"Richie used this place as a mental and physical energizer, claimed that it helped him forget the craziness of his job." Glancing at Sharon, Steve explained, "He was an investigative reporter for the *Times*. Before that he worked for a newspaper in Madison. He was always researching stories on some kind of corruption or scam." Steve chuckled and shook his head. "I think he saw himself as part journalist, part detective." After a pause, his expression turned somber. "Only yesterday afternoon we had an argument about his work."

Sharon didn't interrupt Steve's monologue, deciding it was better to let him talk out his feelings, to express whatever was bothering him.

When they reached the water's edge, he looked out over the lake and thrust his hands into his trouser pockets. "The argument we had was so stupid. His computer was in the shop, so he asked to use mine at the office. Then he accidentally erased some business records I'd spent a week inputting." His jaw set, Steve narrowed his eyes. "I flew off the handle. Now it's all so damn unimportant, but it's too late to take back the dressing-down I gave him."

Taking hold of Steve's arm, Sharon said, "Don't blame yourself for that. You had no way of knowing what would happen."

"No, we never do, do we?" he said, his voice low.

For a few silent moments Sharon's hand remained on his arm. Then she withdrew it and moved to a nearby bench. Placing her hands on the back of it, she gazed at the colorful sails on the boats skimming over the lake, the early-evening silence broken only by muted sounds of throaty tree frogs and clicking crickets.

Steve moved closer, rested against the bench and crossed his arms. As he studied the way the ebbing rays of the sun washed over her lovely features, he tried to understand why he was so strongly drawn to her. The sensation was immensely exciting, but at the same time it was alarming. Why should he expect her to invite him into her private life? Why should she care that he felt empty, that he was desperate for a woman's loving kindness? What if he offered friendship and she rejected him? But she hadn't—so far.

Tilting his head back, he glanced up at the leaves rustled by a gentle breeze. The sweet scent of jasmine drew his attention to a nearby pine tree, where the white blossoms curled around and up the slender trunk. He looked back at Sharon and was about to comment on the weather, but a sudden constriction tightened his chest, and he realized he didn't want to talk about the climate or other incidental things; he wanted to know more about her. Charging ahead, he asked, "Do you ever miss California?"

"No," she said without hesitation. "I've made good friends here."

He recalled she had mentioned that there was no special man in her life, but he needed to make sure.

"Good friends other than Debbie?" he probed, hoping his inquiry would sound conversational.

"As in a man?" she asked, her tone nonchalant.

"When a woman's as attractive as you are, there's usually a man somewhere."

"There was, and there was a divorce...years ago in California." Wanting to change the topic, Sharon tilted her head toward him and said lightly, "We're being awfully serious for a first date."

Impulsively he took hold of her hand. "Is that what we're having?" When Sharon started to draw her hand back, he firmed his grasp on it. "A date is exactly what we're having," he said, easing his thumb over her soft skin. "If you're enjoying it half as much as I am, we could do this again. How does a tour of my greenhouses and a home-cooked dinner sound?"

His warm gentle pressure on her hand and his admission sent another comforting wave of intimacy spiraling through her, a sensation that made her feel giddy. Her unexpected excitement gave way to a stronger feeling of vulnerability, however. She had just met Steve Nordstrom, and she knew instinctively that he would be an easy man to like, perhaps too much, too soon.

Seeing that she was hesitating, he offered her an easygoing smile. "I don't have any etchings to show you, honest...just orchids and a square meal."

"What more could an off-duty nurse ask for?" Sharon said, then felt his hand squeeze hers.

"Good. I'll phone you as soon as I get back from Madison." His eyes settled on her lips, and the agonizing craving for intimacy that he had been living with for so long gripped him like a steel vice. He wanted to take hold of her, crush her in his arms and kiss her long and deeply. A little presumptuous, Nordstrom, he warned.

Fighting the powerful impulse to take her into his arms, he tore his eyes from hers. "We'd better leave," he said huskily. "They'll be closing the park soon."

"Yes," she agreed softly, her pulse racing.

Hand in hand they retraced their steps to his car and he drove her home, neither of them feeling the need to make conversation.

The instant she was alone in her apartment, Sharon realized that, in spite of having had less than four hours' sleep, she was feeling wonderful, light-headed even. Of all the men she had dated since her divorce fourteen years ago, not one of them had affected her the way Steve had.

Not for an instant had she felt she might become involved in a wrestling match after their dinner date, nor had he come up with the "women don't usually understand me" routine she'd heard so often. No, Steve was every inch a gentleman, kind and sensitive. Her eyes fell on the exquisite plant he had given her. He was so thoughtful, too.

As she sat on the sofa, admiring the lovely blooms, her euphoria dissipated when she remembered the reason for the gift: his brother. She slumped back, reproaching herself for having asked Tony to analyze the man's blood. What would Steve think if he learned what she'd done? What had possessed her! Richard Nordstrom went into cardiac arrest. That was it and nothing more.

Well, she determined, heading for the bedroom to get some rest before going on duty, in the morning she would talk to Tony and tell him to forget the whole thing. She hadn't reached the bedroom door when the phone rang.

"Where've you been all evening?" Tony asked. "I stayed after work to analyze Nordstrom's blood."

"Tony, I don't—"

"You were right, Sharon," he interrupted. "Something is very wrong. The guy had enough narcotics in his system to stop an elephant's heart."

Sharon's grip on the receiver firmed until her knuckles whitened. Forcing the words out, she asked, "Can you tell which narcotic?"

"I've double-checked. It's morphine."

"Morphine! But . . . but that was ordered. I gave him the injection."

"No sane doctor would prescribe that much," he said anxiously. "Sharon, I wanted you to know first, but . . . well, damn it, you know I've got to report what I found. There'll be a medical inquiry and probably an autopsy."

"Yes," she whispered, "I know. Thanks, Tony. I'll talk to you tomorrow."

Dazed, she replaced the receiver and sank into the chair next to the phone, her mind's eye seeing the indicators on the syringe before she had injected Steve's brother. The amount of painkiller Dr. Wilson had ordered was normal in Richard Nordstrom's case. She had checked the dosage carefully, as she did routinely. She was positive she hadn't made a mistake!

Mentally reviewing her patient's chart, she knew her memory was correct. He'd been given sixteen milligrams of morphine shortly after 10:00 p.m. when he was still in Emergency. It was almost six hours later when she had given him a second injection. Considering his general physical condition and the time span, the ten milligrams of morphine she had administered couldn't have caused cardiac arrest, certainly not an hour later.

But what would Steve think?

An icy chill tore down her spine, causing her to shudder. What else could he think other than that she had made some kind of mistake—and had caused his brother's death!

Standing, she paced nervously. Then her eyes darted to the phone. Should she call Steve? And say what? *Oh, by the way, your brother's heart attack was probably brought on by an overdose of morphine. I gave him his last injection. I thought you might want to cancel dinner plans.*

For all her glibness Sharon had to fight back the tears that stung her eyelids. She had worked so hard to resume her nursing career five years ago, first as a private-duty nurse and then at the hospital. Now the prospect of serious trouble loomed ahead of her again. Life wasn't fair, she thought, slumping onto the sofa and deciding that some power seemed to have singled her out for special treatment.

AS INSTRUCTED by her chief nurse, a little after four o'clock the next day, Sharon sat rigidly at the oval table in Dr. Samuel Benning's conference room. Second by second she became more tense as the chief of staff announced that after receiving the results of Richard Nordstrom's autopsy, he had felt compelled to notify the police. Sharon had come prepared to face questions from a medical board of inquiry, but not from the craggy-faced homicide detective who sat at the far end of the table.

Her head swung toward the door when it opened and Steve entered. As he sat directly across from her, his tormented eyes held hers for an excruciatingly long moment. Then he faced the balding red-haired detective.

Sharon tried to listen as Detective Al Werner questioned personnel who had attended to Richard Nordstrom. But as the staff members answered his inquiries, she couldn't ignore Steve's mounting distress. It was obvious in the tenseness of his jaw and the cold stare in his eyes as he scrutinized each person the detective questioned.

Checking a paper that lay on the table in front of him, Werner said, "Sharon McClure?"

Steve's alert eyes focused directly on hers.

"Yes," she answered, her response steady but spoken softly.

Werner assessed her for a moment, then asked, "You were the head nurse on ICU when Richard Nordstrom had his heart attack, correct?"

"Yes," she replied again, her voice sounding like an echo to her. "I personally supervised his nursing care when he was brought to ICU from post-op."

Werner glanced at Louella, who sat next to him. Then he looked down at the papers in front of him. "The patient's records indicate you checked on him at 4:50 a.m."

"I did. At that time he was stable and showed no signs of respiratory depression."

"And his heart attack occurred about ten minutes later. Where were you then?"

Moving uneasily in her chair, Sharon's eyes flicked toward Steve, then back to the detective. "I was in the nurses' station, preparing medications for the unit. As soon as Mr. Nordstrom's monitor indicated problems, I instructed Dave Schaeffer to call the code. Immediately I initiated CPR, and Dave assisted with chest compressions until the cardiac arrest team arrived."

Werner nodded slowly, then asked, "Did any of the other nurses on duty give medication to Mr. Nordstrom?"

"No, he was totally in my care."

"And," Werner continued, "earlier you had given Richard Nordstrom an injection of morphine."

"Yes, ten milligrams at 4:00 a.m. The patient was experiencing pain." Sharon glanced at Steve, remembering that she had assured him his brother hadn't suffered. She wasn't certain how to read Steve's expression. Confusion was there, but something else was also. Disbelief perhaps. Or was it condemnation?

"Only the one injection?" Werner asked.

Calmly Sharon answered, "Yes, I only gave him one, just as I charted. He'd also received a previous injection six hours earlier before coming on to my unit."

"Was anyone on the ward that night, anyone who usually wouldn't have been?"

"We were short one nurse for a while, and several nurses from other wards spent some time in the unit. Transport workers brought in a patient and transferred one to another ward." Sharon thought momentarily. "There were several visitors, relatives."

Her eyes swept to Steve and she flinched, now deciding that it was accusation she saw in his face. Her attention swung back to Detective Werner when he asked, "But you saw no one who shouldn't have been there, no one who—"

He cut himself off to take a written phone message from Rachel, the chief of staff's secretary. Sharon couldn't understand why the woman, whom she counted as a casual friend, looked at her so oddly.

The homicide detective scanned the message, glanced at Sharon, then asked Rachel, "Who phoned this in?"

Sharon barely made out the woman's whispered response when she told the detective that the man refused to give his name.

Werner tapped a thumb against the message before putting it down on top of other papers on the table. For seconds he massaged his double chin thoughtfully as he studied Sharon intently. Then he clasped his hands together and fixed his pale green eyes directly on her. "I was told earlier that you're one of the most dedicated nurses in this hospital, Miss McClure. I imagine it's difficult beyond belief to see people in pain day after day, or in your case night after night."

"It is difficult," Sharon replied, her words little more than a whisper.

He took a moment to reread the telephone message before saying, "You were an army nurse in Vietnam. Is that correct?"

Sharon fought hard to dislodge the lump in her throat that nearly choked her. All she could do was nod, but tilting her head slightly she saw that Steve's eyes were riveted on her.

"You had to treat many wounded soldiers who were in a great deal of pain, didn't you?" Werner asked, his words measured, his voice low, almost raspy.

Again Sharon could only nod, feeling the knot in her stomach tighten until it ached. She knew beyond any doubt what was coming next.

The detective read the message for the third time. "Is it true, Miss McClure, that while you were a nurse in Vietnam you gave a hospitalized soldier an overdose of morphine?"

She gripped the edge of the table with trembling fingers. Slowly, as though in a trance, she lifted herself from the chair. Her entire body was quivering, her alarmed eyes swept to Clara Riley, her chief nurse, the only person at the hospital in whom she had confided that information.

"Is it true?" Werner asked again.

Sharon's burning eyes drifted to Steve, who rose from his chair, waiting anxiously for her to answer. His shocked gaze held hers as tightly as a clenched fist. Her head pounding, she forced out her response.

"Yes," she admitted in a tortured whisper.

CHAPTER FOUR

MURMURS OF SURPRISE punctuated by startled gasps echoed throughout the conference room as Sharon stared at the shocked look on Steve's face. Almost immediately, though, his stunned expression gave way to a cold glare, and he slumped back onto his chair. An almost palpable pain wrenched Sharon's heart when what she had dreaded became a reality: Steve suspected her of having killed his brother.

"Miss McClure," Detective Werner said firmly, "please sit down."

She did, her head pivoting toward his end of the table, in time to see the chief of staff whispering in Clara Riley's ear. Commanding her voice to be steady, Sharon looked directly at the detective. "The case you're referring to in Vietnam was totally different from Richard Nordstrom's. There was every reason to believe Mr. Nordstrom would recover. Aside from that—" her eyes lowered to the hospital records in front of Werner "—as I charted, I gave him one ten-milligram injection of morphine, and one only. If he—"

"Yes, yes," Werner said abruptly, "his file indicates that, but the autopsy tells us something else." He leaned back in his chair and assessed her for long, nerve-racking moments. "Somebody gave him an overdose. Who did it and whether it was done accidentally are what we'll have to find out."

Nervously Dr. Benning asked him, "Must the press know you're investigating? We've never had anything like this happen here. It could cause a decrease in the financial gifts and endowments we receive."

The detective's eyes swept over the whispering staff members in the room. Then he glanced at the anonymous telephone message he had received. Facing the chief of staff he advised, "The press is going to find out one way or the other. You'd be wise to announce the investigation yourself."

Benning nodded anxiously. "Yes, I guess you're right." Looking over at Sharon, he said, "Miss McClure, pending the outcome of the police investigation, I've no choice but to suspend you from duty."

Dr. Wilson saw the shocked look on Sharon's face and jumped up. "Is that necessary, Sam? Nobody in this room believes Sharon would have deliberately given her patient an overdose, and she's too excellent a nurse to have done it accidentally."

The majority of staff members voiced their agreement, but Dr. Benning, Clara Riley and Louella, the three people from whom Sharon wanted an expression of confidence, remained notably silent.

Werner gathered the files from the table and stood. "No charges are being brought against anyone at this time," he announced, "but each of you will be called to the station to give a formal statement." Of Dr. Benning, he asked, "Could we go to your office and work up a schedule?"

"Certainly," he replied, casting Sharon a furtive glance as he rose from his seat.

When the staff members began filing out of the conference room, Sharon's eyes met Clara's, and she stood, reaching the chief nurse before she could depart the room.

"Mrs. Riley," she said, her voice low, "when I told you of the incident in Vietnam, it was in confidence. I didn't expect you to use it against me like this."

"I didn't," Clara insisted forcefully, then followed Dr. Benning into his office.

From the doorway Detective Werner overheard the brief exchange. He crossed back to Sharon, inspecting her reaction as he said, "The phone message I received was called in by a man. Any idea who might want me to have this information?"

"No," she answered, her heart sinking even more.

"Whoever he is, he doesn't like you," Werner said, then entered Dr. Benning's office.

Her head throbbing, Sharon leaned a shoulder against the wall, trying to regain her composure. After taking several deep breaths, she turned and saw that Steve had remained behind, his questioning eyes hard on hers.

After moistening her lower lip, she slowly retraced her steps to where she had been sitting and picked up her purse. She tried to appreciate how he felt, but she was sorely confused herself. As Detective Werner had said, somebody had given Richard Nordstrom the overdose. But she knew that someone hadn't been her. Why couldn't Steve give her the benefit of the doubt? Why did he seem so ready to accept that she was the one who had made the mistake?

She forced her weary eyes to meet his unflinching ones. "Steve," she said quietly, "I know what you must think, but believe me, I gave your brother the best nursing care possible."

Still shaken by Richie's death and jolted by what he had just learned at the inquiry, Steve clasped his hands tightly on the table and began rubbing them. Averting her gaze, he said darkly, "I don't know what to believe. All I know is that my brother's dead—" his accusing eyes flicked up at her "—and someone's responsible."

"And you actually think I am? I'm a nurse, for God's sake. I spend my life trying to save people."

"Like that soldier in the hospital in Vietnam?"

Steve's condemning words cut through her heart like a scalpel, and she almost flinched from the pain. "That's cruel, Steve," she moaned. "The situation in Vietnam was totally different. You'd understand if you'd let me explain why I—"

In one quick motion he shoved himself up from behind the table. "The only thing I understand is that Richie is dead. Nothing you can say is going to change that. I phoned my parents yesterday to tell them. They're inconsolable now. How do I explain that their son's death was just someone's mistake?"

"Steve, if you'd give me a chance to—"

"A chance?" he repeated, his throat thickening, the wrenching in his stomach almost a pain. "Like you gave Richie?"

Feeling as though Steve had struck her, Sharon grasped the back of the chair for support as he rushed from the conference room.

FROM THE CURVED BAR in her condo on Clearwater Beach, Debbie glanced over at Sharon, who stood by the open glass door to the balcony, staring out blankly. "Sure I can't fix you something?"

"Uh-uh," Sharon replied dispiritedly. "I'm depressed enough as it is."

Debbie chuckled as she poured herself a Scotch on the rocks. "Must be the difference in our metabolism. A drink perks me up."

"At first maybe," Sharon said, casting her longtime friend a concerned look.

She had met Debbie Weston almost twenty years ago in Vietnam at the Seventy-first Evacuation Hospital in Pleiku when Debbie worked for the Red Cross's Supplemental Recreational Activities Overseas program. Now, at forty, Debbie was still a knockout. Her long, wavy hair glistened with a natural flaxen sheen. Her hazel eyes—at least before the cocktail hour—sparkled clear and alluringly. But if her physical appearance hadn't changed much, Debbie had.

Born into a sheep-ranching family in San Angelo, Texas, she had been raised by strict fundamentalist parents, who thought it wonderful when she went to work for the Red Cross. They were less pleased when Debbie volunteered to go to Vietnam as a "chopper chick," as the workers were called.

She arrived there an enthusiastic, naive young woman, intent on bringing some moments of joy to wounded soldiers by singing while she played a piano or accompanied herself on a guitar. She left Vietnam after a year, no longer enthusiastic, no longer naive, and she never returned home to Texas.

But she still entertained. Debbie Weston's glamorous picture had been posted outside the best cocktail lounges in San Francisco, Reno, Denver, Chicago, New Orleans and finally on Florida's Suncoast. She had a smooth touch on the piano, and she sang and smiled her way across the country, leaving behind a trail of broken hearts and her own shattered dreams.

"What you need," Debbie suggested, joining Sharon, "is a gorgeous man to get your mind off the damn hospital."

Stepping onto the tenth-floor balcony, Sharon stood at the railing and gazed out at the gold and red purple sunset mirrored in the immense swath of the Gulf of Mexico, feeling the late October evening breeze, still warm and humid, wafting over her face. Half turning, she smiled at Debbie. "A gorgeous man, huh? That's the advice I get from someone who preaches that she travels fastest who travels alone?"

Barefoot and clad in white shorts and an oversize Beethoven sweatshirt, Debbie stretched out on one of the two yellow lounge chairs and raised her glass. "Men are good for two things, for dancing—" mischief snapped in her lively eyes "—and to make you forget everyday problems."

"My problem at the hospital can't quite be categorized as an everyday concern. I could lose my nursing license and maybe even face criminal charges."

"That's ridiculous. They're investigating, aren't they? So this hotshot detective will find out what happened, and that will be that."

"I'm not too sure just how hard he's going to look," Sharon said, crossing her arms. "I've got the disconcerting feeling that he thinks he has all the answers now, thanks to that anonymous phone message he got at the inquiry."

"What ever possessed you to tell Clara Riley about what you did in Vietnam?"

"When she interviewed me for the job, I had to explain my five years away from nursing. What was I supposed to tell her—that I finally gave in to my mad desire to work for an insurance company? I told her the truth, that I'd had some problems after Nam. She was a navy nurse there, and we talked about it. God knows I wasn't the only nurse or doctor who made a dying soldier's last hours less painful." Sharon glanced down at the pool below and shrugged. "I don't know why I told her about that one incident. It's preyed on my mind for so many years, maybe I just had to tell someone."

"Obviously the phone message didn't come from anyone in the conference room."

Sharon's brow furrowed as she faced Debbie. "Clara could have had someone else call it in, but I don't understand why she would have. We've always had an excellent working relationship. Why would she dump on me all of a sudden?"

"'Tis a puzzlement." After a swallow of her drink, Debbie set the glass down on a little wicker table. "Maybe the morphine you gave him was bad or something."

"Now don't you start!" Sharon said briskly. "I need someone to believe and trust in me."

"I'm just trying to shed light on the mystery."

"It's no big mystery to me. If I had made a mistake and given Richard Nordstrom as much morphine as the autopsy indicated, in minutes he would have gone into respiratory depression, hypotension and severe nausea." She shook her head. "No. However he got the morphine, it had to be shortly before his monitor signaled trouble, and that's what I'll tell Detective Werner when I'm called to the station." She braced her hands on the railing and leaned back. "I wish I'd had the presence of mind to tell him that at the inquiry, but I was so rattled by Steve being there."

"Who's Steve?"

Sharon chuckled dryly and sat sideways on the lounge across from Debbie. "He's the gorgeous man you're telling me I need right now."

"Aha, the plot thickens," Debbie said, her eyes flashing. "How gorgeous? And is he single?"

"Very and yes, but his name's also Nordstrom. He's convinced I'm responsible for his brother's death."

"Hmm. That could put a damper on a relationship, I suppose."

"A damper? I shiver when I think of the look he gave me just before he charged out of the conference room."

"Bring me up-to-date. You just met this Steve, right?"

"He came by the apartment yesterday with an orchid plant and took me to dinner."

"Orchids...dinner? You must have made one hell of a first impression."

"He was just showing his appreciation for the care he *then* thought I'd given his brother. Right now I wouldn't be surprised if he's broken into my apartment to retrieve his plant."

"Give him time to work things out. Maybe he's not as upset as you think."

"He's that upset, trust me."

"It's possible he only—"

"Please," Sharon begged, "let's talk about something else—like you and Tony. Are you going to set up household together?"

Debbie drew her legs up and hugged her knees. "No, I'm happy just the way things are—uncomplicated."

"And uncommitted," Sharon added.

"That's the pot calling the kettle black, isn't it?"

"If the right man comes along, I'll give marriage another try. As far as Tony goes, though, you're not going to find a more Mr. Right. He's crazy about you, and he's a nice guy."

"Too nice to get too involved with me."

"Oh, knock it off. You make yourself out to be the fallenest of fallen women."

Tilting her head toward Sharon, Debbie grinned. "Let's face it. There can't be winners without losers, and I'm a loser. But look at it this way. I make it possible for some other woman to have a winner's slot in life. Tony will make some lucky lady a dream of a husband."

"If you'd slow down and concentrate on him, you could fill that slot."

"Get off my case, friend. I haven't exactly toured the country on my back, and Tony's the only man I'm dating now. But he deserves better than me. I'm not about to saddle him with my problems."

"Shouldn't he decide that?"

"No. Mr. Noble would take on the challenge willingly, but how long do you think he'd be able to take my occasional benders and my screaming nightmares?"

"I think you're underestimating him, Debbie."

She chuckled halfheartedly. "I think you're overestimating me." Her smile evaporated and she leaned back in the lounge chair. "Look, I don't need the pressure of having a man rely on me. I've been doing pretty good lately. Maybe it's because of Tony, and maybe it's not. But there's still something eating at me inside, something that makes me feel like a machine, not a woman."

Placing a gentle hand over Debbie's, Sharon said softly, "You still haven't gotten over Vietnam."

"Have you?"

"No, but I've learned to cope with the memories."

"The memories," Debbie repeated grimly. "I never believed in that stupid war. I believed in the guys in the hospitals. I wish to hell I could forget the ones who died, but I keep thinking that if I don't remember them, they'll be gone forever, just as if they never existed."

Sharon knew it wouldn't help to push her friend right now. After Vietnam she had never had a problem with alcohol the way Debbie did, but Sharon had gone through other symptoms of PTSD. Many of the women who had served in Vietnam still were. Not least among the symptoms was the difficulty they experienced in forming lasting intimate relationships. Why some women were affected and others weren't, just like the men who served there, was yet to be clearly understood, Sharon knew. But in a way she always thought that coping with PTSD was more difficult for the women because war was supposed to be men's business, and in the aftermath, it was supposedly the men who suffered, not the women.

Moving to Debbie's lounge, Sharon gave her a little nudge on the arm. "Your listening to my problems at the hospital is good for a dinner at Red Lobster."

"You buying?"

"If you leave the tip."

"You're on."

On Friday morning Steve was in one of his six greenhouses, potting the last of the phalaenopsis orchid seedlings that had arrived from Thailand. Listening to a tape of Elvis Presley songs, he hummed along with "Are You Lonesome Tonight?" as he firmed pine bark over the roots of the seedling. Suddenly he reached over and struck the stop button, muttering, "Yes, damn it, I am lonesome."

He added more bark, then set the plant with the others he had potted, thinking of Sharon again. No matter how he tried he couldn't get her out of his thoughts. But what a confusing mixture they were. His mind reeled with recollections of a sympathetic nurse in white, a desirable woman standing by a palm tree on the edge of Lake Seminole and the tense woman he had seen at the inquiry—the one who might have killed his younger brother.

After screwing a nozzle onto a water hose, he began misting the leaves of the blooming orchids on the tiered shelves on the other side of the greenhouse, smirking at himself for having thought Sharon might be the woman who could pull him from his loneliness.

He'd been surprised when she agreed to have dinner with him. Surprised, yes, but then nervous. A woman like her, he'd told himself, could have her pick of dinner dates. At first he thought she had accepted to be kind and sympathetic, but during dinner and the talk they'd had in the park, he believed she had been enjoying his company. After he took her home, all he could think about was seeing her again. The next day the phone call came from the chief of staff's office, advising him of the inquiry.

The inquiry. Detective Werner had all but accused Sharon of giving Richie an overdose of morphine. Accidentally would have been bad enough, but she had done it before purposely to some soldier in Vietnam for whatever reason. But would any reason be good enough to snuff out a life? And why would she have done it to Richie? Everyone seemed to agree that he was going to survive the accident.

He switched off the water and told himself for the hundredth time, *Innocent until proven guilty.* Except that was a hard idea to swallow. Maybe he wasn't being objective enough, but how could he be? It was his brother who was dead.

His tormented eyes swept to the phone on the wall over the potting bench, and he decided he couldn't live with his ambivalent attitude toward Sharon any longer. He rushed to the phone, grabbed it, then froze.

What would he say? *Just wanted to remind you about our date when I get back from Madison.* Or, *how's your conscience and how have you been sleeping lately?*

"Damn!" he muttered, slamming the receiver back onto the wall cradle. *Why would she even want to talk to me after the way I treated her yesterday? Wait a minute,* he told himself. *First you better figure out why you'd want to talk to her.*

But in his heart he knew why. His brain was telling him he should hate her for what he'd learned at the inquiry, yet his heart pleaded for him to be cautious in condemning her, regardless of how guilty she appeared to be. Uncertainty took hold of him once more, and he threw himself back into his work.

He had just begun mixing fir-bark mulch with sphagnum peat for several green Lady Slipper orchids he planned to divide, when from the corner of his eye he spotted a figure at the greenhouse door. Turning, his heart lurched when he saw Sharon standing there, a hesitant smile on her face.

"Hello," she said quietly. "The man in the next greenhouse told me you were in here. I hope I'm not interrupting your work."

"Uh...no, no," he said wiping his hands on a towel, his brain declaring war against his heart again.

Deciding he wasn't going to throw anything at her, Sharon took a cautious step onto the mulch-covered floor and glanced around the long greenhouse with its double side shelves of orchid plants, then at the angled glass roof and glass walls that were dotted with drops of moisture.

"Air-conditioning?" she asked, surprised by the sudden feel of cool air wafting over her face.

"Uh-uh," he answered, still coping with her sudden appearance. His eyes riveted on her, he nodded toward the four-foot built-in fan at the end of the building. "Water drips in front of the blades and keeps it humid and cool in here."

"I had no idea your greenhouses would be this big."

"They're twenty-by-forty feet," he said as he assessed the aqua suit and white blouse she wore.

Sharon wondered if Steve could tell how uncomfortable she felt at showing up unexpectedly. But after a long, sleepless night, she'd decided she had to see him again, to make him understand that she would never have done anything to hurt his brother. Giving herself time to compose herself, she again examined the tiered shelves of healthy green orchid plants, many with blooms of extraordinary beauty.

The cattleya flowers, the ones she had seen used in corsages, presented a rainbow of vibrant colors. Other blooms, some small, some gigantic, she found breathtaking in their exotic shapes and brilliancy. The petals of some flowers spiraled, twisting in foot-long tendrils, others looked like graceful butterflies. One, that she wouldn't have guessed was an orchid, looked more like a white camellia with a tiny white dove perched at its center.

"They're breathtaking," she complimented Steve. "And such exquisite colors." She moved closer to one hanging plant that was almost two feet wide with hundreds of small pale lavender blooms flowing from it like a static fountain. "Is this an orchid?" she asked.

"Yes," he said, not taking his eyes from her. "It's a dendrobium that was awarded a First Class Certificate at the American Orchid Society this year."

He could see the tenseness in her eyes and understood then that it wasn't easy for her to see him face-to-face. He wondered why she had decided to.

After admiring the plant, she glanced at him briefly. "I know I'm a few days early for the tour you suggested, but...well, I'm a lady of leisure now. I hope you don't mind my stopping by."

When he didn't respond, she turned toward him. "I wouldn't blame you if you did, though. I know how things must look to you."

Leaning back against a metal shelf, Steve crossed his tanned muscular arms over his sleeveless gray sweatshirt and fixed his eyes on hers. "I'd be lying if I said I wasn't surprised to see you."

"I appreciate your honesty," she said, lowering her gaze. "Yesterday you didn't give me a chance to tell you my side of the story."

"That would be interesting," he said flatly, immediately regretting his curt tone.

Her eyes flicked up to meet his. "And it would be the truth," she insisted. Her head swung toward the entrance to the greenhouse when a man in jeans knocked on the open door.

"Your father's on the phone," he said. "Do you want to take it out here?"

Steve gave Sharon a concerned look, then answered, "No, Ed, I'll get it in the office." He took hold of her arm and unceremoniously led her from the greenhouse. Outside he gestured toward the rear of the two-story brick house. "There's a patio in the back. Make yourself comfortable and I'll be with you in a few minutes."

More unnerved by the second, Sharon said, "Maybe my coming here was a bad idea."

"Not at all," he said crisply. "I'm anxious to hear your side of the story. I won't be long." He gave her arm a little push toward the rear of the house to let her know he meant what he had said. Then he went into the office to speak with his father.

As Sharon trudged toward the patio, she bolstered her courage by telling herself that she disliked being ordered around. But she was the one who had descended on Steve, not the other way around. And why shouldn't he be a little leery of her, considering the scenario at the inquiry?

Turning the corner of the house, she stepped up onto the redwood floor of the sprawling patio that was rimmed by a white wrought-iron railing. Long redwood beams, entwined with brilliant red bougainvillea and yellow allamanda, extended from the house, lending partial shade from the strong Florida sunlight. Two umbrellaed tables, also white wrought iron with matching cushioned chairs, rested under the shaded portion of the deck. Placing her purse on one of the tables, she walked into the sunlight and gazed out over the free-form pool edged with Chinese fan-palm trees. Her eyes drifted over the lovely garden area strewn with multicolored azalea, rounded hawthorn bushes and trellises of red honeysuckle vines. Near a clump of orange-flowered oleander bushes a family of red cardinals splashed playfully in a terra-cotta birdbath.

She glanced back at the well-kept house and decided that the orchid business must be fairly good. Suspended without pay, she again bemoaned the injustice of it all, but she was troubled by more than that. Steve troubled her.

The man had every right to be hostile, she reminded herself, turning away again toward the garden area and surveying the tall pine trees in the background that assured privacy. His caustic attitude, though, hurt deeply, more so because she liked him. She had decided that when she first met him at the hospital. She'd even allowed herself to imagine that they might become good friends, particularly after the evening they had spent together.

Tilting her head up, she felt the warm sun on her face and recalled the warmth of Steve's hand when she'd held it in the park. Yes, she was definitely attracted to him, and even if he never wanted to see her again, he was going to listen to her if she had to sit on him.

She heard a noise and turned toward the house in time to see louvered shutters being drawn open and Steve placing a tray on a narrow counter. He disappeared and Sharon took note of the ice bucket, bottle of bourbon and two glasses on the tray. Seconds later he slid open a glass door, carried the tray to one of the tables and began mixing two drinks. When she joined him, he handed her one of the glasses.

"No, thank you," she said, thinking him rather presumptuous. "It's a little early for me."

"I suggest you have it," he advised, "and you might want to sit down."

Although annoyed by the tone of his voice and the taut expression on his face, Sharon once more found herself following his thinly veiled command. Taking the offered glass, she placed it on the table, sat down and waited for him to speak.

After a long swallow of his drink, Steve turned the chair on the other side of the table around and straddled it. His arms crossed over the back of the chair, he said evenly, "I'm ready to hear your side of the story."

"You seem to admire honesty, Steve," she said, her chin raised slightly, "so I'll be honest. I don't at all appreciate your setting yourself up as judge and jury."

His eyes narrowed. "All I have to go on so far is your admission of what you did as a nurse in Vietnam."

She could almost feel Steve's sharp, accusatory glare. Averting his eyes, she took a sip from her drink, then set it back down. "Were you in the service, Steve?"

"Yes."

"Did you see any combat?"

"No. When I was eighteen, before they could draft me into the army, I enlisted in the air force. I could type, so I wound up as a morning-report clerk at Harlingen Air Force Base in Texas."

"You were luckier than the young men I knew when I was in Vietnam."

Wondering if he was supposed to feel guilty for not having been in combat, he said somewhat tersely, "I can imagine how rough it was for you and everyone else who was over there."

Quietly she asked, "How could you possibly imagine what it was like? You weren't . . . over there."

"I didn't head for Canada, either. Does that get me any points?"

Absently her fingers crumpled the linen napkin Steve had placed by her glass. Her expression vacant, she said softly, "I wish every soldier we operated on in Vietnam had gone to Canada."

Darkly pensive, she paused briefly before saying, "I got used to the horrible sounds of men in pain and of nurses and doctors shouting over the grating noise of helicopter rotors, but I never got used to young men crying or to the throbbing inside my head. Maybe I just didn't work too well under pressure. Maybe I saw too much of dying and death and had to clean too much blood from under my fingernails. Maybe I just wasn't brave enough or tough enough."

Deeply struck by the agony in her voice, Steve reached over and covered her hand with his. "Maybe you have better qualities than bravery or toughness."

Her shimmering blue eyes rose to meet his. "Like what?"

"Like tenderness and caring."

His words were comforting, momentarily, but then she glanced down at his hand and withdrew hers. Slowly she stood, crossing her arms as her memory flashed awful images of endless hours in the chaotic nightmare of Vietnam. Staring ahead blankly, she said, "As a nurse, I thought death was the enemy, but in some cases—" Cutting herself off in midsentence, she slanted Steve a cool look. "Do you know what triage is?"

Quietly he said, "Deciding which of the wounded get care first."

Her lips formed a pained half smile. "It's more like playing God, only you have to live with deciding which of the wounded would be treated first, which ones could wait a little longer and which ones would probably die...the 'expectants' we called them. One night the choppers brought in mass cals—massive casualties. We'd just started to unload them when another wave of choppers came in with more...more and more expectants, men with horribly burned bodies that didn't even look human. So many others were missing arms and legs." She closed her eyes and shook her head. "They weren't like the amputees I had seen in hospitals here. Their missing parts weren't cleanly cut off and sterile."

As though agonizingly weary, Sharon looked over at Steve. "One of the soldiers was a corporal barely eighteen. His name was Edwards, and he had the biggest puppy-dog eyes. What was left of him was so terribly torn up, and he was so frightened. He squeezed my hand and begged me to help him."

Again she turned away, covering her eyes, trying to blot out the vivid mental picture of the young man's muddied tear-stained face. "He should have been placed with the expectants, but I got him into the operating room. It was a madhouse in there. The doctors took one look at him, said he wouldn't last the hour and ordered me to get him out. 'Please, ma'am, help me,' the boy begged. I knew his pain was horrible."

Slowly her hand slipped from her eyes and she stiffened. "I injected him with fifty milligrams of morphine and held his hand until he—"

Not knowing what to say to Sharon, Steve lowered his head. When he glanced back up and saw that she was trembling, he rose quickly, moved behind her and took hold of her shoulders. "I didn't mean to open up old wounds," he said softly. "When you tell Detective Werner what you just told me, I'm sure he'll—"

Sharon spun around, causing Steve's hands to fall from her shoulders. Her eyes flaring, she informed him, "I just spent two hours at police headquarters, giving a statement and being interrogated by him. He had the same sympathetic look on his face that you do now, but he made it clear that he had his job to do, and that was to find out who gave your brother the overdose." She picked up her purse and faced Steve again. "You still think I did, don't you?"

"Look," he said, raking his fingers through his hair, "right now I don't know what to think. Somehow, someone caused Richie's death."

"I didn't!" she shouted, tired of having to defend herself. "The young soldier in Vietnam was a terminal case. He was in excruciating pain and wouldn't have survived. Your brother's prognosis was good. I wish to God that I knew what happened to him, but I don't, and it's important to me that you believe that."

"I want to... in the worst way, but—"

"But you can't," she said quietly, then exhaled a long, painful sigh before starting toward the patio steps.

Catching up with her, Steve took hold of her arm. "Sharon, there's something I've got to tell you." She half turned and gave him a quizzical look. Hating what he was about to say, he rushed the words out. "My father plans to get a lawyer and... have him file charges of wrongful death against the hospital and you."

Sharon paled. "You agreed to that?"

"No, I told him to wait and see what the investigation came up with."

"To wait until you were sure that I wasn't a murderer, you mean."

She tugged free of his grasp and bounded for the steps, her vision blurred by incipient tears.

CHAPTER FIVE

GRINNING FROM EAR TO EAR, Tony applauded with the other lounge patrons after Debbie executed a rippling piano arpeggio, completing the last number before her break. His dark brown eyes drifted over the slinky mauve gown she wore, then settled on her lovely face, his heart swelling with pride.

Automatically a waiter placed a Scotch on the rocks on the small round table in front of the vacant chair across from Tony.

"Thanks, Sean," Debbie said, sitting down and taking a healthy swallow from her glass.

"It's a good crowd tonight," Tony remarked, observing that there wasn't an empty seat in the elegantly appointed room.

"Friday nights are always good," she said before sipping her drink again. "Two more sets and I'm out of here. I'm ready for it, too. I'm beat."

Sean placed another drink next to her glass, saying in his lilting Irish brogue, "From the gentleman over there, the one grinning from ear to ear." He nodded to her right, where a blond-haired man in a three-piece suit raised his glass.

Debbie pushed her half-finished drink away and lifted the other glass to acknowledge the gesture, causing Tony's eyes to darken even more.

"Fortunately," he said lightly, "unlike most Italians, I'm not the jealous type."

"A little jealousy can be very engaging in a man."

He flashed her one of his easy smiles. "All right, then, I'm so jealous that I wish you were a Muslim so you'd have to wear a veil."

She chuckled softly, her silky golden hair catching the soft light from the chandelier above. "When the male customers stop looking, I'll be out of a job."

His eyes swept briefly to the blond-haired man, who was still gawking at her. "If they don't stop looking, I'll go out of my mind."

Debbie didn't miss the anxiety in his voice. Reaching into her velvet evening bag, she withdrew a pack of cigarettes and lit one with the gold lighter Tony had given her on her fortieth birthday.

"You smoke too much."

"You nag too much," she replied, and blew a stream of blue haze out to the side.

"Only because I love you."

Not looking at him, she tapped the tip of her cigarette on the crystal ashtray. "When I was growing up in Texas, I used to believe everything anybody told me, but that was a long time ago."

"When I was growing up in Orlando, my mamma taught me not to lie, so you can believe me when I say I love you."

"Why?" she asked, smiling impishly. "Do I remind you of your mamma?"

"No. Because you're sassy, smart and sexy. I love those qualities in a woman."

She rested an elbow on the table and stared at the wisp of smoke coming from the cigarette. "There was a song I used to do in Nam, Tony." Softly she sang,

"Don't let the stars get in your eyes. Don't let the moon break your heart. Love comes at night, by daylight it dies..." Her words trailed off. "It went something like that. The guys really loved it."

"I don't want to talk about the guys back then. I want to talk about us here in the present."

She glanced at her watch, then placed a gentle hand over his. "It's almost midnight, and you've been working all day. Why don't you go to my place and get some sleep?"

"I can sleep in, in the morning." He emptied his glass and signaled Sean to bring him another. "My sleeping arrangements are something else we need to talk about. It's a crazy way for us to live, my spending some nights at your place and some in my apartment. I'm never sure where home is. With my working days and your working nights, we hardly spend any waking time together."

"From nine to five there's not a big demand for what I do." In jest she suggested, "You could get a night job at the hospital."

Not amused, he said, "Advancement in my field comes to day employees. Look, Debbie," he added, his tone warming, "I want to be successful, not just for me, but for both of us. If you won't marry me, at least move in with me, or I'll move in with you if you want. We just can't go on with the way things are."

"Then we don't," she said, vigorously snuffing out her cigarette.

He leaned back in his chair and studied her impassive expression. "Just like that, huh?"

Curtly she asked, "What is it you want from me, Tony?"

"A commitment," he said, leaning forward. "That's what I want from you."

"You want too much."

"You want too little. Why are you so afraid of a commitment?"

"It means you can't walk away when things get tough."

"Do you give up that easily?"

"It's you I'm thinking about. These circles under my eyes aren't exactly from too much reading."

"Circles and all, you're beautiful."

Her lips curved in feigned amusement. "The kind of beauty that comes with self-respect?" Immediately her simulated smile evaporated. "For a number of years now my sense of propriety has been slightly impaired by this." She lifted her glass and emptied it.

"That's a very unattractive trait you have, Debbie."

"Drinking?"

"No. Putting yourself down like you do."

"Old habits are hard to break."

"Honey," he said softly, "we all have our demons to cope with, and from what little you've told me about your wartime experiences, I know you have yours. But we can work through anything, if we do it together."

Shaking her head slowly, she said, "You are a glutton for punishment, aren't you?"

"I don't have a choice. I love you."

Again she chuckled, but with little heart. "You have a gift for loving, and if you keep saying you love me, you're going to wind up believing it eventually."

"If I say it often enough, maybe you will, too."

"Then we'll both be in a lot of trouble."

"I can handle it."

"You just think you can."

"I also think you could, if you'd give it a try."

"Believe me, I've tried, but Cupid can't quite find my heart."

"I have."

"Have you, Tony?" she asked, a dim ray of hope in her question.

"Yes, and your heart's good and warm and it beats in perfect harmony with mine."

Dropping her cigarettes and lighter into her evening bag, she asked quietly, "Why couldn't I have met you twenty years ago?" Her long lashes flicked up and she smiled ironically. Then her voice turned hard. "That was a stupid thing for me to say. Twenty years ago you would have been eleven."

"That bothers you a lot more than it does me."

"You're absolutely correct." She picked up her bag as she stood. "I've got to get back to work, but there's no point in your sitting here all night."

"I'll wait for you. We Italians also have a stubborn streak when we know we're right."

Her eyes held his for a silent moment before she said softly, "This time I'm afraid you're wrong, Tony, very wrong." Then she headed back to the piano.

THE WARM MORNING SUN bore down on Sharon as she carted a sack of groceries from the parking area next to her apartment building. She stopped in her tracks, spotting Steve who was casually dressed in jeans and a blue sweatshirt. He was leaning lackadaisically against his car, which was parked in front of the entrance. Deciding she wasn't going to let him put her through another session of grief, she was about to turn and make for the back door, but before she could he headed toward her, carrying a small white paper bag.

"Morning," he said brightly, taking the grocery bag from her.

Unceremoniously she jerked it back from him. "I can handle this just fine. The lifting we nurses do makes for strong backs."

He grabbed the grocery bag from her again, ripping the top edge of the paper a little. "I was raised to be a gentleman."

"Then act like one."

"I will if you'll give me a chance," he shot back, then lifted the small white bag and tempered his tone. "I stopped by a bakery and got some lemon Danish. They'd go well with a cup of coffee."

"Aren't you afraid I'll poison it?" she asked as she swept past him and strode to the entrance of the building.

"No," he hollered, catching up with her and entering when she held the door open.

At the elevator she punched the button and glared at him sideways. "To what do I owe this chivalry? Some dark need of yours to hassle me again? Or did a good night's sleep make you mellow?"

"I didn't sleep worth a damn," he admitted as he followed her into the elevator.

"I suppose you want to blame that on me also."

His eyes slanted toward hers. "Apparently you didn't sleep very well, either."

She chuckled wryly. "Why shouldn't I have? I've been suspended without pay, I'm being investigated for murder and your father wants to press criminal charges against me."

"He's not going to." When Sharon glanced at him dubiously, he explained, "After you left yesterday, I called him back and had a long talk with him. Then I visited Werner at the station.''

The elevator door opened, and Steve followed Sharon down the carpeted hallway, noting that her hand was shaking and she had trouble unlocking her door. Inside her apartment he carried the grocery bag to the kitchen and put it down on the countertop.

''Thanks,'' she said begrudgingly, and started to unload the groceries.

''You're welcome,'' he returned pleasantly, thinking she looked as appealing as a spring day in the floral sundress and the sandals she wore.

''Can you boil water?'' she asked as she put a container of milk and a package of cheese in the refrigerator.

''It is part of my culinary repertoire,'' he returned sweetly.

''The kettle's on the stove. You've invited yourself to instant coffee.''

''How about instant civility?'' he asked, running tap water into the kettle.

Slamming the refrigerator door shut, she spun around. ''This schizophrenic routine of yours is getting to me! One minute you treat me as if I belong behind bars, and the next you want to be my bosom friend. Make up your mind.''

''Sharon, you've got to understand my frustration.''

''You've got to understand mine!'' she retorted, and stormed from the kitchen.

''I'm trying to,'' he mumbled to himself as he switched on the burner under the kettle. Then he checked the cabinets, located the instant coffee and two mugs with grinning Snoopies on them. After arranging things on the counter, he went to the archway, braced a shoulder against it and looked across the room to where Sharon was sitting on the sofa, pumping her foot.

"How about we start over again?" he suggested. "Good morning."

"Good morning," she said icily.

Moving to the sofa, he sat at the other end and propped a knee on the cushion between them. "As I started to say, I called my father back and convinced him he was wrong. He's not going to bring a suit against you."

"You convinced him I was innocent?" she asked tightly.

"Yes."

"And you believe it yourself?"

"I believe that whatever happened was an accident."

Sharon's expression turned grim. "So we're right back to square one."

"Not exactly. I talked to Detective Werner. We both understand why you did what you did in Vietnam."

"That is *wonderful* of the two of you," she said caustically, and started to rise from the sofa.

Steve leaned over and took hold of her wrist. "Will you please listen for a minute?"

The kettle started to squeal. "I'll fix the coffee if you'll let go of me."

He did, and when she returned, he took the mug and plate with a Danish on it that she offered, watching her position herself stiffly on the easy chair across from the sofa.

"You don't like lemon pastry?" he asked, noting that she had only coffee for herself.

Disregarding his query, she said crisply, "So you and Detective Werner have decided I'm not the monster you both thought."

"I never really thought that."

"You gave a good impression of thinking it."

"I was still in shock."

"And now you're clearheaded."

"More so." Setting his Danish and mug down on the coffee table, he propped his forearms on his knees and interlaced his fingers. "Werner and I talked about you at great length. He's interviewed some of the staff from the hospital, and everyone says you're a class A nurse, too good to make that kind of a medication mistake."

"That's reassuring."

Ignoring her sarcasm, he continued. "Then he brought up a possibility that never crossed my mind. He said that if Richie's death hadn't been an accident, there could be only one other explanation." Steve saw he had her complete attention now. "He was murdered."

Sharon bounded from the chair. "What?"

"That was exactly my response. I can't believe anyone would want to kill Richie."

All feelings of animosity toward Steve vanished as Sharon sat down next to him on the sofa, recalling Tony's having suggested murder jokingly when she asked him to check Richard Nordstrom's blood. "Is that what Detective Werner is investigating now...a murder?" she asked.

"He says he has no motive and no evidence for that, and I couldn't come up with anything."

"Steve," she said, totally serious now, "I know I gave Richie exactly ten milligrams of morphine, and when I checked him at 4:50 a.m., he showed no signs of distress. Sometime, minutes after that, an overdose got into his system. None of my nurses went near him.''

''As far as you know,'' Steve remarked.

''I know they didn't. They were too busy with their own patients.''

''But if this theory of murder is to be taken seriously, someone did it. The question is who and why.''

''That's what the police will find out, isn't it?''

''If they see it as a homicide. Right now Werner is willing to call it—'' he hesitated ''—an accidental death.''

''That I caused,'' Sharon added quietly, sinking back against the sofa. After a poignant silence, she looked Steve square in the eye. ''Be honest with me again, please. Do you still think I made a medication error?''

He took hold of her hand and shook it gently. ''It's as hard for me to believe you did as it is that someone hated Richie enough to kill him.''

''But until the police find out one way or the other you won't really be sure, will you?''

''You said you wanted me to be honest,'' he reminded her.

''I know,'' she said uneasily, ''but you have a way of telling the truth that can really hurt.''

A stillness hovered between them. Then Steve eased his thumb over the smooth skin on the back of her hand. ''Accidents do happen...in any field.'' He managed a meager laugh. ''I had a dentist put a drill into my lip once.''

Sharon responded to his false lightheartedness with a sad smile. ''It was an accident you recovered from.''

Moving his hand to the side of her cheek, he brushed it with his fingertips. ''There is one thing I am sure about. I don't want to lose you as a friend. Maybe I'm not as clearheaded as I think yet, but this business with Richie will work itself out, and when it does, I'd like us to—"

Suddenly Sharon drew back from Steve and pushed herself up from the sofa. She glanced down at him, then half turned. "Maybe we shouldn't think that far ahead right now. I'm unsettled and so are you."

"Not so much that I can't see how special a lady you are."

A dull ache welling around her heart, she looked back at him over her shoulder. "If the police investigation does decide Richie's death was accidental, will you still think I'm special?"

"I'll deal with that when the time comes."

"And how do I deal with it until then?"

"You try to understand that I'm between a rock and a hard place, and not very comfortable."

"Move over," she said tensely, unable to disguise the conflicting emotions she felt. "I'm right in there with you."

Steve glanced at his watch, then stood and took hold of her hands. "I'm flying to Wisconsin this evening with Richie. I'll be gone for several days, but when I return, can I see you again?"

"Why, Steve?" she asked, wanting to say no. "Every time you'd look at me I'd know doubt would be lurking behind your eyes. Just how comfortable do you think I'd be?"

"Please," he asked, his word a desperate plea. "Couldn't we at least try? Would having one dinner with me hurt you so?"

After long vacillating moments, she shook her head almost imperceptibly, then said, "I still owe you a dinner."

"You accepted an invitation to my place, remember? I actually can do more than boil water."

Once again Sharon experienced that nagging warning not to get deeply involved with Steve. She knew instinctively that it wasn't just the matter of his brother's mysterious death. It was something else, some silent admonition she couldn't understand, and it took great mental effort for her to discount it.

"I'll try to make it back by Wednesday," he said, forcing her from her troubled thoughts. "How about I phone you Monday or Tuesday evening?"

"All right," she agreed, then remembered she had plans for Monday night. "Make it Tuesday, okay?"

"Tuesday," he repeated before following an impulse too strong to be denied. He leaned down and touched his lips to hers, softly and briefly.

Perhaps it was his gentleness, or perhaps it was the comforting warmth that Sharon felt in his kiss, but whatever it was, all of her hesitancy dissipated and her heartbeat seemed to tinkle like a little silver bell that sent echoes resounding through her body.

"Tuesday," Steve said once more when he lifted his head and took a moment to savor the shining light in her lovely eyes.

Quietly Sharon saw him to the door, then leaned back against it for heart-pulsating seconds after he departed. Missing him already, she hurried across the room and gazed out the front window onto the street. She watched him walk to his car, get in and drive off. Her fingertips on the windowpane, she murmured softly, "Until Tuesday, Steve."

Turning from the window, she thought the room dismally quiet. Her apartment had always been a comfortable haven for her, but now that Steve had gone the silence weighed heavily on her. She began counting the days until she'd hear his voice again, then her Monday get-together came back to mind. Considering her suspension from duty, she phoned Anna to let her know the invitation was still good.

CHAPTER SIX

ALWAYS READY TO PARTY, Debbie was the first to arrive Monday evening, her night off at the lounge.

In the kitchen, as Sharon arranged crackers around a bowl of cheese dip, she glanced at Debbie, who was fixing herself a drink. "Tony didn't look thrilled when he dropped you off."

"He's sulking because he wanted me to watch *Carmen* on cable with him tonight."

"You're really broadening his musical taste."

"For a man who used to think Bach's 'Air on a G String' was an accompaniment to a striptease, he's come a long way."

"Maybe you should have spent the evening with him," Sharon suggested, really hoping that Debbie and Tony would settle down permanently.

"And miss meeting Anna, another graduate of America's police action in the boondocks? No way. I want to see what five years in that hellhole can do to a woman."

"She seems to be in great shape. I thought it'd be good to remind ourselves that not every lady came back wacko."

"Probably she's in one piece because she was a civilian and didn't have to put up with the crap we did."

"You were a civilian," Sharon reminded her, smiling.

"I kept trying to tell the Red Cross that, but it didn't sink in." Debbie snared a square of cheese with a toothpick. "My boss was a clone of that colonel who ordered you not to wear earrings on duty."

"Colonel Furtwangler," Sharon said, readying a plate of Vienna sausage for the microwave. "She was always on my case, couldn't understand that the guys on the wards liked to see us looking like females. Those grungy fatigues sure didn't help."

"Yeah. I can still smell the perfume I used to pour on myself before visiting the wards. The noses of the guys with bandaged eyes would twitch, and they'd smile before I even got to their bedsides. They liked it when I wore my hair in pigtails, too. I never figured out why."

"It made you look cute. Here," Sharon said, handing her the cheese dip and crackers, "put this on the coffee table, would you?"

"Sure." The door buzzer sounded. "I'll get that on my way in."

Plate in hand, Debbie swung the door open to find a smiling Marge Graham, an ex-air force flight nurse who was now a surgical nurse at a hospital in St. Petersburg. Her father was a retired USAF lieutenant colonel; her mother had been a nurse on Corregidor and a POW of the Japanese. Forty-five now, Marge had three ex-husbands to her credit and was working diligently on a possible number four.

"All for me?" Marge asked, her Alabama accent vivid as she took a cracker from the plate Debbie held and scooped up some dip.

"Thought you were on a diet."

"I'm voluptuous, not fat," she insisted, munching on the cracker as she swept into the living room. "Where's our hostess?"

"In here, Marge," Sharon called from the kitchen.

At the archway the new arrival's dark eyes sparkled. "Do I have news for you!"

"You're going to marry Ted," Sharon guessed.

"How did you know?"

"I didn't. I was kidding."

"Marriage is *not* a thing we black women kid about."

"For a three-time loser you have to be kidding," Debbie teased, eavesdropping. "You stink at being married. Why would you dream of trying it again?"

Snatching a piece of cheese from the plate Sharon was preparing, Marge placed her other hand on her hip. "Because a sexy body is a terrible thing to waste."

"Oh, please," Debbie moaned on her way to the fridge. "Want your usual?"

"Maybe just one ... to begin with."

As Debbie retrieved a can of beer and snapped the pop top open, Sharon warned, "I want the two of you to be on good behavior this evening. I don't know if Anna shocks easily."

"Is she still fillin' in for you on ICU?" Marge asked.

"Dave's acting head nurse," Sharon said, exiting the kitchen, "and Anna has agreed to take on my schedule temporarily."

Dropping her handbag on the floor next to one of the matching easy chairs, Marge said, "Your chief of staff must be a wimp."

"Dr. Benning's okay. Considering that anonymous phone message, he didn't have much choice except to suspend me."

"Without pay Debbie told me. If you need some money, holler."

"Miss Rich Bitch," Debbie commented, cocking her head. "Are all three of your castoffs paying you alimony?"

"It's called settlements, darlin'." She took a swallow of beer and put the can on the small plastic tray on the table next to her chair. "Where's Julia?"

"She'll be here," Sharon said. "I called her this afternoon."

Marge leaned back in the chair and wrinkled her forehead. "I'm worried about that child. She's a nervous wreck. We had lunch Saturday, and when a busboy dropped a tray, she literally jumped up. And her nails are chewed to the quick."

"There must be a full moon or something," Debbie said. "Sharon's in trouble, Julia's acting up again and Tony's giving me a hard time."

"Tony!" Marge gushed. "That sweet boy?"

"Boy is right."

After a sip of her beer, Sharon said, "Say hello to the nineties, Debbie. His being nine years younger than you is irrelevant."

"Almost ten," she remarked morosely.

"Too much horizontal dancin' for you, honey?" Marge asked, a wicked glimmer in her eyes.

Sweeping up the back of her long golden hair, Debbie struck a seductive pose. "I am just beginning to reach my sexual peak."

"Don't you wish," Marge groaned.

"Wishing has nothing to do with it. Making love gives me a powerful feeling," she said dramatically, "fills me with the grand illusion that I'm in charge of my life." She grinned. "Besides, I like to have a good time."

"If Sharon is to be believed, when the two of you were on R and R in Thailand, you were havin' such a good time, she had to drag you back to Pleiku screamin'."

"Did she also mention that half the guys on leave in Bangkok serenaded us at the airport?"

"Listen, you two," Sharon said, sitting on the arm of the sofa, "when Anna gets here—"

Her head spun toward the door when the buzzer announced another arrival—Julia Delgado.

Petite, her brown hair framed a shy face with large dark brown eyes. A hint of an accent suggested her having been born in Puerto Rico. Julia had been an army decoder in Vietnam, where she met Carlos, a Marine at the time. He was now a construction worker, and they had two children: Luis, eleven, and Elena, eight.

"How are the kids?" Sharon asked, handing Julia a cup of coffee once she had settled next to Debbie on the sofa.

"Fine," she said with little enthusiasm.

Debbie glanced over at Marge, then laid a comforting hand on Julia's shoulder. "You look tired, honey."

She smiled weakly as she put her coffee cup down. "With two energetic kids it's easy to get tired. Some mornings I can hardly drag myself out of bed. When I do, it seems like even the smallest decision is a major chore."

"Are you sleeping all right?" Sharon asked.

"Carlos says I sleep too much, but—" she squeezed her hands together "—sometimes it's all I can do to get the kids off to school."

"And everything you do takes twice as much energy as usual," Sharon said, knowing Julia was prone to periods of depression.

"But I always feel better after I talk with all of you."

Slipping down next to her on the sofa, Sharon took Julia's hand in hers. "We feel better, too, but I think it's time you talked with someone at the Veterans Administration and got some professional help."

The buzzer announced Anna's arrival, and once introductions had been made she opted for a soft drink. The women assailed her with questions about her long service in Vietnam, and she in turn asked them about theirs.

"I used to think I was one of the lucky ones," Julia said, her voice a monotone. "I mean, there I was working in an office in Saigon, not in the field or in one of the hospitals where I'd actually see the casualties. All I had to do was encode and decode messages. But I knew when some of the fighting was going to happen, and I knew that in a few days I'd been decoding messages that gave the body counts. They were just numbers when I was working, but at night I felt I had to create faces in my thoughts so the guys wouldn't just be numbers."

"Yeah," Marge said to Anna, her cheerful facade fading. "When I volunteered for Nam I thought I was goin' to live an excitin' life in a foreign country."

"Give us a break, Marge!" Debbie cried. "You told us the same thing when you volunteered to go to the Persian Gulf."

"You were there, too?" Anna asked Marge.

"For four months. First as a flight nurse on a Medevac helicopter. Then I was assigned to the 807th MASH unit on the Kuwaiti-Iraqui border. Girl, I had sand in places you wouldn't believe!" She paused for a sip of beer. "It wasn't a picnic in the desert, but it wasn't like Nam, either. I expected Vietnam to be a rough job, but

I sure wasn't prepared for the emotional wringer I went through over there.''

"None of us were,'' Julia said softly.

For tense moments each of the women reflected silently, then Marge continued. "Durin' my first tour at the evacuation hospital in Da Nang, I tried to think of the wounded as patients, period, but I couldn't manage that cool, professional distance. We just kept the guys overnight until they were flown out to Japan or the Philippines, but even in that short time I became attached to each one of them. When they did leave, I'd never know if they eventually made it or not, and that really got to me. There were times when I didn't know whether to cry, throw up or scream. I usually cried...at night in my hooch, never on the wards. I thought it would be easier emotionally as a flight nurse, so that's what I did durin' my second tour. In those cargo planes we had those poor guys on litters stacked four high, but even in a six- or eight-hour flight I got so damn attached to each and every one of them.''

Debbie smacked her lips, then said, "You were crazy to go back for a second tour.''

"Honey, I wasn't plannin' to, but I felt so damn guilty leavin' the hospitalized guys after the first one that I had to do somethin' to help.''

"That's how I felt,'' Sharon said. "After my first two weeks of eighteen-hour shifts at Cu Chi, I was a basket case. All I wanted was my mother and a way to get back home. I made a little calendar and began counting the days till I could get out of there, but when the time came to be rotated home, I just couldn't leave. After a year's experience in that hell, you knew that your replacement wouldn't be able to do as much or function as quickly as you could, regardless of how good she was when she arrived. It was a crazy ambivalent feeling. I wanted to stay and help the guys, but I wanted to get out of there so I'd stay alive. I mean, you don't hear about it a lot, but nurses as well as doctors and medics and civilian women were also shipped home in body bags. I guess I just felt too guilty to leave after the first year, though.''

Marge shook her head. ''Talk about a bunch of weirdos. Why were we going around feeling guilty?''

''I don't know,'' Julia said quietly. ''Maybe because we were surviving when so many others weren't.''

After finishing her drink, Debbie set the glass down. ''The guilt got to me, too. There was this one blond kid from Brooklyn who was really out of it. I was holding his hand, and he thought I was his wife. He kept saying, 'Susan, Susan.' And I'd say, 'I'm here. You're going to be all right.' But I knew he was going to die.'' She chuckled bitterly. ''Those were the early days when I thought that lying was a sin.''

''There were good times, too,'' Sharon said, trying to lighten the mood.

Marge laughed. ''Yeah, no hot water and those stinking cubicles in the bug-infested sandbagged hooches we lived in, not to mention the snakes and rats in the bunkers.''

''Ugh, those bunkers. They were like swamps!'' Sharon moaned as she shivered, then she faced Anna. ''When we had incoming fire, I usually just shoved on my helmet and flak jacket, dived under the bed and screamed. There was no way I was going into those bunkers.''

As though speaking to herself, Anna said, ''In the countryside there weren't many places to hide. After the bombings, some of what were villages looked like moonscapes.''

"All that was years ago," Julia said softly, "but I still think about those fatality numbers and the faces I created. Whenever I do, I begin shaking and I tell them to go away. 'Everyone go away,' I say, but they don't. They just stare back at me.'' She lifted her moistened eyes toward Sharon. "Why can't we forget about it?''

"It's the nature of the beast," Sharon said quietly. "None of us can completely forget what we've lived through. All we can do is try to cope with the memories and our feelings about them.''

Marge began a rhythmic tapping on the arm of her chair. "We sure didn't have time to talk about our feelings over there.'' She paused for a moment. "Or maybe we didn't want to. We were too busy being earth mothers, caretakers and helpmates.''

"The patients' feelings came first," Sharon said. "There just wasn't time to ask for emotional support for ourselves.''

Anna nodded in agreement. "Most of the nurses I knew, civilian and military, had built up a lot of fear, anger and hurt, but they internalized it because they had a job to do, taking care of others...never themselves.''

"That's exactly how I felt," Debbie said, gripping her empty glass. "I was always some soldier's sister, mother or girlfriend, and when I came home from Nam, I didn't know who I was supposed to be. I just didn't fit in anywhere, nothing made any sense. It was like living in a dreamworld.'' Dragging her fingers through the side of her hair, she said abruptly, "Let's talk about something else.'' Quickly she shifted the conversation to the sale a local store was having on designer swimwear.

An hour later Tony arrived to pick Debbie up, and after deciding to get together again at Debbie's condo, the women went their separate ways. But Anna stayed behind.

"We really miss you on ICU," she told Sharon.

"I miss being there. Cleaning out my closets isn't all that satisfying. How's Dave holding up?"

"He prays for you to come back, says Louella's driving him crazy. Also, he asked me to pass on a bit of gossip."

"That's my Dave," Sharon quipped, carrying two plates into the kitchen.

Anna picked up several glasses and followed. "A friend of his in Personnel told him Louella changed her home address. She's moved in with Dr. Wilson."

"Humph! Must have been some wild weekend in the Bahamas," Sharon remarked. "I imagine she's grinning from ear to ear."

"She wasn't Friday afternoon, not when I saw her coming out of Detective Werner's office."

"Has he called you in, too?"

"There wasn't much I could tell him. I don't know people on sight yet."

"Anna, I feel so much better with you helping out on the unit while I'm gone."

"It's what I really need, I guess . . . to get busy again. This evening was good for me. Josh and I used to talk about our Vietnam days, and I miss that. Since he died I've been thinking about those kids more and more."

"Being able to talk about it with him over the years probably helped more than you realized." Leaning back against the sink, Sharon crossed her arms. "Sometimes I think we women have a problem feeling like real veterans of that war. Maybe we didn't go into the bush and shoot the enemy, but we went through a kind of hell ourselves, and some of us have to deal with symptoms of PTSD just like some of the men do.''

"I saw that, particularly with Julia. She's really feeling down."

"She has bouts with depression, and I'm afraid her husband isn't a lot of help. Carlos was a Marine in Nam, but he shuts out the memories and tells Julia that her coming here to talk about hers is causing her troubles, bringing them all back.''

''Debbie doesn't seem to be having any problems.''

''Don't let her wisecracking fool you. She uses it to cover up her pain. When I first met her in Pleiku, she was too sweet and naive to be believed. She left the country a different woman, hardened and cynical. Since then she hasn't been able to keep a relationship with a man going for very long. She's petrified that if she loves someone, she'll lose him just like she lost so many of the guys she made friends with in Nam.''

Sharon crossed to the small kitchen table and sank down on a chair. ''And look at Marge. She'll swear that she doesn't have any problems. True, she's never gone through what some of us have—the flashbacks, nightmares and the depression that seemingly comes out of nowhere—but in her own way she has the same problem Debbie does. Only Marge marries the man and then can't keep the relationship going.''

Sitting across from Sharon, Anna asked, ''How did you come through it all without the scars?''

''Oh, I have them,'' Sharon replied, smiling uneasily. ''They just don't show now. Soon after I left the army I married an intern, but I was really screwed up. No one knew what PTSD was then. My marriage to Sam lasted for a year and a half.''

"I was fortunate to have Josh for the twenty-four years I did. I guess we used each other to hold ourselves together. These meetings of yours are really like group therapy."

"It helps, but I'm worried that Julia is getting beyond just talking things out. I hope she does get the professional support that's available at the VA."

Anna glanced at the wall clock. "Let me give you a hand in here, then I'd better leave."

"Thanks, but it'll only take me a few minutes." She rose and walked Anna to the door. "Say hi to everyone on ICU for me."

"I will," Anna promised, then, after thanking Sharon again, and saying good-night, she left the apartment.

As Sharon carted the remainder of the glasses and plates to the kitchen, her thoughts centered on Steve. She wondered if he was in Madison now and if he had thought of her at all since leaving Florida. She doubted it. He had too many other things to deal with—his brother's death, his parents' reaction and the police investigation.

She reminded herself that she had a lot of thinking and planning to do, as well. How long would the investigation take? she wondered. Her savings wouldn't last very long. What if the police came up with nothing? Would the finger of guilt still be pointed at her? Would she ever be reinstated at the hospital? Would any other hospital hire her?

Mulling over the problems that faced her, she rinsed the last plate and placed it on top of the others, then reached for the towel hanging on a hook. "Think of this as a time of R and R," she muttered, "a chance to do the things you don't have time for ordinarily." Returning to the apartment door, she locked it and pushed the dead bolt in place. *Think of it as being on a well-deserved vacation.* But if it was a vacation, why did she feel so damn miserable?

SHARON SPENT MOST of Tuesday lounging on Clearwater Beach, trying to convince herself she was enjoying her mandatory vacation. That evening, nursing a glass of iced tea as she was writing checks for the monthly bills, the phone rang, and she hurried to the living room, sure that it was Steve.

"It's cold up here already," he reported. "I miss the Florida sunshine."

Sitting in one of the easy chairs, wearing shorts, her bare legs draped over the arm, she twirled the phone cord around a finger. "I spent the day at the beach," she teased.

"Don't rub it in," he said, then his voice softened. "How have you been?"

"Fine," she lied. "I no longer set the alarm clock, and I watch late-night TV shows I haven't seen for ages." After a brief pause, she forced herself to ask, "How are your parents doing?"

"There are good moments and bad, but they're holding up fairly well. The funeral was this morning. They've gone to bed now. I had a long talk with my dad, and he's willing to let me decide about...well, you know."

"Whether or not to bring charges against me," she added for him, tensing.

"Or the hospital."

"What will you do?"

"I don't know," he replied honestly. "Nothing will bring Richie back, but my father wants someone to pay

for what happened. I don't think he'll rest until someone does. Look," he said quickly, "I'm not telling you
this because I don't understand how much it hurts you.
I just want things between us to be out in the open. It
won't do us any good to wonder what the other is
thinking."

"You're right, I suppose," she said quietly.

"I'll be back Thursday afternoon. We're still having
dinner at my place, right?" When she hesitated, he said,
"I want us to, Sharon, very badly."

"Okay," she replied hesitantly. "What time should I
come by?"

"How about six, six-thirty?"

"All right."

"It'll be good to see you again. I've thought about
you a lot."

Especially when you were talking to your father, she
thought uncomfortably. She was just about to renege on
his dinner invitation when he spoke again.

"I guess I'd better let you go now. Sleep well."

"You, too, Steve," she said, her voice little more than
a whisper.

She held the receiver to her ear until the line went
dead. Then she cradled it, telling herself hopefully that
if Steve really thought she had accidentally killed his
brother, he wouldn't want to set eyes on her again. But
she suspected that still tucked away in some corner of
his mind was the belief that she had been responsible.

Well, what was he supposed to think? It did look bad
for her. In her heart she yearned for Steve to trust her,
to believe in her and support her now when she needed
support the most. Sam hadn't had the time, or the in-
clination, apparently, to support her emotionally when
she had needed it years ago, and the hurt remained to

this day. His lack of support had been the real reason their marriage had failed. But if she had been the guilty one then, she wasn't now, and she wanted Steve to believe that. She needed him to desperately.

As SHARON WAS RINSING her breakfast dishes the next morning, the door buzzer sounded. Her curiosity turned to surprise when she saw Detective Werner on the landing, an iffy smile on his face.

"Good morning," he said, pushing at the bridge of his metal-rimmed glasses. "Can you spare me a few minutes?"

"Sure," she said with little enthusiasm, brushing back a stray lock of hair from her forehead. As she closed the door after he entered, she wished he'd phoned first to give her time to slip into something other than the neon-green shorts and the purple polo shirt she was wearing. But then what difference did it make, really? The man hadn't dropped by for a social visit.

"Nice place," he remarked, his alert eyes scanning the neatly kept living room.

"It's comfortable," she said, then asked, "What is it you want to talk to me about?"

"May I?" he asked, gesturing toward one of the upholstered chairs.

"Please." As he sat down, she did, also, on the sofa across from him.

He drew a leg up and propped an ankle over a knee. "I had a talk with Tony Catalano yesterday afternoon. Did he tell you about it?"

"Yes, he phoned me."

"Your friends are very loyal, and your co-workers speak highly of you."

"Without exception the staff at the hospital are dedicated people," she stated flatly, anxious for him to get to the point.

"Mr. Catalano, in particular, is extremely devoted to you." Werner snickered, his ample stomach vibrating as he did. "He was somewhat incensed at some of my questions."

"Concerning me," Sharon guessed.

Nodding, Werner said, "He wanted to make it clear that you were the one who asked him to run the tests on the victim's blood." The detective saw her wince. "Nordstrom was someone's victim, Miss McClure, accidentally or deliberately."

"Let me make your job a little easier for you," she said in a no-nonsense tone. "Neither I nor any of my nurses on ICU *accidentally* injected Richard Nordstrom with an overdose of morphine. That should narrow down your list of suspects." She paused. "You do have a list by now, don't you?"

Werner crossed his hands over his stomach. "To be frank I've got zilch, no leads and no motive for murder. Nordstrom lived here for only a few months. From what his boss at the paper tells me, he was a hard worker and apparently he wasn't involved with anyone's wife. His brother's got only good things to say about him and can't accept that anyone would have wanted to murder him."

"You have a way with words, Detective Werner," she said, her tone slightly petulant.

"If you didn't make a medication error, your patient was murdered. The doctors who worked on him all say he was banged up inside, but considering his age and general health before he was run down, they were all optimistic about his recovery. You've had time to think things through. What's your opinion?''

Sharon lowered her eyes and drew her fingers across her forehead. The man was giving her a first-class headache. Looking back at him, she said, ''I wouldn't have asked Tony to check Richard Nordstrom's blood if I hadn't been bothered by the way he died so suddenly.''

''From what I've learned the time element is important. The medical examiner's report indicates that considering the amount of morphine found in the body, cardiac arrest would have occurred minutes after the man was injected. As far as I can tell from talking to people, you were the only one in the isolation room for a good half hour before his death.''

''If someone did deliberately give my patient an overdose, that person isn't going to admit being in the room.''

''I've checked out ICU, Miss McClure. Anyone entering the isolation room would have to go by the nurses' station and pass through the ward. Nobody remembers seeing anyone out of the ordinary wandering around ICU that morning.''

''That entire shift was hectic, and my nurses are trained to keep a sharp eye on the patients they're caring for and the sensitive equipment they're attached to, not to keep a lookout for strangers.'' Her gaze unwavering, she asked, ''If I had anything to hide, why on earth would I have asked Tony to check the patient's blood?''

''Yes,'' he commented noncommittally, ''why would you?'' He stood. ''I guess that's about all for now, Miss McClure. We'll most likely be talking again.''

Joy! she thought, rising and opening the door for him.

Outside on the landing, Werner peered at her. "By the way, you didn't know Nordstrom before he was admitted to the hospital, did you?"

"Of course not."

"Just wondering," he said pleasantly, then tipped two fingers to his forehead and sauntered away.

After closing the door, Sharon shook her head, surprised by the detective's final question. But then, she told herself, it was his job to check out every possibility. And that was good. The sooner he discovered just what had happened, the sooner she'd be in the clear. Wouldn't she?

CHAPTER SEVEN

PLEASANT BACKGROUND MUSIC, coming from two speakers placed high under the redwood beams, flowed over the patio as Steve charbroiled steaks on the antique brick barbecue pit. Wearing a pink sundress, Sharon rested on one of the two cushioned redwood lounge chairs that were now set under the cover of red bougainvillea and yellow allamanda.

She had arrived fifteen minutes ago and, as she had predicted, she was uneasy and wondered what she was doing there.

In her heart she wanted to believe Steve was as attracted to her as she was to him—and attracted she was. She was having a difficult time not staring at him as he barbecued dinner. Wearing white shorts and a blue-striped tank top, he moved with an easy grace, his trim but muscular body flexing much like that of a tennis player at work. But her attraction to him was more than just physical.

He was sensitive and he was honest, even when it was difficult for him to be so. And under trying circumstances they had shared lighter moments together. She also found Steve intriguing. He had a great deal to offer a woman, but apparently he hadn't been in a rush to reach out to one, although she suspected he yearned for someone to fill the void in his life left by his wife's death.

"Won't be long," he said, turning and smiling at her. "Would you like some more wine?"

"I'm doing fine," she said. Her wineglass remained half-filled. "Can I help?"

"Salad's in the fridge. You could give it a toss and bring it out here."

From inside the kitchen she glanced through the window, thinking how handsome Steve looked in the soft glow of the lamplight next to the barbecue pit. As she tossed the salad, she wondered if the brief kiss he had given her before going to Wisconsin had just been a spontaneous reaction to her concern for him, or if he had followed through on a more personal impulse.

The wooden salad bowl in hand, she returned to the patio and set it down on the slab of white marble that served as a worktable next to the barbecue pit.

"You certainly can do more than boil water," she complimented him, savoring the beefy aroma of the sizzling steaks. "That smells heavenly and this salad looks scrumptious."

"Hope you have a good appetite," he remarked as he peeled back the aluminum foil from the baked potatoes.

"Embarrassingly so."

"Good. I like a woman who's not a constant slave to diets."

Sharon smiled. "Then we're going to get along famously."

His eyes slid toward hers and his voice became velvety smooth. "I've known that all along."

A powerful emotional energy crossed the distance between their steady gazes. It surged through her, vibrating every nerve in her body, and try as she might, she couldn't break eye contact with him. His unwavering eyes held hers until she thought he was actually speaking to her. But she wasn't prepared to respond in kind; she sensed his unspoken words to be too intimate, too binding. When he finally returned his attention to readying their baked potatoes, she almost slumped with relief, happy to shed the emotional tension that had gripped her so suddenly.

With a finger he slid a tray on the marble table nearer to the grill. It held bowls of sour cream, chopped bacon and onions mixed with parsley. Casually he said, "I like everything in the refrigerator on my potato. How about you?"

"Same here," she agreed. Then she added, "I'm not used to being waited on like this. I feel so unnecessary."

"Don't *ever* think that," he remarked as he forked the sizzling steaks onto the plates. "If you'll pour the wine, I'll finish here and bring dinner to the table."

Steve had already set napkins, woven place mats and silverware on one of the wrought-iron tables. She picked up his wineglass and refilled his and hers, sitting when he joined her.

"This is a feast," she said sincerely, looking down at her plate.

"Enjoy," he said, then raised his wineglass in a toast.

Sharon lifted hers, clinking it against his. "To the chef."

"To the future," he said before sipping the wine, his eyes again holding hers over the rim of his glass.

Once more she felt the full impact of his intimate gaze, then rallied quickly and tasted the wine, wondering how much fluttering her heart could take.

As they cut into the two-inch-thick steaks, the evening silence was broken only by the soothing music wafting over the patio. After her first bite, she closed her eyes momentarily and breathed, "Mmm, heavenly! If you ever want to branch out from the orchid business, you could open up a steak house."

"I wish you could have sampled my grandfather's barbecue. He had a small dairy farm in Wisconsin. When I was a kid I used to spend summers there, helping him out and having an all-round good time doing it. He's the one who taught me how to barbecue. The secret's in the basting sauce."

Sharon waited, then smiled. "Going to share the family secret?"

"A dash of mustard powder."

"My compliments to him."

"He and Grandma are gone now. Dad was an only child, and he sold the farm and enlarged his business. Now he imports flowers from Europe and South America and distributes throughout the northeast."

"My grandparents had a mom-and-pop grocery store in Laguna Beach. That's where my cousin David and I spent summer vacations and I got hooked on desserts. Grandma was the best cook in the world. David used to tease me, call me pudgy."

"You!" His smiling eyes roamed over what he could see of her svelte form, which was clad in a pink sundress with spaghetti straps.

"You should have seen me then. I could look at an éclair and gain five pounds. One of the good things about nursing is that I get eight straight hours of physical exercise at least five nights a week." Her cheery tone suddenly became serious. "Or I used to."

To change the subject Steve said, "While I was in Wisconsin I put the vacation home that Laura and I had up for sale."

Sharon wondered how she was supposed to reply to that, but Steve continued.

"It's on Door Peninsula. Ever been up that way?"

Her mouth full of salad, she shook her head.

"We also spent Christmases at the house when we lived in Madison, and until last year we would go up each summer for a few weeks. Right now it's just sitting there. The real estate woman handling the deal said she wouldn't have any trouble selling it."

This was only the second time Steve had mentioned his wife, and the first time he had, Sharon recalled, he'd said she'd been a semi-invalid during the last years of their marriage. For how many years? she wondered. Not wanting to ask, she said, "I imagine it's difficult to sell a house that holds so many memories for you."

"I'm not a man to live in the past, and I don't think it's any good to ruminate over memories."

Something in the resolute way he said that sounded almost cold to Sharon, very unlike him, and his thinking was contrary to what she believed. "I believe just the opposite," she said. "We all have memories, some good and some bad, that we have to deal with or else they have a way of coming back to haunt us."

"Not if we keep busy enough."

Again alerted by his tone more than his words, Sharon wondered what it was in his past that he wanted to forget. Her belief that he wouldn't succeed in forgetting came not from the psychology courses she'd had, but from her own experience in having to deal with the memories of Vietnam that had so complicated her life.

"Are you familiar with the term PTSD, Steve?"

"Uh-huh. Posttraumatic stress disorder. Something they used to call delayed shell shock."

"Exactly. It can happen to people after any severe shock—a fire, an earthquake, a loved one's death or a war. Some people aren't seriously affected, others are to various degrees. Pretending that something didn't happen by putting it out of your mind doesn't always work."

"That's not why I'm selling the house," he said, a weak smile on his face that slowly ebbed. "And I've come to terms with Laura's death. We had a good marriage, and her being diagnosed as having rheumatoid arthritis shook the hell out of both of us. Her years of decline were devastating, but we dealt with it together. If I have any regrets, it's that—" He stopped abruptly. "I told you I don't like dredging up the past. Can we talk about something else...please?"

"I'm sorry, Steve. I didn't mean to upset you."

"Let's talk about you," he said, smiling. "After you get a good suntan, what are your plans? Werner's investigation could take a while."

"It'd better not take too long," she said anxiously, then wiped her mouth with a napkin. "I'm not on a paid vacation."

"That's something I thought about during the flight back. This is my busy season. Would you consider giving me a hand here in the office? I'd pay you, of course."

Surprised by his sudden offer, Sharon stared at him briefly before asking, "How do you think that would look? Detective Werner told me he has no suspects...other than me. And I'm the one the hospital is going to throw to the dogs to avoid a million-dollar lawsuit."

"No one's going to sue you or the hospital," he said adamantly. Then he lowered his voice. "Accidents happen."

"Steve," she said, her tone crisp, "that's the second time you've explained away Richie's death as an accident, meaning that you still think I caused it."

"If you did, Sharon, persecuting you isn't going to help Richie now."

She jumped up and glared at him. "Why are you so willing to hire me if you believe I could have killed your brother?"

He shot up, too. "Damned if I know!" After a thoughtful moment he said calmly, "No, I do know why." He placed his napkin on the table, took a few steps and grabbed hold of the wrought-iron railing.

For a while he stared blankly out over the pool area, then looked back at her as she stood immobile. "During the past four years, Laura and I were husband and wife in name only." He paused and the silence was heavy. "I did love Laura and she loved me, but four years is a long time for a man my age to have to settle for loving companionship. If that sounds cold and selfish, I'm sorry, but a man doesn't die of too much love. He wastes away slowly from a lack of it."

Taking a deep breath, he ran his fingers through his hair, then turned completely around, leaned back against the railing and crossed his bare arms. "These past six months haven't turned out the way I thought they would. I imagined that I'd eventually be able to pick up the pieces and begin living again. I'm not an ogre, I'm financially in good shape and it hasn't been because women haven't been attentive, but I...I haven't been able to reach out to anyone...not until I met you. I was suffocating, and you were like a breath of fresh air. I couldn't believe it when you said you'd have dinner with me that first night. I told myself you were just being sympathetic, that you felt sorry for me."

"Steve, I never—"

"Don't say anything," he directed, raising a hand. "Let me get this out while I can." He paused, then continued. "After I drove you home, I came back here, but I couldn't sleep. I felt like a college kid after he's really fallen in love for the first time. I paced out here for hours, knowing that everything was happening too fast. I told myself that I wanted to love and be loved so badly that I was trying to make it happen with you. But damn, I wanted to believe it! Then at the inquiry, when Werner got that phone message, reality struck and I felt the same miserable way I did when Laura died—alone again. And I knew you couldn't possibly have felt about me the way I did about you."

Sharon saw the pained look on his face, heard the despair in his voice, and her heart went out to him, ached for him. She moved closer and placed a gentle hand on the side of his flushed face. "You're wrong, Steve, so very wrong. I decided you were special the first time I met you. I wanted us to be friends, even more eventually. You didn't imagine anything. There was something between us from the very beginning. It's still there now . . . if you want it to be."

She felt his arms rush around her and pull her up against his hard body as his lips molded to hers hungrily, feverishly, his frenetic moist tongue probing hers wildly, as though he were attempting to devour her. Instinctively her arms clasped his waist for support. Then she slid her hands up under his loose tank top and pressed her fingers against his warm, muscular back.

Like a man possessed, he drank from her lips and moved his hands wildly over her body, pressing her against the hard ridge of his burgeoning arousal.

Needing air, she tilted her head back and gasped deeply, trying to fill her depleted lungs.

With his lips at the side of her neck, Steve moaned, "Oh God, it's been so long since I've held a woman like this. Your softness and warmth and the way you smell so sweet make me dizzy."

Limp in his arms, Sharon reached up and took hold of his shoulders. "I'm feeling rather heady myself," she admitted, very aware of his broad chest pressing against her now-sensitive breasts.

He gazed down at her flushed, lovely face, feeling his throbbing maleness swelling even more, stretching his shorts until he ached. Too long unsatisfied, he knew he had to do something quickly or he was going to have an embarrassing orgasm then and there. Easing her backward, he glanced over his shoulder and knew what he had to do.

Sharon gaped as he took hold of the railing, leaped over it, darted to the pool and dived in, sending arcs of water splashing up.

When he didn't surface, she scurried down the steps leading to the moonlit garden. Just as she reached the pool, his head and shoulders shot up at the far side, his hair slick, water streaming over his silly grin.

"Come on in," he called breathlessly. "It's refreshing."

"Are you crazy?" she called back, then began laughing.

Her laughter died when he tossed his tank top and then his shorts and briefs onto the stone walkway that edged the pool.

He swam toward her with strong, even strokes, then gripped the green tiles near her shoes and gazed up at her. "Well?" he asked, a mischievous twinkle igniting his blue-gray eyes.

Sharon stepped back. "I didn't bring a swimsuit," she said, her pulse racing as her gaze roamed over his smiling, moonlit face and broad, tanned shoulders. An unexpected warmth curled inside her breasts, tingling her entire body.

"We have complete privacy here," he assured her. "Come on, Sharon...please."

Come on, Sharon! She moved back even farther, her mind playing a cruel trick on her, re-creating Doug's voice as he had called to her from the turquoise water on the beach at Phan Rang in Vietnam so long ago. Ensnared by the sudden memory, she saw herself clad in a one-piece swimsuit, running toward him, diving, surfacing, caught in his arms. She could even feel his lips on hers.

"What's the matter?" Steve asked, his arms crossed on the tiles at the pool's edge.

Wide-eyed, Sharon stared down at him, then rushed back up the steps to the patio, where she covered her face with her hands.

Steve bounded out of the pool, and after he slipped on his soaked shorts, he took hold of her shoulders, shaking her gently. "What's wrong? Please tell me." When she didn't respond, he eased her hands from her face, exposing her reddened eyes and tear-stained cheeks. Confused, he said quietly, "I didn't mean to embarrass you. Forgive me."

She shook her head. "It wasn't you."

Trying for humor, he smiled. "My cooking was that bad, huh?"

Sharon managed a mirthless chuckle as she drew her fingers over her moistened cheeks. ''Dinner was delicious.''

He wanted to take her into his arms and comfort her but knew she'd wind up as wet as he was. Instead he asked, ''Would a glass of wine make you feel better or worse?''

''Better,'' she said, moving to the table where she had laid her purse. She took out a tissue and wiped her eyes, turning to accept the wineglass he offered her. ''Thanks,'' she said, feeling a little ridiculous.

''You relax. I'll be back in a minute.''

She watched him enter the house and close the sliding glass door after him. Sitting sideways on one of the lounge chairs, she chided herself for having behaved so stupidly. What must Steve think of her? she wondered. And why had memories of Doug surfaced just at that moment?

For several years now she had been free of the flashbacks and nightmares of her Vietnam days. She had thought them gone forever. Were they going to start again? Why now? Yes, she was stressed out because of the situation at the hospital. Was that the reason? It had to be. Certainly it wasn't Steve's swimming in the altogether. She and Doug had occasionally done that at night when she was able to steal away to Phan Rang to see him.

But this wasn't Phan Rang, and Steve wasn't Doug, she reminded herself, rising quickly, intent on grabbing her things and rushing off.

Just as she rose from the lounge chair, Steve walked out onto the patio, and she sat back down. He now wore denim shorts and an unbuttoned white shirt, its cuffs rolled up over his forearms. His damp brown hair was slicked back and looked even darker in the dim light of the patio.

After pouring himself a glass of wine, he sat down on the lounge chair opposite hers. "Feeling better?" he asked, sincere concern in his voice and attentive eyes.

She nodded and smiled slightly. "Some guest I turned out to be. I'm sorry, Steve. I don't usually fall apart like that."

He reached over and placed a soothing hand on hers. "I don't usually jump into the pool with my clothes on. So we're even, okay?"

"Even," she repeated, feeling a coolness on her hand when he withdrew his. Silent moments followed, and she was fairly sure he wouldn't press her for an explanation, but she decided she owed him one. "When I saw you in the water—" she shrugged "—I don't know why, but you made me think of someone I knew in Vietnam."

"Someone special?"

"Doug was special," she said, her voice soft but shaky. "Doug Kowalski . . . he was a medic." A hint of a smile curved her lips. "He taught me to dance the limbo on the terrace bar of the Continental Hotel in Saigon. That was the wonderful thing about Doug. He could make me temporarily forget all the misery that we lived with over there. He was a sergeant, though, and I was a lieutenant. I wasn't supposed to get involved with an enlisted man." She smiled more openly, but it was somewhat bittersweet. "My commanding officer was constantly reminding us nurses that we weren't to become involved with any of the men. She said if the U.S. Army had wanted us to have a love life, it would have issued us one."

"And you were in love," Steve said huskily, realizing he was more than a little envious of this Doug Kowalski.

Putting her wineglass down on the redwood table between the lounge chairs, Sharon nodded. "Really in love, for the first time in my life. I was only twenty-one and hadn't been in Nam very long. I didn't know then how foolish it was to care that much about someone over there, but I soon learned."

She suddenly felt chilled to the bone, although the night air was balmy, and she hugged herself. "One night in Cu Chi—that's where I was stationed then—we'd been working in surgery for what seemed like three days straight. The stretchers were lined up everywhere. I had just changed gloves and was readying the instrument tray. They shifted the next patient—what was left of him—onto the table. Automatically I began cutting away his burned battle fatigues. Usually I tried not to look at the patient's face, not unless—" she struggled with the aching lump in her throat "—not unless there was facial trauma to be dealt with. I don't know why, but something made me look at this soldier's face. It was...Doug."

Steve slipped next to her on the lounge and placed a comforting arm over her shoulder. "I'm sorry," he said softly, feeling her quivering.

As though unaware of Steve's holding her, she continued. "My heart seemed to stop and I wanted to run when I recognized him, but I knew I couldn't. Too many lives depended on all of us working as fast as humanly possible. In a split second I decided that the only way I could continue to function was to block out my feelings. I can still remember the strange sensation, just as if it were yesterday. I felt cold, numb, as if I were ex-

isting in a heavy fog, but I worked as quickly and as ef-
ficiently as I usually did. All our efforts didn't save
Doug, though.'' As if in slow motion, she rose and her
voice turned hollow. "When they wheeled him toward
the morgue, I thought I would die, too, and at that moment I swore that I would never again become close to
anyone.''

Standing, Steve took her in his arms, feeling the thud
of her heartbeat against his chest. As he stroked her
hair, he said softly, "It's hard when we lose someone we
love, someone who loves us. I know how empty you
must have felt.''

Her head resting on his shoulder, she moved her arms
around his waist, absorbing his soothing warmth.

"But loving and losing doesn't mean we can't love
again," he whispered. "I could love you, very easily...if you'd let me.''

The resolve Sharon had made long ago took hold of
her automatically, unconsciously, and she eased back
from Steve's embrace. She met his gaze briefly, then
looked away. "You're saying that because you need
someone to fill the void you feel, Steve.''

Gently he placed his fingers under the smooth curve
of her chin and tilted her face back toward his. "I said
it because I meant it.''

"Are you sure you're not trying to convince yourself
that you could love me for fear of hating me?''

Gripping her shoulders, his eyes searched hers. "I
could never hate you no matter what you might have
done.''

"No matter what I might have done,'' she repeated,
strangely relieved by his remark. "That doubt of yours
always surfaces, doesn't it?''

"Apparently just as your decision not to let anyone get close to you again does."

"Then we have two strikes against us."

"We still have one to go," he said darkly, and kissed her with a fury that made her head spin.

Caught in his strong arms, her breasts molded to his bare chest, his tongue surging against hers, Sharon's already stirred need for him soared. In spite of her long-practiced resolve her body became vibrant and sparkled under the pressure of his hands moving over her back and below.

"Steve," she murmured breathlessly against his lips, but he disregarded what he wrongly thought was an objection. He couldn't have stopped if he had wanted to. She made him feel more alive and vital than he had ever felt in his entire life, made him rejoice in his maleness, in her femininity. When he felt her fingers digging into his taut biceps and then his shoulders before raking through the hair at the back of his head, he realized she wasn't objecting and he came close to the edge of losing his fragile control again.

Years of desperate need welled up deep inside his deprived body, constricting his chest and causing havoc in his aching groin. Not willing it, one hand cupped her breast, its supple warmth burning his palm. He had to have her, lose himself inside her sweet body, drive her to need him as much as he needed her, make her want to love him! And he would—now!

A sharp moan pierced his awareness, and he pulled his mouth from hers, watching horrified as she covered her lips with a hand.

"Dear God," he groaned, "did I hurt you?"

She drew her trembling fingers over her bruised lips, saying, "No, no, you just surprised me."

"I surprised myself," he said honestly, almost dazed, feeling his entire body tingling. "I guess I'd better take another dive in the pool."

The ridiculousness of the moment made Sharon smile weakly. "Maybe it would be simpler if I left."

As she started to, he caught hold of her arm, then freed it immediately. "That won't happen again, Sharon. I promise...not unless you want it to."

On the verge of admitting she did, she said quickly, "Yes, I should leave right now."

When she moved to the table to get her purse, he followed, commanding his arms to remain at his sides. "You haven't said if you'll give me a hand here in the office."

Facing him, her palpitating heart skipped a beat as her gaze slipped over his imposing manly form, but for all of his strength, she saw the ardent plea in his eyes and sensed his exposed vulnerability. He made her feel so needed that her years of caring as a nurse got all mixed up with her personal caring for him. She felt a deep urge to comfort him, to help soothe away his anxiety, just as she had done for so many people throughout her nursing career. But, she warned herself, this evening with him made it obvious that they were being drawn to each other so strongly and at such a pace that there could only be one inevitable consequence.

With effort she called forth all her emotional strength and said quietly, "Thank you for trying to help me, Steve, but I don't think our working together is a good idea." She started across the patio, heading for her car.

Steve caught up with her and matched her stride. "I think it's a great idea," he persisted, again ordering himself not to touch her. "We could help each other, Sharon. God knows I need your help right now, and not just in the office, and what's wrong with my helping you a little?" He manufactured a boyish grin. "Your salary would be a tax write-off."

Oh, how she wanted the excuse to be near him, and even as she fought the temptation to accept his job offer, she felt her resolve weakening. "You don't even know if I can type," she pointed out.

"Can you?"

She nodded. "I worked in an insurance office for a few years."

He raised his hands sideways, palms upward. "See, you'd be perfect for the job."

Arriving at her car, she glanced at his pleading expression, then stifled the warning voice in her inner ear. "It would be a purely business arrangement?"

"Purely," he said, opening the car door for her. "How soon can you start—tomorrow morning?"

"No. I want to talk with my chief nurse and see if she can get Dr. Benning to reconsider my suspension."

"Tomorrow afternoon?" he asked hopefully, closing the door after she slipped onto the car seat.

Sharon looked up at him through the open window. "Are you really that far behind in your work here?"

"You're going to be a godsend. Two-thirds of the statements that the last person I hired as temporary office help sent out were all screwed up. They came back from my customers with less than flattering comments."

"Well, I am pretty good with figures," she said nervously as she turned the ignition key.

His hands braced on the car door, he smiled down at her. "I was sure you would be."

Over the hum of the engine she said, "Good night, Steve, and thanks for the lovely dinner."

"I'll see you tomorrow afternoon. Plan on having lunch with me."

"You said it would be purely business."

"You'll find I'm a good guy to work for."

Sharon didn't doubt that for a second. "I'll try to get here by noon," she said uneasily, then quickly backed out of the parking area near the greenhouses.

As she did, her headlights rayed over Steve, who was waving at her. *Sharon,* she asked herself, *what are you getting into? Isn't your life complicated enough right now?*

Glancing in the rearview mirror, she saw that Steve was now standing at the curb, still waving. She was sorely tempted to swerve the car around and throw herself into his arms again. Instead, she switched on the car radio and turned up the blaring rock music.

CHAPTER EIGHT

THE FOLLOWING MORNING disappointment shaded Sharon's face when Peggy, Clara's secretary, told her that her boss was attending a medical conference in Chicago and that Louella was acting chief nurse in Clara's absence.

With a nod toward the closed door to her left, Peggy said, "She's in there if you want to talk to her."

"No point in that." Sharon knew she wasn't one of Louella's favorite people.

Just then the office door opened. Louella spotted Sharon, then handed Peggy the file she was holding. "I won't sign off on this, and I doubt if Clara will when she gets back. When Dr. Wilson returns my call, put him through right away." Slipping her hands into the front pockets of the long white medical jacket she wore over a plum-colored dress, she fixed cool eyes on Sharon. "Good morning," she said rigidly. "Did you want to see me?"

What was there to lose? Sharon thought. Then she answered, "If you have a minute."

Louella glanced at her watch. "That's about all I do have. C'mon in." She entered her office and closed the door after Sharon. "Have a seat," she directed, and sat down in the leather-backed swivel chair behind the desk. "Well?" she asked, her chin tilted up even more than usual.

"Actually," Sharon said as pleasantly as possible, "I came by to see Clara, but—"

"And you got me," Louella commented.

"Since you're acting chief nurse, I'll ask you the same thing I had planned to ask Clara. I'd like you to intercede with the chief of staff for me."

"You want him to lift your suspension, right?"

"Yes."

After leaning forward and clasping her hands, Louella asked, "Are you ready to admit that you made a medication error?"

"Of course not! If I did, why would I even think Dr. Benning would entertain the idea of reinstating me?"

"What makes you think he would now?" She raised a hand toward Sharon, effectively cutting off her response. "Detective Werner and his men have all but memorized Richard Nordstrom's file. They've interrogated everyone who had anything to do with the patient from the moment he was admitted. He was in your charge when he was transferred to ICU, and you yourself stated that none of the other nurses on the unit were involved in his care."

Sharon focused on the woman's icy hazel eyes. "It would have been easy for anyone to slip into the isolation room for a few seconds. ICU was a madhouse that night, and you know it."

"What I know is—" The buzz of the intercom drew her attention, and Peggy reported that Dr. Wilson was on the line.

Louella removed the large pearl earring from her left ear, picked up the receiver and swung her chair around a quarter turn.

"Hi, Jimmy," she said, her voice now sounding more like an ingenue's. "Rita said she'd take the four-thirty meeting, so I'll pick up the hors d'oeuvres and the liquor on her way home." She listened for a moment, then giggled.

Nonplussed, Sharon thought that maybe Dave had been right; perhaps Louella was a different woman outside the hospital. She wished, though, that the woman would exhibit some of that oozing sweetness toward her.

"Yes," Louella continued, seemingly unfazed that Sharon was within earshot, "that's how I feel. See you later... bye."

When she swiveled her chair back around and cradled the receiver, Sharon was again taken by surprise. The woman was actually blushing. But that wasn't the extent of Sharon's amazement. Louella's tone softened, too.

"I'm sorry, Sharon. I know this is a difficult time for you, and if I thought it would do any good, I would talk to Dr. Benning. We desperately need you on ICU. I'm not taking anything away from Dave, but you do have the courage to make decisions you should make, and you have the sense not to make those you shouldn't. Dave's driving Jimmy... Dr. Wilson crazy up there at night. He won't give a patient an aspirin without a written order."

Sharon seized the opportunity to get through the chink in the aloof armor the woman usually wore. "I appreciate your telling me that, Louella, but after what happened to me I'm sure Dave feels he has to be extra cautious. And believe me, please, I didn't make a medication mistake. Granted, Nordstrom was given the morphine by someone, but it wasn't by me."

Before her eyes Louella's expression reverted to the cool look Sharon was used to. "Are you implying that there's a homicidal maniac skulking around this hospital at night?''

"That's for the police to find out. I'm only saying that it's very unfair for me to be suspended while they investigate. And if you honestly believe I'm the nurse you just said I am, it's also unfair to the patients on ICU.''

Rhythmically Louella tapped her plum-lacquered fingernails on the desktop as she regarded Sharon pensively, then she said, "All right, I'll talk to Dr. Benning." She saw Sharon's face light up. "But don't get your hopes up. His fear of scandalous publicity or a lawsuit overshadows his loyalty to anyone here at the hospital.''

Standing, Sharon blurted out spontaneously, "Louella, I could kiss you!''

The woman reared back. "Let's not get carried away." She glanced at the wall clock. "I have a supervisors' meeting right now. I'll phone you and let you know what Dr. Benning decides.''

"Here,'' Sharon said, excitedly digging into her purse for the business card Steve had given her. "You can reach me at this number during the day.''

Louella glanced at the card, and her eyes shot up. "Nordstrom Orchids?''

"It's a temporary job. Being suspended without pay isn't easy for me financially.''

"This Steven Nordstrom... he's the brother, isn't he?''

"Yes, he is." Immediately Sharon wished she had simply jotted down the phone number on a piece of paper.

An enigmatic smile reshaped Louella's wide lips. "He must be a man of great understanding.''

Deciding to get out before Louella changed her mind about talking to the chief of staff, Sharon said, "I don't want to keep you from your meeting, so I'll leave." At the door she glanced back over her shoulder. "Thanks again."

The second Sharon closed the door behind her, Louella buzzed Julie and told her to notify the supervisors in the conference room that she would be there shortly. Then she checked the phone directory and quickly dialed a number. After a moment she said, "Detective Werner, please." Her long eyelashes flickered impatiently when she was informed he was busy and couldn't be interrupted. "He'll talk to me. Tell him I have information concerning the Richard Nordstrom case."

Anxiously she waited for him to come on the line. When he finally did, she lowered her already deep voice, saying, "If you're still looking for a motive for Richard Nordstrom's death, you should know that the nurse who gave him the overdose now works for his brother, Steven Nordstrom. You might check to see who Richard Nordstrom's beneficiary was."

That said, Louella hung up and leaned back in her chair, extremely thoughtful.

HER SPIRITS HIGH, Sharon sailed into the hospital lab, looking for Tony. Told that he was in the employee lounge, she rushed down the corridor and found him munching from a bag of potato chips.

"Hey!" he exclaimed, grinning up at her, "are you back with us?"

"Not yet," she said, sitting next to him on the vinyl sofa and crossing her fingers. "But soon maybe. Louella's going to talk to Dr. Benning on my behalf."

His eyebrows arched. "Frowning Frawley is going to bat for you?"

"Don't burst my bubble, Tony. She said she would and I believe her. I have to."

"Want some?" he asked, extending the bag of chips. When she declined, he said, "If you've won her over, you might be doing as well with Werner."

Attentive, Sharon asked, "What do you mean?"

"He called me down to the station again yesterday afternoon, wanted to rehash exactly what you said when you asked me to do the blood work on Nordstrom."

"And?"

"It's my guess that he either thinks you're a grown-up Nancy Drew or a very shrewd killer."

"That's supposed to mean I've won him over?"

"At least he's beginning to wonder if maybe you're not the one who shot the overdose into Nordstrom."

"Did he say how the investigation is coming along?"

"I got the impression he's at a dead end. You know, kind of grasping for any little clue. I don't think he has motive one for foul play, though."

"Great," she moaned. "That leaves me swinging in the breeze with a sign hanging around my neck saying case closed."

"Sweet lips, I don't think he's ready to close the case, but if you didn't, somebody gave the overdose to Richard Nordstrom."

Sharon slumped sideways and leaned a shoulder against the sofa. "Steve can't think of anyone who would have a reason to kill Richie."

"Well, you're a deep one. Who's Steve and just how well did you know 'Richie'?"

"Steve's his brother, and I never laid eyes on Richard Nordstrom until they brought him up to ICU. Steve calls him Richie all the time."

"All the time?" Tony repeated with a smirk. "What are you doing, rooming with the guy now?"

"Cute, Tony. I only met him the night his brother died. Right now he's not sure if I'm Florence Nightingale or Lucrezia Borgia."

Munching on the last of the potato chips, Tony wadded up the plastic bag and flipped it into a trash basket. "I've got a similar problem with Debbie. Half the time she treats me as if I'm the world's greatest lover. Then she turns around and acts as if I'm a distant relative. It's like tossing a coin. I'm never sure which side of her is going to come up. Any suggestions about how I get through to her?"

"If you really love her—"

"Love her? I can't sleep or eat when she gives me the distance treatment."

"As I started to say, if you really love her, be patient. She went through her own private hell in Nam, and she's still carrying around a lot of hurt. She lost guys on the wards that she thought a lot of, and Alice, her roommate, went down in a chopper. After that Debbie changed from a sweet, caring young woman to an icy workhorse who got most of her energy from a bottle. What she needs right now is your support."

"She knows she has that."

"Maybe so, but she's going to test you time and time again, not because she doesn't believe you love her, but because she doesn't want to believe anyone could. It's her way of protecting herself from being hurt again."

"I've had Psych 101, too, but that doesn't make a lot of sense. I know she had a bad time over there, but why would she beat herself about it? Hell, she volunteered to do a job that she didn't have to."

"Get a book on PTSD, Tony. You'll find that low self-esteem is high up on the list of symptoms, along with alcohol. It's a way of drugging out the memories."

"You're not dependent on it."

"Different strokes for different folks. I had my own problems, believe me, and my ex-husband didn't support me the way Debbie needs you now."

Tony mulled that over before shaking his head. "I want to be supportive, but sometimes she can make it mighty difficult."

"There are good times with her, too, aren't there?"

"You'd better believe it. She can be so damn sweet and thoughtful. She keeps me thinking positively about my getting the promotion to chief of lab services, she's trying all kinds of Italian recipes just because I like them and she makes me laugh a lot."

"Dwell on those times," Sharon suggested, rising from the sofa. At the open door she glanced back at him and smiled. "If you can get back just half of the Debbie I first knew, you'll find out that the effort was well worth it."

As SHE PULLED into the parking area next to Steve's house, Sharon saw him loading several large orchid plants into a station wagon. He chatted briefly with a man whom Sharon assumed owned the car. Then Steve patted the man's shoulder and headed toward her car.

"You're early," he said, smiling broadly. "Trying to make an impression on the boss?"

"You may not be my boss for much longer," she advised, closing the car door. "There's a chance the chief of staff may rescind my suspension."

"Oh," Steve said, not too enthusiastically as they started toward the side of the house. Then he brightened his tone. "That's great news."

After he opened the office door, Sharon stepped inside, scanning the large, carpeted room, the wooden desk and filing cabinets, the bookcase holding rows of tomes on orchids and the computer station at the far end. Scattered haphazardly on a long table against one wall were sloping stacks of papers.

As he began putting the stacks in order, Steve said, "I've been trying to get these files computerized, but I just don't have the time." He sent her a sideways glance. "Ever work with a computer?"

"Daily in the insurance office."

He beamed and folded his hands as if in prayer. "You're due for a raise already."

"Then I'd better get to work," she said, placing her tote bag on one of the filing cabinets.

In between phone calls Steve gave Sharon an overview of the system he'd developed in the office, assuring her that any suggestions for improvement would be welcomed. Then he took her on a tour of the six greenhouses, introducing her to Ed and Willie, his two full-time employees, and showing her the large workroom built onto the last greenhouse, where he received and packed plants for shipment throughout the States and Canada.

Duly impressed, Sharon asked, "How many orchid plants do you have?"

"At any one time the count runs about three thousand, but we're constantly shipping some out and receiving others. On the average I sell about fifteen hundred plants a month, mostly to other orchid businesses. I've computerized all recent transactions. It's the older records I'd like to get into the machine now to cut down on the paper files.''

Back in the office he glanced at the clock on the wall. ''Hungry?''

''You know, Steve,'' she said, smiling, ''you don't have to feed me, too.''

He guided his eyes over the cheerful floral-print sundress she wore. ''If I'm going to work you hard, I want to keep you in prime condition.''

After he switched on the answering machine, he led her from the office into the adjacent spacious living room decorated in eclectic Early American, not pretentious, but comfortable and inviting. They passed a wide archway that led to a dining room with a wood and brass chandelier, then they entered the kitchen, a long room that ran the length of the patio.

''Hope you like chicken and cheese sandwiches,'' Steve said as he took a platter from the refrigerator. Placing it on the countertop, he glanced at her. ''I can rustle up something else in a minute, though.''

''That looks great.''

''Iced tea or a cola?''

''Tea, please.''

As he removed a glass decanter from the fridge, he said, ''Grab the platter, would you?'' Then he carried the iced tea to the breakfast nook by a wide window that overlooked the patio area.

Following him, Sharon examined the nicely arranged table: the crystal vase of yellow tea roses, the yellow linen napkins and glass dishes containing lemon wedges, sugar and assorted pickles.

"You're too good to be true, Mr. Nordstrom."

"I've had years of practice," he said casually.

His explanation took on more import to Sharon, though. She guessed that since his wife had been a semi-invalid, Steve probably had taken over many of the household chores. Her estimation of him rose considerably.

"Dig in," he said, pouring iced tea for both of them. "There's more mayonnaise there if you want."

"This looks perfect," she remarked, slipping half a sandwich from the platter onto her plate.

As he forked a slice of dill pickle from a bowl, Steve said, "Laura liked chicken sandwiches."

"David did, too. For a while after his accident that was about the only thing he'd want to eat, that and dessert, which he ate first."

Steve smiled. "Your grandmother's fault, right?"

"Exactly. It used to drive my parents crazy, but I guess adults think most children have strange eating habits."

"Children," Steve said, as though to himself. "One of the regrets Laura and I had was not having any, but that was out of the question."

Hesitantly she asked, "How old was Laura when the arthritis was diagnosed?"

"Twenty-seven, three years after we were married. Out of the blue she started to eat less and began to tire easily. It passed and we thought that was it. Then she began having tenderness and swelling in some joints, and we found out what the problem was."

Sharon imagined the rest, knowing that life was equally hard for the families of arthritic patients, since they were usually involved in the afflicted person's daily heat treatments and exercise routines. In some cases psychotherapy was required, since there was no cure and the disease was chronic and disabling. She didn't know how long Steve and Laura had been married, and she wasn't about to ask, but she guessed he had probably lived under a terrible strain for a decade or more. In her eyes Steve was fast becoming a saint.

Wanting to change the subject, he transferred another sandwich onto his plate and asked, "How come you left nursing to work in an insurance office—to get a crack at lower premiums?"

"Wrong, but that's a long story, and my boss is a stickler for keeping strict lunch hours."

"He sounds like a curmudgeon."

"He has his good moments."

"What would you say if the old guy asked you to have a drink with him after work?"

"I'd have to think about it."

"For a long time?"

"Pushy, aren't you?"

"When I want to know something badly enough."

The wall phone jangled, and Steve answered it. "Okay, I'll be right there." Returning to the table he said, "Got some live customers. You take your time and finish. There are some éclairs in the fridge."

"Trying to see if I'll actually gain five pounds?" she asked, smiling.

"Something like that," he said playfully, and took a quick swallow of tea.

"Before I report for duty can I have a few minutes to straighten up in here?"

He leaned down, flattened his palms on the table and grinned. "Miss McClure, I was only kidding about the raise."

"I either pay for lunch or I clean up afterward."

"There'll be a white-glove inspection."

"I can handle that."

"I bet you can," he said, stroking the tip of her nose with a forefinger before sauntering out of the kitchen, whistling.

As the afternoon progressed, Sharon made friends with Steve's computer and began transferring some of his accounts receivable information onto disks. She found herself running back and forth across the room each time the phone rang and decided one improvement would be to either get a longer cord or have another phone put in. By five o'clock she was dead set on wearing low-heeled shoes on Monday.

"Quitting time," Steve announced, coming through the outside door and locking it.

"Just a second," she said, peering at the warning note on the computer screen. "The little man in there says I'm running out of space on this disk. I have to start a new one."

Steve reached into a filing cabinet and took out an unopened box of disks and a plastic case containing ones he'd used before. Flipping up the plastic top, he said, "These are all good, but I screwed up on them. If you erase what's on them, they'll be as good as new."

"You'd better check one while you're here before I erase it. It might be something you'd want to save."

"No work after closing hours. Your boss is a stickler about that, too. Besides, you have an engagement to keep with that curmudgeon," he said, flicking on the phone answering machine.

"The plight of the working girl," she complained, instructing the computer to shut down.

As they entered the living room, he asked, "What's your pleasure? I've got a good assortment."

"Umm . . . a gin and tonic?"

"Two coming up. Make yourself at home and kick off your shoes if you like. I'm going to."

Sorely missing her comfortable nursing shoes, she mumbled, "A man after my own heart."

"You got *that* right," he said halfway to the kitchen.

His offhand remark struck a nerve, and as he exited the living room, Sharon sank onto the upholstered chair by the fireplace. She used the toe of one shoe to push off the other, then a stockinged toe to rid her aching feet of the second high-heeled shoe. Bending, she massaged the ball of each foot in turn, pondering Steve's comment.

He was certainly all male, and from what she had learned of him so far, he hadn't been painting the town during the past six months. She thought herself a fairly attractive woman, and she could understand that he might have unfulfilled masculine needs. But "a man after her own heart"? Was it just a phrase, or had he meant that as a signal that he was ready to embark on a serious relationship? Just how serious, she pondered, and was she ready for that?

If last evening was any indication, she realized she would have to decide quickly. Extending her legs, she wiggled her toes, thinking that she had just about moved in with him already. Dinner, lunch, working in his office, and now she was perched in his living room, waiting for him to serve her cocktails.

All very well and good, she mused, except for the little matter of why she was working for him. After the conversation she had with Detective Werner, there was a good possibility that she'd soon be employed in the laundry of a women's prison.

She forced that idea away immediately, ordering
herself to look on the bright side. Which was? she asked
herself, and waited for a hopeful response.

None came.

Well, she decided, she'd made it through two years in
Vietnam. What lay ahead of her could in no way be as
bad as that.

Steve returned with an aluminum tray, which he
placed on the oval coffee table in front of the long sofa.
"C'mon over and join me," he suggested, then arranged their drinks on napkins and placed a small bowl
of mixed nuts next to each ice-filled glass.

Sharon settled in the corner of the sofa and curled her
legs under the flare of her dress.

"Worn out?" he asked, shedding his sneakers.

"I don't think I've adjusted to the day shift yet," she
admitted, then took a sip of the refreshing drink.
"Umm, this hits the spot."

After a good swallow of his, he picked up the bowl of
nuts and began munching. "When I was in your apartment, you weren't hiding a dog or a cat, were you?"

"No," she said, looking at him quizzically.

"Good."

"Don't you like animals?"

"Sure, but knowing you don't have one means you
don't have to rush home to take care of it. I thought we
might go out to dinner."

Yes, Sharon reminded herself, she was going to have
to decide just how deeply she wanted to get involved
with Steve, and fast. "When I was unemployed," she
said lightly, "it was okay for you to feed me, but I've
got a paying job now."

Concentrating on his bowl of nuts, he said matter-of-
factly, "The man you were here with last night wan-

dered a little out-of-bounds. I gave him a good talking to. He's seen the error of his ways and promises to be a perfect gentleman from now on.''

Sharon put her glass down on the napkin, then rested an arm over the back of the sofa and regarded Steve. ''The man I was with last night was a perfect gentleman.''

His surprised eyes slanted toward her. ''He was?''

''Neither of us are teenagers, Steve. If you did get a little carried away last night, you caught yourself quickly and apologized. I've dated some men who presumed too much and then got angry when they didn't get their way. I'd say you were a gentleman.''

''I'd say you're an angel.''

She chuckled softly. ''In my nursing uniform maybe.''

''Dinner is on the schedule?''

Her thoughts raced for unsettling moments before she said honestly, ''I'm not ready for a serious involvement, Steve.''

''Sharon,'' he explained quietly, ''I'm asking you out to dinner. I'm not saying we should hit the sheets, running.''

She felt her cheeks warm. ''I . . . I didn't for a moment think that you—''

''Don't misunderstand me,'' he cautioned her. ''The thought has crossed my mind, but I'm not the macho type who's going to get you into a wrestling match. Wherever our friendship leads us, we'll travel the road together.''

Already feeling halfway to ''wherever,'' she reached for her glass and took a long swallow, eyeing him sideways. ''I'd love to have dinner with you, but it's my treat this time.''

"You're on," he said, jumping up. "I'm going to shower. How about you?" When she stared up at him, he pointed at the ceiling. "Separate bedrooms, separate showers."

CHAPTER NINE

IF SHARON HADN'T BEEN busy digging into the luscious lasagna on her plate, she would have seen the totally absorbed expression on Steve's face as he watched her eat. The flame from the candle stuck in the top of the wicker-wrapped Chianti bottle cast a yellow gold glow over her lovely features, highlighting her sensual lips and long eyelashes. Again he felt that insistent tug deep within his chest, that desperate desire to touch her, even casually.

What's happening to me? he demanded silently, excited and fearful that she had become so important to him so quickly. *Hit the sheets running. I actually said that to her. Where the hell did those words come from?*

At that moment she looked up and smiled. He did, too, his heartbeat escalating to a heroic pounding. She had reminded him that neither of them were teenagers, he recollected. *Then why do I feel the same earthy cravings I did then? You're forty-four, Nordstrom. Your days of feeling like a rutting stag are long behind you.*

So why does her slightest smile set me on fire?

He hadn't experienced feelings like this in a long, long time. The first seven of his fifteen years of marriage to Laura had been every man's dream. He had loved her with all his heart, and she had returned his love in kind. She had been his companion, his best friend and his exceptionally satisfying lover. Her physical decline changed all that, though, and during the last four years of their marriage only their companionship and loving respect survived. Caring for Laura became the reason for his entire existence.

Throughout those last years he had blocked out his own physical needs and had buried the hopes he and Laura had had for children. He'd wanted to watch their children grow up, marry and have children of their own to bring added happiness to his and Laura's golden years. But her illness shattered their dreams, and he sublimated his own by throwing himself heart and soul into his task as his wife's caretaker. He had succeeded royally—until that one damnable night in Costa Rica.

At Laura's insistence he took a week to comb the Sarapiqui Canyon, looking for the fabled blue cattleya orchid that rumor claimed grew wild deep in the jungle. Destiny smiled on him and he found it. Then destiny exacted its price.

If only he hadn't celebrated and drunk so much that night in the cantina. If only the smiling, seductive young woman with the raven hair hadn't beckoned to him with her midnight dark eyes. If only she hadn't been so alluring, so soft, so willing.

"Steve?" Sharon said, interrupting his painful ruminations. When he looked up at her, seemingly startled, she asked lightly, "Where were you?"

He saw that he was holding his fork in midair, the black olive shaking slightly. Quickly he put the fork down, took a hefty drink of his red wine, then explained, "I was thinking of my last trip to Costa Rica."

"Are you going again soon?" she asked conversationally.

"No," he said, his response quick, edgy. "Never again."

The tone of his voice and the lightninglike flash in his eyes made Sharon wonder if he'd had a bad experience there. To brighten his mood she said, "Enough of the snakes and creepy crawly things, I take it."

His eyelashes flickered nervously. "Yes...it's not a place I ever want to see again." Realizing his voice had roughened, he forced a conciliatory smile. "I'm no Gene Kelly, but would you like to dance off some calories later?"

"You get the best ideas. Now I can appease my sweet tooth and have the tortoni for dessert."

After dessert and cappuccino, Sharon suggested they go to the club where Debbie worked. During the drive there, she gave Steve some background on her friend, telling him that Debbie had been born in Texas and had volunteered to go to Vietnam the week after her twenty-first birthday.

"With her guitar strapped on her back," Sharon said, "she'd hitch rides on anything that moved, chopper, truck or jeep, to sing for the guys out in the field on firebases. She wasn't supposed to go alone, though. The Red Cross gals always traveled in pairs. Not Debbie. She had more guts than a lot of us. In Pleiku, when we'd have incoming fire in the middle of the night, you could see her running to the bunkers with that guitar on her back. She claimed she used it to beat the rats away."

"Sounds like a winner," Steve said. "I haven't kept contact with the friends I made while I was in the air force," he admitted, feeling strangely uncomfortable that he'd sat at a desk while Sharon and other women had been in combat zones.

"Friendships," Sharon said, her thoughts drifting back, "were important to us over there, essential even. That's what held me in one piece. Debbie and I laughed and cried a lot together. There was so much misery, pain and ugliness in both our jobs that after a while we just felt empty, but she kept me sane and would give me a hug whenever I needed it. She was someone I could lean on, someone who kept reminding me that it would all be over soon and I'd still be human."

"You did the same for her, I'm guessing."

"I tried to, but in a way Debbie always seemed stronger than I was at the time. It wasn't until she came back home that she—" Sharon cut herself off, feeling it wasn't right to tell Steve all about Debbie now. Seeing that they were approaching the lounge, she said, "That's it on the right. You can pull into the next driveway."

As they entered the dimly lighted, elegant room, the hostess greeted them and led them toward one of the few available tables by the wall. Steve glanced at the captivating woman playing the piano. She was singing, "It's very clear. Our love is here to stay," a song he hadn't heard in ages. Her jade-colored dress and her long blond hair shimmered in the ray of light that came from above the piano.

Just as he and Sharon were about to sit down, a man called her name softly. Two tables over one of the men he'd seen at the inquiry motioned to her.

"It's Tony," she said. "He wants us to join him."

As they headed toward his table, Steve's memory informed him that Tony was the microbiologist who had discovered that Richie's body had been laced with morphine.

Sharon saw Tony's smile freeze as he rose from his chair, and she realized he must have remembered Steve from the inquiry. Tony shifted his eyes from Steve to her, then back to Steve, who extended his hand, reading the question in the dark-haired man's ebony eyes: *How come you're so chummy with the woman you think killed your brother?*

The two men shook hands and introduced themselves, and as the trio sat down, Steve said, "I remember seeing you at the hospital. You're a microbiologist, aren't you?"

"One of the best," Sharon remarked. "Tony will be running the lab fairly soon."

Steve ordered white crème de menthe and soda for Sharon and himself, then Tony asked him, "What kind of work do you do?"

"I import and ship orchid plants."

"Steve's my new boss," Sharon added, watching Tony's expression turn quizzical again. "I'm working in his office temporarily."

"That's . . . uh, nice," Tony allowed, then took a sip of his bourbon and water, his eyes darting down to the college ring on Steve's left hand.

"Sharon's going to get me organized," Steve said, smiling at her.

"With her nursing skills, she shouldn't be doing office work," Tony said, meaning it as a compliment.

Concerned that Steve would take his remark as a not too subtle jab, Sharon said, "I appreciate having something constructive to do, Tony. The busier I am right now, the better."

"Well sure . . . I just meant—"

"I agree with you," Steve interrupted, suspecting that Tony resented him. "Sharon should be working in her chosen field."

"Until the police find out what happened that night," Sharon said to Tony, "I really don't have a choice in the matter."

"Benning's suspending you was stupid as far as I'm concerned. It makes you look as guilty as hell."

"I don't think so," Steve said with a certainty that surprised him.

And he did want to believe it. He had wrestled with the problem until he had become mentally exhausted, but try as he might he couldn't totally dismiss the possibility that Sharon had given his brother an overdose accidentally. The only alternative would be to accept that someone had murdered Richie, and that seemed so irrational. What motive would anyone have to kill him?

As Steve mulled that over, his words echoed in Sharon's thoughts. "I don't think so," he'd said. She felt an overwhelming sense of relief, realizing that in his mind he had finally exonerated her. Her relief swelled to a joyous feeling that threatened to bring tears to her eyes. She had sorely needed to hear Steve say that he believed in her and that he trusted her absolutely. Now he had.

She was tempted to lean over and kiss him, but instead she placed her hand over his, saying, "Thank you for the vote of confidence."

"Don't I get to vote?" Debbie asked, a wide smile on her face as she gave Steve the once-over.

Sean was right behind her, setting down her usual Scotch on the rocks. He checked the other glasses and asked, "Are you ready yet, Tony?"

"Thanks, no. I'll nurse this a while longer."

Her inquisitive hazel eyes settling on Sharon, Debbie asked, "Aren't you going to introduce me to your friend?"

"Debbie Weston, Steve Nordstrom."

"You play and sing beautifully," he complimented her sincerely.

"The requests tonight have been for golden oldies. I don't hit my stride until I get to country and western music." She raised her glass, but paused and set it back down. "Nordstrom?" she said, turning the name over in her mind.

Quietly Tony said, "Richard Nordstrom's brother."

"The man who—?" Debbie stifled her words and looked at Sharon.

To break the tension Steve said, "Sharon told me you also play the guitar."

"And a musical saw when I want to empty this place out and leave early," Debbie joked, then sipped her drink.

"The saw went over real big in Nam," Sharon said, eyeing her, "but she gave it up after the thing snagged most of her nylons."

"Even in torn stockings I still looked more fashionable than you did in those grungy fatigues of yours." Debbie turned to Steve. "In Bangkok she went crazy buying every dress that would fit, knowing she'd rarely get to wear any of them."

"I had to have something to do while you took afternoon-long bubble baths in the hotel."

"Ah!" Debbie gushed, closing her eyes. "Hot water finally and a toilet that flushed."

Sharon turned to Steve and shook her head. "You should have seen her during the monsoon season, standing ankle-deep in mud and shampooing her hair in the rain with a towel wrapped around her."

"I can picture that," Tony said, a twinkle in his eyes.

Debbie nudged him with her elbow. "Rainwater's good for your hair." To Sharon she said, "Don't pretend you were Miss Prim and Proper." She faced Steve. "This one was famous for the parties she gave in her hooch. When the air force guys flew in the hospital supplies, they always brought special Care packages with her name on them. French wines, tins of caviar and all kinds of cheeses."

"It was their way of making sure they were invited," Sharon explained.

"And that rakishly handsome pilot, the one who brought you the electric frying pan and pizza mix. You remember, the captain who was the spitting image of Tyrone Power."

"That's how you remember him."

"How do you?"

"As an octopus," Sharon said, smirking at Debbie. Then she rose and smiled warmly at Steve. "You offered to take me dancing, remember?"

He led her to the small dance floor and took her in his arms as the relief pianist played slow, soothing music. "I like your friend," he said as he drew Sharon closer.

"It's difficult not to . . . most of the time."

"Tony seems quite taken by her. He can barely keep his eyes off her."

"You're very observant, Mr. Nordstrom."

"And you're very nice to hold like this, Miss McClure."

I like you holding me, she admitted silently, snuggling even closer, catching the pleasant aroma of the after-shave he'd used. It had a woodsy scent, reminding her of wildflowers in the spring.

His cheek nestled against her forehead, Steve said, "It's been years since I've danced like this."

"You're doing just fine."

"That's something else I have to thank you for."

"For dancing?" she asked languidly, lulled by his comforting warmth and soothing voice.

"That and for changing my life." When she tilted her head back slightly and gazed up at him, he said, "You've done that, you know. Before I met you I felt isolated, so alone, but now I'm beginning to believe that the future can be brighter."

Lowering her head again, she felt his warmth against her temple once more, felt his arms tighten around her, his firm thighs brushing hers as they moved slowly to the music. She closed her eyes and gave in to the relaxing comfort of his embrace, more than content to let him guide her with his easy rocking movements.

Without thought she slipped her left hand over his shoulder and eased her fingertips along the back of his neck, sensing his warmth and the soft hair at his nape. His foot missed a musical beat, his arm stiffened around her, and she felt his chest rise as he took a deeper breath and exhaled a little sigh.

He wondered if she had any idea what her slightest touch did to him, and he longed to tell her that his entire body ached for wanting her—but he had promised that no repetition of the scene by the pool would ever happen again unless she wanted it to. And he was determined, no matter what it cost him, to keep his word.

It had been torture while he had taken his shower earlier, knowing she was in the next room taking hers. He had imagined the soapy lather running over her smooth shoulder and down over her breasts and thighs. Turning off his hot water and letting the cold spray pelt his face hadn't helped at all. Finally he'd had to charge out of the stall before he tore through the wall to get at her.

"Steve," she said, breaking into his erotic reverie.

"Yes?"

"The music has stopped."

"Oh," he said, somewhat flustered, then followed her back to the table.

"I thought you two were going to go to sleep out there," Debbie remarked, smiling knowingly at Sharon.

"I'm not used to being up all day."

"Tony just told me you're working again." Her eyes sparkled mischievously. "Poor thing, I imagine you're exhausted and you're anxious to get home and rest."

"She's just trying to get me alone for a while," Tony said, taking hold of Debbie's hand and flashing her a brilliant smile.

Standing, Debbie ruffled his hair. "If Sharon and Steve leave, you're going to be alone. I've got to get back to work."

"I think we will go," Sharon said to Debbie.

"Give me a call tomorrow afternoon—" her eyes lingered on Steve "—and we'll chat."

As she headed back to the piano, Tony said, "Sunday, Debbie and I are driving up to Tarpon Springs for dinner. Why don't the two of you come with us?"

"I'd like that," Steve said quickly.

Hoping she'd soon hear from Louella about Dr. Benning's lifting her suspension, Sharon said, "I'll let you know, okay, Tony?"

He nodded and gave her and Steve a little wave as they departed.

Pulling out of the parking lot, Steve said, "You have some pretty good ideas yourself. I enjoyed that."

"Thank you for a nice evening."

He glanced at the car clock. "It's still early. Can I talk you into stopping by the house for some coffee?"

"Sure," she said brightly.

Not long after she was resting back on a cushioned lounge chair on his patio, sipping from her coffee cup while listening to the haunting call of a whippoorwill in one of the tall pine trees. Putting her cup down on the little table between her chair and the one Steve was lying on, she glanced over at him and smiled. "I could get used to all this service."

"I could get used to having you here," he said quietly, his eyes closed as the evening breeze rustled the fronds of the palm trees surrounding the pool.

Her gaze drifted over the verdant garden area on the other side of the patio railing. "How do you find time to keep everything looking so picture perfect and run a business, too?"

"I make sure I plant things that don't require a lot of pruning and fuss, things like the azalea and hawthorn bushes, and a woman comes in once a week to see to the house."

"You really have your life organized," she said, chalking up another plus on the already long list of things she admired about Steve.

"I suppose so." He lifted himself onto an arm and tilted his face toward hers. "But lately I'm realizing how empty my life really is. There should be more to living than working and being organized."

In the dim patio light Sharon thought his blue gray eyes the most beautiful she had ever seen, and she felt a quivering sensation tease her breasts. Suddenly, though, she questioned the wisdom of spending so much time with Steve. *Don't go getting strange,* she cautioned herself. *All you're doing is relaxing and having a cup of coffee.*

"Don't you agree?" he asked, wondering what she was thinking so hard about.

"With my job at the hospital I work hard and have to be organized. That doesn't leave a lot of time for much else."

"Time," he repeated, his voice low. "Why does it go by so quickly when you're happy and so slowly when you're miserable?"

"Are you unhappy?" she asked, searching his unreadable expression.

"I was . . . until you—"

"Don't, Steve." Feeling unnerved and not sure why, she rose from the lounge chair, crossed to the steps leading to the pool area and started down.

He followed and stopped on the top step. "Don't what?" he asked, sensing the sudden tension between them.

Turning, she looked up at him. "Every now and then I get this feeling that you'd like me to be responsible for your happiness. It makes me uncomfortable. I have a difficult enough time with my own."

"Isn't that what friends are for—to help bring a little happiness into each other's life?"

"Yes," she said, glancing away again, "if that's the kind of friendship you're talking about."

"I'm not talking about the kind of friendship you have with Debbie or with Tony." He took the two steps down and placed a hand on her shoulder. "I think you and I are capable of something more personal. I know I am."

"I'm not, Steve," she lied, feeling the tantalizing warmth of his hand through the cotton material of her dress. It almost scorched her skin, yet it caused her to shiver. A wonderful paradox, she realized, and had to admit she did yearn for his touch. So why was she fighting him? Because something warned her that her emotional well-being depended on her doing so.

He moved in front of her and examined her evasive eyes. Unable to control his hand he ran his fingers along her bare upper arm, its silky smoothness a delight to his touch. "There's something special between us, Sharon," he said softly, "something I can't even understand, never mind explain. We can pretend it doesn't exist, but that's not going to make it disappear."

Her heartbeat quickening, she attempted to reason with him. "The only thing between us, Steve, is something that you want to believe is there."

"Do I imagine the excitement I feel whenever I see you? Did I just want to believe the way you kissed me last evening? Did I imagine the way your fingers caressed my neck while we were dancing?"

She edged her way past him and followed the stone pathway along the curve of the pool, wishing she had told him to take her directly home when they left the lounge. She almost jumped when she felt his hands take hold of her shoulders.

Standing behind her, his lips close to her ear, he said, "I can't pretend any longer. You're driving me crazy. I think about you before I go to sleep and when I awake, and in between I dream about you. When you're not with me, I wonder what you're doing, what you're thinking." Kissing the side of her neck, he murmured, "For God's sake, tell me what I'm supposed to do."

With her eyes closed she tilted her head a little, wilting under the exquisite feel of his lips on her skin. But when she felt his hand slip around her waist and then his thumb brush the underswell of her breast, she knew she was the one who had to think sensibly and quickly.

Facing him, she said, "Sorry, Steve, but this worked for you before."

Using all her strength, she shoved him backward.

Wide-eyed and gaping, he stumbled, then tottered, his arms rotating wildly as he splashed into the pool.

CHAPTER TEN

THE MOMENT STEVE surfaced Sharon knew this was *not* the time to be amused, but she couldn't stop herself from smiling at the amazed look on his wet face. When he sputtered water, she doubled over and planted her palms on her knees, tears welling up in her eyes as she began to laugh.

His movements were swift, and it was in her bent-over position that Sharon felt herself hitting the cool water.

Bobbing up, she squealed, soaked strands of hair screening her shocked expression, her nostrils sucking in the odor of chlorine. "You jerk!" she spit out with a spray of water.

Drenched, he thrust his hands onto his hips and grinned. "What's good for the gander, et cetera."

"I'll gander you," she threatened as she dog-paddled to the side of the pool.

He crouched down and put a large hand on top of her straight, wet hair. "Apologize," he ordered playfully, "and I'll let you out."

She raised her hands to swat at him and sank under the water. Quickly he reached down, grabbed her descending arm and pulled her up. "Are you all right?" he asked, seriously concerned now.

"Help me out of here," she said between clenched teeth, then took hold of his wrist with both hands.

"You idiot!" she yelled, tugging his arm with all her might.

He landed half on the water and half on her, submerging her as he went under again. When he came up this time, he drew her up with him. Finding that he touched the bottom of the pool now, he encircled her waist with his arms, crushing her to him, feeling her heart pounding against his chest through their soaked clothes.

"I didn't know you were into water sports," he said with a wide-mouthed grin.

"You want water sports?" she hissed, then kneed him in the groin.

The motion was less than effective, since her feet were dangling and the water cushioned the blow. But he was not to be outdone by her theatrics.

"Ohh!" he moaned, and backed away.

She started to go under again, then grabbed hold of the side of the pool, gaping and wondering if she had lost her sanity. "Steve!" she cried when his head submerged.

Immediately she dived, took hold of him and brought him to the surface. In the best lifeguard tradition she struggled but managed to get him to the curved tiled steps at the shallow end of the pool. As though half dazed, he slumped onto a step, half in the water, half out, leaning against the round aluminum handhold, his head tilted down.

"Did I hurt you?" she asked, really worried as she perched next to him.

"I'll be all right," he said dramatically. Then, eyeing her, he added, "I think."

"Well, it's all your fault," she chastised him, parting the wet hair from her eyes.

"You try to make a soprano out of me, and it's *my* fault?"

"I said I was sorry. What more do you want?"

His eyes lowered, drawn to the wet dress that clung to her breasts and outlined her nipples. "This," he said huskily, then took hold of her shoulders, pulled her against his saturated shirt and kissed her soundly.

Sharon didn't attempt to struggle, nor did she want to. She moved her arms over his shoulders and kissed him back with a passion that stunned him. If she had been thinking, it would have amazed her also, but she was too busy doing what she had been tempted to do for a long time.

Moved emotionally, Steve found himself being moved physically, as well. Sharon was so into the kiss that she had maneuvered him onto his back against the slippery steps, and she was showing no signs of letting up.

When she finally did, he stared up at her and grinned as he moved a hand over her wet backside. "Now this is the kind of water sport I like."

"What am I going to do with you, Steve?" she asked, smiling and shaking her head slowly.

"I have a suggestion."

She eased back the wet tendrils that stuck to his forehead. "Be careful what you ask for, you may get it."

A seriousness settled in his expression and his voice. "I'm asking."

"There can't be any strings attached, Steve," she said, matching his earnest tone. "I'm not ready for that."

"Your rules all the way," he promised, then took hold of the railing and pulled himself up. His pulse racing, he gazed down at her. "We've got to get out of these wet clothes."

"Uh, Steve, I seemed to have lost my shoes."

"I'll get them." Quickly he raised a hand. "This time I'll jump in myself."

In seconds he returned with her high-heeled pumps. "Are these yours?"

"Is female traffic here that heavy?" she asked, now standing on the pathway, her smile more of a question.

"That's another thing I like about you," he said, water pouring off him as he ascended the steps. "You have a sense of humor."

"They're ruined," she moaned, taking the shoes from him.

His arm around her shoulder, they started toward the house. "I'll buy you a new pair."

"Do you have any idea what these cost?"

"Maybe my accountant can chalk it up to a business expense."

He slid open the glass door to the kitchen and locked it behind them.

"We're going to ruin your carpeting," she said, taking note of the pool of water they were dripping onto the linoleum.

"Not if we do things my way."

Before she could ask how he stripped down to his jockey shorts, then swooped her up in his strong arms and carried her upstairs to his bedroom, where he set her down in front of the shower stall.

"That chlorine won't do your hair any good," he advised. "Let me have your dress. I'll put our clothes in the dryer downstairs." As Sharon began to disrobe, he half turned. "Give me your lingerie, too." It wasn't that he thought either one of them would be all that embarrassed, but he knew that if he didn't look aside, he'd make love to her on the spot.

"Here," she said softly, then stepped into the shower and closed the glass door.

Her wet clothes clutched in his hand, he risked a quick glimpse of her slender form through the glass, then hurried downstairs to the utility room. After placing their wet garments, including his jockey shorts, in the dryer, he bounded up the steps again and opened one of the louvered doors to his closet that ran the length of the bedroom. He withdrew a tan terry robe, shrugged into it, then pulled a white one off a hanger. As he laid it across the bed, his gaze drifted to the photograph of Laura on the dresser. Dark-haired and green-eyed, she smiled at him. A heaviness filled his chest, and his stomach knotted as a silent accusing voice—his own—taunted him.

He slumped down on the bed, closed his eyes and lowered his head, trying to fight the gnawing guilt that still haunted him because of his one act of infidelity. In his heart he knew Laura would have forgiven him, but he couldn't forgive himself. The sound of pelting water filled his ears, and he inclined his head toward the bathroom, imagining what Sharon would think of him if she learned what he had done that night in Costa Rica.

She would recoil from him, he decided with merciless self-condemnation.

Heavyhearted he rose from the bed, went downstairs and poured Courvoisier into two brandy snifters, taking a hefty swallow from one before slumping onto the sofa and staring blankly into the darkened fireplace.

"All finished," Sharon announced a while later.

He turned toward the staircase. She was halfway down, wearing the white robe, her hair looking silky and shiny now.

"I used your hair dryer and your brush," she said, a soft smile on her face as she descended the remaining steps. "I hope you don't mind."

Crossing to the foot of the stairs, he gazed at her, his eyes filled with longing. "No, I don't mind," he said quietly. "I poured us some brandy. I won't be long."

"I'll wait for you," she said, touching his arm, her smile evaporating when he pulled away.

"Uh…if you hear the buzzer go off, would you take our things from the dryer? It's in the utility room next to the kitchen. After I shower, I'll get dressed and then drive you home."

Shocked, Sharon watched him bound up the steps and disappear into his bedroom at the top of the stairs. A flurry of questions whipped through her mind. Why had he changed so suddenly? Was it something she had done, something she had said? Just a short time ago in the pool he had made her think she was so very important to him, and now he couldn't wait to take her home. And she had all but thrown herself at him!

Her face flushed and she felt ridiculous wearing his robe. She darted to the utility room, jerked open the dryer door and checked the clothes. "Dry enough," she mumbled, searching for hers. Then she dressed quickly, feeling more humiliated by the second.

Minutes later, wondering what Sharon thought of him now, Steve returned to the living room and saw that she was standing by the front bay window, her back to him. He glanced down at the brandy snifters, noting that she hadn't touched hers.

"Sharon," he said quietly, and she turned, a taut smile on her face.

"Ready?" she asked, picking up her purse.

"Could we take a minute and talk?"

Her precarious control weakened. "About what?" she asked dourly.

"About this evening."

"There is *nothing* to talk about. Please take me home or call me a cab."

"Can't the two of us sit down and calmly—"

"There are three people in this room, Steve. Me, the man who was in the pool and the one who couldn't wait to show me the door. Which one of you wants to sit down and talk now?"

"I know how you must feel," he began.

"No, you don't. I feel like a fool, which is how I was about to act tonight. Luckily you saved me from making a big mistake. Now—" she started for the front door "—if your offer is still good, I'd like to go home."

It took some fast moving, but he beat her to the door and opened it for her.

The short drive to her apartment building was made in tense silence, but when he parked in a visitor's space, he twisted his body sideways and stretched his arm over the back of the car seat. "Please, just give me a minute."

"Why, Steve?"

"Because we're friends."

"All three of us, huh?"

"Don't keep saying that. You make it sound as if I'm two different people."

"The words split personality keep coming to mind."

"Maybe that's how it looks to you, but it's not the way I feel . . . not deep inside, anyway."

His words and expression seemed so troubled and sincere that Sharon modified her sharp tone. "You don't owe me an explanation. In fact, you don't owe me anything. Let's just leave it at that and call it a night."

"Still friends?" he asked hesitantly.

Just wanting to get the evening over with, she looked straight ahead and nodded.

"Can I ask a friend a favor?" When her eyes slanted toward him, he said, "Tomorrow I have a shipment of orchids arriving from Java. It's Ed's wedding anniversary and Willie has tickets for the homecoming game in Jacksonville. I can't ask them to come in. Would you give a helping hand?"

She peered at him suspiciously. "How much help could I be? I don't know the first thing about handling orchids."

"I'll show you what to do. It shouldn't take us more than two hours. Please... I'd really appreciate it."

Against her better judgment, she asked, "What time do you want me to come by?"

"I'll pick the boxes up at the airport around eight o'clock. They've already passed the Department of Agriculture inspection, so I should be back by nine. How about nine-thirty? Is that too early?" He was about to say they could have lunch afterward, but wisely decided against it.

"No, that's okay," she said, reaching for the door handle.

"Thanks," he said quietly, and she glanced back at him briefly before getting out of the car.

Her heels clicked on the pavement as she took quick strides to the building entrance, but the only thing she heard was that little voice again, warning her that she was asking for trouble, big trouble.

IN THE MORNING Sharon found Steve already busy at the workstation in the last greenhouse. Dressing comfortably was one of the benefits of being your own boss and working at home, she thought as her gaze slid over the sleeveless white T-shirt and denim cutoffs he wore. Four large, sturdy cardboard boxes with air holes in them were on the long worktable. One was open, and he was removing the shredded packing material. Four long rows of small black plastic pots half filled with previously soaked fir bark were lined up on the table.

"Morning," she said casually, putting her tote bag down.

He turned toward her and smiled, scanning the jeans and pale green pullover she wore. "You're right on time," he said, thinking how attractively cute she looked with her hair pulled back and held in a curly ponytail by a wisp of green scarf.

"So far so good," she quipped, trying to give the impression that last evening had never happened. "What do you want me to do?"

"These are vanda seedlings," he said, removing a two-inch plant from the box and placing it in one of the plastic pots. "Vanda *sanderiana* actually." When she looked at him blankly, he smiled, then took hold of her hand. "C'mere, I'll show you a mature plant."

In the greenhouse section he removed a three-foot-high potted plant from a shelf. Each of three long spikes bore six large blooms, five inches across. The upper half of each flower was pink with a yellow, red-veined lower portion. "For orchid growers," Steve explained, "the vanda *sanderiana* is one of the most important species of its genus because it can be used extensively for hybridization. I can't keep enough of them in stock. Half of the seedlings that just came in are sold already."

He replaced the plant on the shelf and reached for Sharon's hand again, but she started back to the workstation, saying briskly, "Show me what you want me to do."

Still touchy, he decided.

At the worktable he picked up the seedling again. "Put each one in a pot, like this, and cover the roots with moist bark." He took a handful from the square plastic tub that was on the table behind the pots. "That's all there is to it. Here—" he handed her another seedling "—try potting one."

She did, slowly and very delicately.

"They aren't real fragile," Steve said, potting another quickly and with firm finger motions as he pressed the newly added bark into the pot. "Okay?"

"If you say so," she commented, eyeing him suspiciously.

Sharon soon began to get the hang of it, and work progressed smoothly. The second box contained larger, more mature plants, and Steve showed her how to attach wire pins to the side of a clay pot to hold the plant securely in the bark.

Two hours later, after they potted and transferred the remainder of newly arrived plants to other greenhouses, he had her spraying them with liquid fertilizer.

"Now," he complimented her, "you're ready to go into business for yourself."

Sipping the cola he'd given her from the small refrigerator in the workstation, she said, "I have a feeling that taking care of all these plants isn't as simple as you make it out to be."

"Like people, they can get sick and spread a virus if you're not careful."

A deep voice said, "They all look pretty healthy to me."

Both their heads pivoted toward the greenhouse door, where Detective Werner stood, the top button of his white dress shirt open, his gaudy tie hanging loose.

"Working overtime?" Steve asked, tensing because he knew the sight of the man would upset Sharon.

"The nature of my job, like yours, apparently," he answered, inspecting the blooming orchids. Moving close to one white flower, he said, "My wife has one something like this pressed in our wedding scrapbook."

Sharon seriously doubted that he had come to buy an orchid for his wife. Nervous energy giving her courage, she asked, "Is this a social call, Detective Werner, or are you here on business?"

He assessed her with inspecting green eyes. "I was just about to ask you the same question."

Steve stepped forward and hooked his thumbs on the front pockets of his denim cutoffs. "Miss McClure is working for me temporarily, just until she's reinstated at the hospital."

As Werner stroked his double chin, Sharon knew what he was wondering: why would the brother of the man she was suspected of killing hire her?

"You know a lot about orchids, Miss McClure?" Werner asked.

"I work in Steve's office."

"Steve's, huh?"

"That's my name," he said, not liking the look the detective was giving Sharon, nor his attitude. "Mind telling us why you're here?"

"Just trying to put some pieces together." He chuckled as he cocked his head. "This case is like a puzzle that's almost complete, but the few pieces that are left don't seem to fit. I hate when that happens."

Sharon's grip tightened around the can of cola she was holding. "I hate it more than anyone, but I'm sure you can understand that. If there's any way I can help make the pieces fit, tell me how."

"How long have you two known each other?"

"I met Steve at the hospital the night his brother died."

Werner pondered that for a few silent seconds. "Steve," he said. Then he asked quickly, "Do you mind if I call you Steve?"

"Not at all. What's your first name?"

The red-haired man frowned. "Aloysius. A mouthful, huh? Just call me Al. Steve," he said again, "did your brother have a life insurance policy?"

"Yes."

Sharon glanced at Steve momentarily, wondering where the detective's questions were leading.

"How much?" Werner asked.

"A hundred thousand dollars."

"And naturally your parents were the beneficiary."

"No. I was."

"You were? Have you filed the claim yet?"

"Al," Steve asked with a crooked smile, "why do I have this feeling that you already know I have?"

"Because you're sharp, Steve." Bluntly he asked, "How come your brother made you his beneficiary and not his parents?"

"That was his decision."

"But why you?"

"We were very close."

"Oh. He only moved here four months ago, right?" Steve nodded.

"When did you see him before that?"

"At my wife's funeral, six months ago."

"And before that?"

"A year maybe."

"You call that close?"

"He was my brother. We grew up together."

"I've got a brother. I don't particularly like him."

"That's your problem, Al."

Werner faced Sharon. "Before signing on at the hospital I understand you worked for a year locally as a private-duty nurse."

"Yes."

"For Laura Nordstrom, by any chance?"

"Your memory is faulty," Steve said sharply. "Sharon and I both told you we met the night my brother died." His thumbs hooked onto the waistband of his denim shorts, he eyed the detective. "Look, *Al*, more than anyone else I want to know what happened to Richie, and I want to help you do your job, but you're barking up the wrong tree and wasting time with these questions."

"How am I gonna get any answers if I don't ask questions?" He tilted his head toward Sharon. "Right, Miss McClure?"

"This is one answer you should remember," she said firmly. "Steve and I have never been, nor are we now, involved intimately."

Werner's eyes darted to Steve to catch his reaction, which didn't allow him to put too much stock in what the lady had just told him. "That's a shame," he said, shaking his head. "The two of you make a nice-looking pair." Before Steve could say a word Werner raised a hand. "That was meant as a compliment." He started toward the greenhouse door, then glanced back, his smile a mere horizontal crack in his lips. "We'll be talking some more."

When he disappeared from view, Sharon asked, "What was that all about?"

"The guy's grasping at straws, trying to make it look as if you and I concocted some scheme to get hold of Richie's insurance money." Steve guessed what Sharon was thinking. "Richie knew how much Laura's years of illness cost, even with our medical insurance. My parents are well set now, so he named me beneficiary. It was a gesture more than anything else, and he planned to change the beneficiary whenever he got married. Neither of us dreamed what would happen. Now Werner's probably toying with the idea that I could have run him down and finished him off in ICU."

"Welcome to the suspect club," Sharon said uneasily. "Now you know how I feel."

Angry with Werner, Steve blurted out, "Where the hell does he think I'd have gotten morphine from?"

His rhetorical question hit Sharon the wrong way. "Because I dispensed it every night, that makes me a logical suspect. Is that what you're saying?"

He stared at her. "Of course not. All I said was—"

"What you can't keep yourself from thinking—that I'm responsible for your brother's death."

"Sharon, please. Let's not go over that again."

"Tell me honestly that you don't believe I am."

"I don't!"

"Then face it, Steve. Someone murdered Richie!"

Her words buzzed in his head like a nagging mosquito. Steve had long realized that was the only possibility if Sharon hadn't mistakingly given Richie an overdose, but the idea that his brother had been murdered always seemed so preposterous that he could never consider it seriously. Now he had to.

Slumping back against the metal shelf that ran the length of the greenhouse, he crossed his bare arms. "Let's say someone did kill Richie. Who, besides you, went into the isolation room?"

Sharon had gone over that question innumerable times, so her answer came without hesitation. "As far as I know, only Dr. Wilson and the night nursing supervisor, but it's ludicrous thinking that someone at the hospital had a grudge against your brother. What about his personal life or his job? Did he have any enemies that you knew about?"

"No. Richie got along with everyone."

"Not everyone apparently," Sharon said, thinking desperately. "Did you ever meet the people he worked with?"

"He had a few of them over to his apartment for a housewarming. I met them there, but they seemed a normal bunch."

"What about his job as an investigative reporter? Could he have made any enemies?"

"In only four months that's unlikely, and the stories that Richie mentioned he was working on didn't seem as if they would give anyone cause to murder him. Also, Werner told me a few days ago that he'd followed up on that possibility with Richie's boss at the paper. He came up with nothing."

"Well," Sharon said, "either he's overlooking something or we are."

Steve thought hard, then said, "The police have already gone over Richie's apartment, but maybe we should take a look, too."

"For what?"

"Damned if I know," Steve admitted. "I'm beginning to sympathize with the job Werner has, though."

Two hours later, after using the duplicate key Richie had given him, Steve closed the last of his brother's personal work files. Rising from the small round table in the dining area, he mumbled, "Not a thing."

"What about his mail?" Sharon asked.

"It's being forwarded to my place, but there's nothing unusual there, either. Richie's life was very uncomplicated."

"I wish mine were," she said glumly. "No one's mentioned it yet, but if Werner doesn't come up with something, he could send the case to a grand jury to see if there's enough evidence to bring a charge of wrongful death against me."

"There's no real evidence to warrant that," Steve insisted, wanting to believe it.

"Considering what he now knows I did in Vietnam, Werner might think so."

"That was totally different."

"He's willing to believe you and I are having an affair. Why wouldn't he believe I'm hooked on putting patients out of their misery?"

"For one thing, our having an affair is completely rational."

"To whom?"

"Me. And if you thought about it seriously, you'd—"

"I'd commit myself."

"Is that a comment on your mental stability or mine?"

"I'm not the one with a split personality, Steve."

"I said I was sorry about last night. I just had something on my mind."

"I thought I was."

"You were." His voice lowered. "Then I began thinking about Laura."

"Laura?" Sharon repeated, knowing that the death of a spouse was disastrous for most people, but she had thought that after six months Steve had come to terms with his loss.

"Yes. While you were showering I saw a picture of her, and I . . . well, it brought back a lot of memories."

"So you decided we shouldn't—"

"Make love," he completed for her. "But that was yesterday."

The need she saw in his eyes was unmistakable. "And today you've changed your mind."

"Yes."

Sharon wished that she could draw upon the hardness of heart she'd felt last evening after Steve drove her home, but now she was unable to. All she could feel was confusion, emotional exhaustion and, God help her, sympathy for the dejected look on Steve's face. But she was also tired of riding an emotional roller coaster.

Calmly she asked, "How many times will you play mental tennis with my feelings, Steve? I have a few hang-ups of my own to deal with. A little insecurity here, a little regret there."

"I do also, but I meant it when I said I thought we could help each other."

"I'm not sure making love would help either of us in the long run."

"We could give it a whirl," he suggested.

"We could stick our fingers in a live light socket, too."

"Is that a definite no, or are you willing to think about it?"

"Right now I think you'd better take me back to my car. I told Debbie I'd stop by before she goes to work."

"Okay," Steve said, always the optimist, "I'll take your answer to be a maybe."

CHAPTER ELEVEN

ON HER WAY to Debbie's condo Sharon decided to see if Dr. Wilson was at home in his Belleair Beach house. She thought that if he also approached Dr. Benning on her behalf, as well as Louella, she would have a better chance at being reinstated.

Turning left off Gulf Boulevard, she pulled into the driveway of Dr. Wilson's home, a sprawling Spanish-style beachfront residence. Sharon had been in his home only once before, when he had open house for the ICU staff and their families. As she closed her car door, she heard the surf rolling in from the Gulf of Mexico and smelled the salty ocean spray. It was sunny, warm and breezy, and she wished her visit could have been as cheery as the day.

She rang the bell. A moment later the door swung open, and Sharon was face-to-face with Louella, who was wearing a blue bikini that, if folded, could have been hidden under a dollar bill. Sharon instantly remembered that the acting chief nurse was now living with Dr. Wilson.

Louella appeared as disconcerted as Sharon felt. "This is a surprise," she said, pulling in her tummy a little.

"Forgive me for not phoning first," Sharon apologized, "but I was driving by and thought Dr. Wilson might be home."

"He is, but is it something that can't wait for a workday?"

"Who is it, Lou?" Wilson's voice rang out from somewhere in the distance.

Louella's eyelids slipped shut and she muttered, "I hate it when he calls me that." Turning her head, she hollered, "It's Sharon."

"I can come back another time if he's busy."

"You're here, so you might as well come in."

Sharon entered the living room, almost afraid to step on the plush white wall-to-wall carpeting.

"He's out back," Louella informed her, and Sharon followed the woman's sway through the house and onto the sun deck at the rear.

Dr. Wilson was lying facedown on a floral beach mat, a tall glass of something close at hand. Glancing up, he said, "Hi there. Have a drink."

From the why-is-everything-moving look in his bloodshot eyes, Sharon guessed he'd had enough for the three of them. "No, but thank you." *Sweet*, she thought, noting that the color of his blue bikini matched Louella's.

"Well," he asked, rolling onto his side and propping his head with a hand, "to what do we owe this pleasant surprise?"

"Dr. Wilson, I was wondering if you'd talk to the chief of staff about lifting my suspension."

"Sharon," Louella cut in, "I told you I would."

"But I thought if both of you did, it would help even more."

"Sure I will," Wilson said agreeably.

Annoyed by Sharon's intrusion, Louella lit a cigarette and blew a stream of smoke directly toward her. "If a hundred people talk to Benning, it's not going to change his mind. The last thing he wants at the hospital is a nurse who can't be trusted with drugs.''

"That's not fair, Louella," Sharon said, stiffening.

"What you did to Corporal Edwards wasn't exactly fair and hardly ethical, either.''

Remembering that Detective Werner hadn't mentioned the soldier's name, Sharon asked her, "Did Clara tell you about Corporal Edwards before or after the inquiry?''

Put off balance, Louella's eyes darted to Wilson, then back to Sharon. "What difference does it make?''

"You could have been the one who saw to it that Werner received that anonymous phone message.''

"Don't be ridiculous.''

"Ladies, ladies," Wilson groaned, "this is too nice a day to argue.''

"Dr. Wilson, I haven't had a nice day since Richard Nordstrom died on ICU.''

"Not enjoying playing with plants?" Louella asked stiffly.

"I'm a trained nurse," Sharon reminded her. "My job is to help save lives, not plants.''

"She got you there, Lou." Wilson focused on Sharon. "Listen, I've got a doctor friend whose nurse is in a big way." He flattened a hand on his hairy stomach. "She's going to be out for a while after the baby's born. I could talk to him, maybe get you a job in his office.''

"Thanks, but I'll keep the temporary job I have. It shouldn't take the police very long to find out what really happened.''

"We know what happened," Louella said pointedly.

"Not if Richard Nordstrom was murdered," Sharon retorted.

Wilson sobered instantly, shoved himself up from the deck and planted his hands on his hips. "What the hell are you talking about? Who's calling it murder?"

"His brother, for one, and Detective Werner for another," she lied, enjoying the shocked look on Louella's face.

After crushing out her cigarette, she peered into Sharon's eyes. "What evidence do the police have that he was murdered?"

"That's what they're working on now."

Bending down for his drink, Wilson took a big gulp, then said, "Werner never mentioned murder to me."

"That's the only possible explanation," Sharon said flatly. "I did not make a medication error."

"Can you prove it?" Louella asked.

Sharon shot her a narrow-eyed look, then faced her housemate. "Do you think I did, Dr. Wilson?"

"Of course not, but if we take this business of murder seriously, neither can I believe anyone on the staff at the hospital would be involved." He paused to chew on his lower lip. "Unless there's a psychotic employee wandering around intent on mercy killing. Remember what happened at that St. Petersburg hospital last year?"

"The orderly," Louella said, "the man who thought he was the angel of death. It's a possibility."

Dubiously Sharon asked, "Why would a psychotic just pick out Richard Nordstrom?"

"Maybe," Wilson proposed, "Nordstrom was just the first victim."

Louella turned pale, and her fingers shook as she lit another cigarette. "That's all we'd need at the hospital. Really, Jimmy, you're sounding quite morbid, thanks to our uninvited guest."

Taking the caustic hint, Sharon quickly made her goodbyes, exiting through the side yard rather than going back through the house. She could hardly wait until she told Debbie how she had ruined Louella's day.

AT THAT MOMENT Debbie was concentrating totally on Tony, who shuddered once again, then let his head fall into the curve of her shoulder as they lay in bed.

"You make me feel so good, it's sinful," he murmured.

Her eyes closed, her breaths still coming with effort, she smiled as she ran her fingers through his curly black hair. "I doubt if saints are very good lovers."

Tony raised his head and smiled back at her. "Is that what I am . . . your lover?"

"Aren't you?" she asked, easing her fingertips over his lips.

He kissed them and his easy smile waned. "Lover has a temporary sound to it that bothers the hell out of me. I want more than that for us."

"You want too much," she said quietly.

"Maybe, but I knew what I wanted the first time I laid eyes on you in Sharon's apartment. You were the most beautiful woman I'd ever seen. That's why I walked right up to you and touched you. I had to, just to make sure you were real."

Debbie laughed softly in remembrance. "You were grinning like a Cheshire cat."

"I felt more like a horny alley cat."

"The twinkle in your bedroom eyes suggested as much."

Nuzzling the side of her throat, he mumbled, "Turned you on, huh?"

"No. It was your nervous embarrassment that did."

He reared his head up again. "I wasn't embarrassed."

"Hell, you weren't. Your Adam's apple was dancing a tarantella."

"Don't burst my bubble. I thought you were attracted by my smooth talk."

"Wrong again."

"My good posture?"

"I thought you were old-fashioned and cute."

"Babies are cute. What was it about me that really drove you into a frenzy of incontrollable desire?"

"Well, I thought you were sweet, kind and...funny."

"Funny?"

"Any man who'll tell a lady he's just met that he wants her to be the mother of his children is definitely a little funny, if not strange." She reached into the drawer of the bedside stand, took out a small gift-wrapped package and handed it to him. "Because you're you," she said softly, smiling as he tore into the box and withdrew a gold pen. "It's for your office when you get the promotion."

"You're so damn sweet and thoughtful," he said before kissing her gently. His shining eyes lingered on the pen for a moment as he twirled it in his fingers. Then his gaze settled on her shining eyes. "Know how you could really spoil me?"

"You want the pencil to go with it."

"No. I want you to marry me."

Her soft smile withered. "That's not in the cards, Tony."

"Why not?"

"Because I'm not into that kinky stuff."

"What have you got against living in a house with some grass around it for our kids to play on?"

She smiled, barely, then averted her eyes. "You have a rich fantasy life."

"Real children would drag me back to reality fast. Just ask my parents. We kids didn't give them much time for fantasies. Of the five I'm the only one who hasn't come up with grandchildren for them yet, and they're starting to wonder about me."

"Want me to give you a note to take them?"

"I want to take you to them."

"They'd be thrilled, I'm sure. Speaking of your parents, did you mail your mother's birthday gift?"

"Yesterday. She'll love the pearls you picked out, and she'll love you, too."

"Why wouldn't she? We could swap stories about growing up in the fifties, a decade before you were born."

"You know," he said, kissing the tip of her nose, "you've got a real hang-up about this age business."

"That's easy to say when you're thirty-one."

"So what's nine years?"

"In two months it'll be ten. Get serious, Tony. Picture yourself with me the rest of your life."

"Picture me without you."

She tilted her head to the side and chuckled painfully. "That's the problem. It's very easy for me to do just that."

"Sure it is," he teased. "Next you'll be telling me that you'd be happy and so would I."

"Tony," she said, gazing up at him as she smoothed her hands over the back of his thighs, "let's not talk about the future. I'm happy just the way things are now. Aren't you?"

He rolled off her, positioned his hands behind his head and stared up at the ceiling. "I'm all for making love in the daylight, but having to schedule it takes a little of the romance out of it. When you get off work at two in the morning, you're wide awake and I'm trying to keep my eyes open. Saturday nights I'm ready to let loose a little and you're working. Sundays are the only days we get to see each other more than in passing.''

"About tomorrow," Debbie said hesitantly, propping herself up on an arm, "I can't go to Tarpon Springs. I have to work."

"What?" He jerked himself up to a sitting position. "Sunday's your day off."

"The relief pianist is sick."

"Will you have to work Monday night also?"

"I hope not."

"Well," he said, trying to hide his disappointment, "we'll drive up to Tarpon Springs then."

"I can't," she said regretfully. "The girls are coming over."

"Damn it! You make it pretty clear just where I am on your list of priorities," he fumed, throwing back the sheet. He swung his legs over the side of the bed and dug his fingers into the edge of the mattress.

Debbie eased herself behind him, wrapped her arms around his body and laid her cheek on his bare shoulder. "Don't be angry with me," she pleaded.

"I'm not angry. I'm frustrated. If we were living together, at least we'd have some semblance of a home life. The way it is now . . . well, I don't know how much longer I can take it."

She kissed his shoulder once, then again. "Too much thinking makes anyone crazy," she said, feeling his heartbeat thudding against her palms. His silence increased her growing anxiety. She hated these scenes with

Tony and she hated hurting him. "Say something. Anything," she pleaded.

"Right now if I don't, we'll both be better off."

"Better off, better off." His words echoed in Debbie's thoughts over and over again, dragging her back to a day long past, to the evacuation hospital in Pleiku, to the letter she was about to read to the young soldier whose eyes were bandaged.

She was sitting on the bed beside him, scanning the first paragraph:

Dear Ernie,
    You'll be better off knowing the truth in the long run. It's hard for me to write this letter, and I know you'll be hurt, but by the time you receive this, Frank and I will be married.

"What did...Sarah say, Debbie?" the young soldier asked, his voice weak and sluggish from the pain-killers a nurse had just given him.

Debbie glanced up at the nurse, who shook her head. Then Debbie took hold of the soldier's hand, squeezed it and began reading softly. "Dear Ernie. It's hard for me to...to be so far away from you. I think of you all the time and pray that you'll be home very soon. Everyone sends their—"

When the young man's fingers loosened their grip on hers, Debbie stopped reading and stared down at his limp hand. She didn't have to look at his face to know that he had slipped away, just as she had watched so many others do.

"Debbie?" Tony asked, feeling her body trembling against his back. He twisted around and saw the tears streaming over her cheeks. Quickly he took her in his

arms, rested her head on his shoulder and began stroking her hair. "Another one of those flashbacks?" he
asked quietly.

Holding him tightly, she murmured through her
tears, "They're like movies...playing in my head, over
and over."

As he rocked her in his arms, he said, "You've got to
get some help, honey."

"Just hold me a while longer."

"I'd hold you for the rest of my life if I thought that
would make them stop."

She uncurled her arms from around Tony's neck and
wiped her reddened eyes. "I thought they had. It's been
weeks since the last one."

"The last waking one, you mean. Sometimes at night
I know your dreams aren't good ones."

"I don't remember them," she lied, drawing her fingers through her tangled hair.

His heart going out to her, he watched anxiously as
she slipped from the bed, put on her robe and started
toward the bedroom door. Knowing what she was going to do, he jumped up and followed her, stopping at
the bedroom door.

"That's not going to help in the long run," he said as
she went directly to the bar cart.

"In the short run it will," she said, pouring herself
some Scotch. She emptied the small glass in one long
swallow, then took a long, deep breath.

Bracing a shoulder against the door frame, he crossed
his arms. "Someday I'd like to show you what too
much of that does to a person's liver."

Still holding the empty glass, she tilted her head toward him and smiled grimly. "Something has to get
us."

"It doesn't have to be that stuff."

"There you go, nagging again," she said, pouring herself another drink. She only took a sip this time, then gazed down at the glass. "And you want us to live together? It wouldn't last very long."

"So now you see into the future," he remarked, then backtracked into the bedroom.

The glass in her hand, Debbie stepped barefoot to the door and watched him dress. "I'm doing you a favor, Tony. You just don't realize it. I tried cohabitation twice already. Both times the relationship went downhill, fast."

As he buttoned his dress shirt, he said, "Obviously you picked the wrong guys."

"They picked me," she corrected him, beginning to feel the effects of the alcohol. "I've always been a sucker for a man who claims he needs me."

"I don't *need* you," he said, jerking up his trouser zipper. "I happen to love you—" he looked over at her and softened his voice "—very much."

"Love . . . need . . . what's the difference?" She lifted the glass and finished it off.

"There's a big difference," he said, taking the glass from her and going to the kitchen, where he readied the automatic coffee maker. After pouring a glass of orange juice, he took it into the living room, where Debbie was curled up in an upholstered chair.

"Drink this. The Vitamin C will do you good."

She took the glass, painfully aware that she had disappointed Tony once again. "Why do you waste your time with me?"

"You make funny little noises during sex. I find that alluring in a woman."

When the door buzzer sounded, Debbie said, "That's probably Sharon. I asked her to come by."

At the door Tony greeted her, saying quietly, "You just missed the early cocktail hour."

Sharon got the message. Dropping her purse on the end of the table by the sofa, she eyed the pink silk robe Debbie was wearing and smiled. "Am I interrupting anything?"

"Only the daily lecture I get from Tony."

"Someone's got to talk some sense into you. Coffee, Sharon?"

"Please." When he went to the kitchen, she sat on the sofa and looked over at Debbie. "He has your interests at heart, you know."

"If I had his at heart, I'd never see him again."

Lowering her voice, Sharon said, "That's dumb. Tony's the best thing that ever happened to you."

Debbie rose, crossed to the bar cart and poured a shot of gin into her orange juice, then sat sideways on the sofa next to Sharon. "At times he drives me crazy, makes me feel as if I'm suffocating."

"He's just trying to help you clear up that crazy thinking you do sometimes."

"My crazy thinking? He's the strange one, always wanting us to play house."

"You're doing that now, only you have two homes."

"It's better this way."

"Safer, you mean."

"A human's first instinct, isn't it?" Debbie asked, then drank from her glass.

"You know, friend, if you gave yourself half a chance you might find yourself being really happy for a change. I know you'd fight it tooth and nail, but what would it cost you to try it?"

"I'm more concerned about what it would cost Tony. The man's talking about meeting his parents and marriage."

"That's not a dirty word."

"It's not any kind of word in my vocabulary." Setting her glass down, Debbie drew her legs up onto the sofa and covered them with a corner of her robe. "Get real, Sharon. Can you see me wearing a cutesy apron, frying eggs at seven in the morning and then waving goodbye to hubby from the window?"

"You could do worse."

"And Tony could do a damn sight better than me."

"That bothers you more than the domestic picture, doesn't it?"

"Shouldn't it? I know him. He's the marriage-for-real type—children, the whole bit. He'd replace my birth control pills with little sugar-coated ones."

"You're still young enough to have children safely."

"Sure, and then Tony would be up half the night trying to keep them from crying and the other half he'd be trying to keep me from screaming."

"Are you having nightmares again?"

Debbie covered her eyes with a hand and her voice shook. "Just about every time Tony stays over."

Gently Sharon eased Debbie's hand from her eyes and held it. "You know why, don't you? You're terrified that you're going to lose him the way we both lost so many friends in Nam. You're going to have to find the courage and the strength to allow yourself to love him, even though it seems so risky for you."

"I can't do that to Tony. He's—"

Coming from the kitchen, he finished for her. "He's witty, charming, at times a man of mystery and he makes great coffee."

"Thanks," Sharon said, accepting the cup he offered.

Debbie exchanged her orange juice glass for her cup and chuckled softly. "Witty and charming. I love a man who wears his humility with pride."

"You bring me to my knees," he quipped, slipping his suit jacket from the back of a chair at the dining area table. "I'll leave you two ladies alone to sing my praises." Leaning down, he planted a kiss on Debbie's forehead. "I'll see *you* later at the club."

After he closed the condo door behind him, Sharon eyed Debbie. "If you weren't my best friend, I'd steal that man away from you."

"Getting greedy in your old age, aren't you, or is Steve the understanding type?"

"I can't really type him one way or the other," Sharon said wistfully, her expression clouding over. "There are times I think he wants to ravish me, then at others he's so very distant."

"Still not sure you didn't do away with his brother, huh?"

"He says he doesn't believe I did, but every now and then his doubt is obvious. Also, I think he still has unresolved feelings about his wife."

"You said she died only a few months ago."

"Six." Sharon took a sip of coffee. "But she'd been ill for a long time. It's been my experience that the shock isn't as great as it is when death is sudden. Some people even feel a sense of relief if a loved one's been suffering." As though thinking out loud, she speculated, "That could bring a feeling of guilt with it, though. Maybe that's bothering him."

"You'd be good for Steve, Sharon. You're so damn smart. Marry him. That way I'd have a constant supply of orchids for wrist corsages."

"Marry him? I haven't even slept with him."

"Yet," Debbie tacked on. "The way he looked at you at the lounge even got me excited. And, my dear, if he hadn't been cheating on his wife, your Steve must be ready to explode."

"He's not *my* Steve. He's my employer."

"Ha! And I'm Rebecca of Sunnybrook Farm. Don't I wish," she remarked dryly, and stood. "More coffee?"

"No thanks. I've got a million things to do at the apartment."

"Hang around for a few more minutes, will you?" Debbie asked, glancing at the bar cart before she went into the kitchen.

"A few minutes," Sharon agreed.

Alone in the room she leaned back against the sofa, her thoughts drifting to Steve as she pondered what she had said about his possibly feeling relieved after his wife's death. Sharon had been certain he had intended for them to make love after their foolishness in the pool, but just the picture of Laura had made him change his mind. How could he feel so guilty, though? she wondered. Apparently he had been very caring toward his wife for years. However, Sharon knew from experience that even unwarranted guilt could be an insidious and often devious companion.

Returning to the living room with her refilled coffee cup, Debbie said, "I like Anna. She seems to be in pretty good shape for having spent so many years in Nam. Kind of makes the rest of us look like crybabies."

"I'm sure she has her scars, but she and her husband had each other. A little support can go a long way after any traumatic experience."

"You know," Debbie said, lowering herself onto the sofa, "sometimes I think I'm using Vietnam as a crutch, something to blame for some inherent weakness I must have."

"That's the PTSD talking, not you. For whatever reason, self-esteem is one of the first things to go, and we blame ourselves for something we had no control over. I mean, look at you. When I first met you, the strongest thing you ever drank was a Coke. Are you going to tell me you started to hit the bottle because of some genetic screwup? You claim your parents haven't had a drink of alcohol to this day. Uh-uh, you began using it to forget."

"It does help."

"Too much of it can ruin your life, physically and emotionally."

"You sound like Tony now. He wants me to check out a diseased liver."

"Listen to him. He sees enough of them every day in the lab."

After a sip of coffee, Debbie looked at Sharon with quizzical eyes. "Do you honestly believe there's a chance that Tony could be happy with me?"

"I think he'd be miserable without you."

"I don't know. There are hordes of women on Clearwater Beach who are his age and better looking than I am. They'd fall in love with Tony in a minute if he'd make himself available. What the hell does he see in me?"

"What you don't. You're lovely, Debbie, and locked inside you is that great twenty-one-year-old lady I knew, the one who sticks her head out every now and then to look over the territory. You got a little screwed up in Nam and decided you weren't lovable. Now you sit there and prove it by asking if Tony could be happy with you. That should tell you something.''

Shaking her head slowly, Debbie said, "I don't know. Whenever I think about anything seriously, it gives me a headache and I need a drink to cure it.''

"You're going to have to suffer through a few headaches on your own steam, but you don't have to do it alone. You've got Tony and you've got your friends.''

"Like you,'' she said, reaching over and touching Sharon's hand. Brightening, Debbie said, "Okay. Let's make a deal. I'll start sewing a trousseau if you get Steve into bed.''

"On that excellent suggestion,'' Sharon said, standing, "I'm getting out of here.''

"Don't forget Monday night,'' Debbie reminded her as they walked to the door. "My turn to host the hen-house club.''

"I wouldn't miss the expression on their faces for the world, not when I tell them you're getting married.''

"Marge would be thrilled, but let me live with the idea a little longer before you blurt it out.''

Her hand on the doorknob, Sharon said seriously, "Think about asking Tony to move in with you.'' She knew he would be so good for Debbie.

"A trial run?''

"We all have to learn to crawl before we can run.''

Debbie smiled softly and nodded, closing the door after Sharon left. Then she returned to the living room and sat down at her apartment-size grand piano to go over some new songs. As she played, her gaze kept slipping toward the bar cart, and finally her fingers rested motionless on the keys.

In the ensuing silence, though, she heard music from long ago, the sound of a guitar being strummed to the tune of "Silent Night." Closing her eyes, she also heard the off-key singing of war-weary boys in helmets and jungle fatigues that were crisscrossed with ammo, smiles brightening their unshaven faces. In her mind's eye it was Christmas Eve once again, and Debbie, dressed in a Santa Claus outfit, had hitched a ride in a chopper and taken bottles of wine to the soldiers in several firebases that were under attack. Dawn had winged over Pleiku before she returned to her hooch.

A tear slipped over her cheek as she again heard Alice's chipper voice, the twenty-one-year-old Red Cross worker from Iowa who had been her roommate.

What's the big deal? I'll take your run to Cong Tum today while you nurse your Christmas Eve hangover. Tomorrow you can take mine to Dac To.

As Debbie sat at the piano, she squeezed her eyes shut, trying to blot out the memory of seeing Alice's bruised body in the morgue after the chopper she had been in was shot down.

"Alice," she groaned, the memory an almost constant agony, "I'm so sorry. It should have been me, not you."

Her burning eyes sought the bottles on the bar cart again, and she was about to drag herself up from the piano bench when Tony's voice echoed in her thoughts. *I happen to love you, very much. We can work through anything, if we do it together.*

"Can we really, Tony?" she whispered, desperately wanting to believe it.

Drawing heavily on his words for support, she tore her eyes from the bar cart, took a long, deep breath and forced her attention back to the piano music.

CHAPTER TWELVE

DUSK WAS SETTLING IN as Steve began to repot one of the orchids from his private collection, a prize-winning pure white cattleya that he had named Alba. When blooming, each flower was six inches wide and seven inches high with not a hint of coloration in its ruffled lip.

He removed the large clay pot from the bucket of water it had been soaking in and tugged at the plant gently. Wanting more light, he switched on the over-head neon lamp, then, with a knife, he carefully dislodged the roots that had attached themselves to the outside of the pot before pulling the plant free.

As he worked, his thoughts returned to Sharon, as they did so often. She'd said she wasn't sure that their making love would help either of them in the long run, but she hadn't argued with the "maybe" he'd had to settle for.

"That's something, anyway," he murmured, then began whistling softly as he turned the water on over the deep sink and fingered the old potting media from Alba's roots. Using the sharp knife again, he cut through the rhizome to divide the plant in two, wondering where an intimate relationship with Sharon would lead. Where would she want it to lead? Where would he?

At the worktable he half filled two large clay pots with fresh, moist pine bark, his mind lingering on

Sharon as he went through the motions he could have done blindfolded.

He placed the newest growth of the orchid plant into one pot and added more bark, careful not to cover the rhizome completely. Then he attached a metal stake to the side of the pot and secured the plant's pseudobulbs with string. As he repeated the process with the back bulbs of the orchid plant, he pictured one scenario: boy meets girl, they fall in love, marry and live happily ever after.

Just a glitch or two in the pretty picture, Nordstrom, he reminded himself. *For one, what if Werner does send Richie's case to a grand jury?*

The wall phone rang and he answered, his tone businesslike. "Nordstrom's Orchids."

"Mr. Nordstrom! Lillian Auger."

"Yes," he said to the real estate lady who was trying to sell his house in Wisconsin.

"Great news. I've got a buyer. No quibbling about price at all. He and his wife love the place, not that I blame them. It's a beaut! He's been stationed overseas, so your selling the furniture is just perfect for them. How soon can you come up here and close the deal? Or I could send you the papers and you could have a lawyer handle it from Florida."

"No," he said, rubbing the back of his neck, "there are too many personal things I have to decide what to do with." He switched the receiver from one hand to the other. "I didn't think you worked so fast."

"I told you I wouldn't have any trouble selling it, but my advice is to strike while the iron is hot. The buyers want to move in before Thanksgiving if that's possible."

"Okay, Mrs. Auger. I'll fly up there next week."
Planning out loud, he said, "If I get there on Thursday, we can take care of the paperwork and I can finish what I have to do at the house by Sunday. Monday it will be all theirs."

"Oh, that would be wonderful! They'll be thrilled. I'll call them right back."

"Good. See you Thursday afternoon in your office. Bye."

Steve replaced the receiver, not looking forward to making another trip to Wisconsin so soon, nor at having to look through the personal things he and Laura had collected over the years and had left at the house. But it was something he wanted to do. He hoped that by cutting himself loose from the past, from the house in which he and Laura had shared so many good times, he might feel more free to think about the future.

Remembering something, he put a call through to Madison.

"Hi," he said when his father answered, "it's me."

Nordstrom senior chuckled. "Steve, we've talked more on the phone in the past few weeks than we have in a whole year."

"How's Mom doing?"

"Pretty good. Today she went through Richard's and your baby things, wondering if she should pass them on to somebody who could put them to good use. I told her you might still give us the grandchildren we want so badly. That really cheered her up."

"If you think it'll help, tell her I said to hold on to them."

"What's that mean, son? Have you met someone special?"

"I think so, but that's not why I called. I've got a buyer for the house on Door Peninsula."

"If you're not going to live in it, it's about time you sold it."

"I was thinking how much Mom likes the set of Limoges china. I thought I'd pack it up and send it on down to you, that and the silver stuff. I'm not much for keeping it polished."

"Want me to drive up and help you?"

"Naw, I can take care of it. With the holidays coming up I know you've got your hands full there."

"Mother sure would enjoy the china."

"Good, that's what I needed to know."

"When are you coming up, Steven?"

"I'm closing the deal on Thursday, probably spend a few days at the house. Let me say hi to Mom."

"You can't. This is her bridge night at Wanda's."

"Well, if either of you think of anything else you want from the house, give me a call."

"Okay, son, and you take care of yourself. I'll tell Mother the news."

After hanging up, Steve eyed the phone, wondering if he should call Sharon.

AT THAT MOMENT Sharon was lying sideways on her bed, her chin propped on her palm as she thumbed through a photograph album. Turning a page, she smiled at the picture of Debbie, herself and four other nurses wearing makeshift "girlie" costumes. They had thrown them together when the USO couldn't get to the hospital for the New Year's Eve show because of enemy fire.

"The good ol' days," she murmured with a touch of sarcasm, then flipped over a page and shook her head as she scanned the snapshots taken during one of the parties in her hooch. Seymour, the prematurely balding neurosurgeon with the magic hands, had a drink in one hand, a mammoth cigar in the other, celebrating the birth of his second daughter, whom he hadn't held yet. Next to him sat a girl named Patty, fresh out of OR, still in her green scrub dress. Sweet Patty, who never had a chance to have children; an incoming mortar shell had had her name on it as she'd run to the bunkers only hours after the picture had been taken.

Sharon's gaze lingered on the nurse for a few quiet moments. Then she looked across to the opposite page, smiling wanly at the picture she had taken of Doug sitting on the hood of a jeep, a cowboy hat tilted rakishly over his tanned handsome face. In the photograph to the right he was stretched out on a blanket, sleeping peacefully on the beach at Phan Rang. Below that was the picture of the two of them in a bar in Saigon. He had his arm around her, grinning at the photographer, while Sharon was gazing at him adoringly.

Lying back on the bed, she rested a hand over her forehead and closed her eyes, remembering sitting next to Doug in the jeep the night the picture had been taken and recalling his words, *You're gonna love living in Sand Springs, honey. It's a nice little quiet town, a great place to raise kids, but close enough to Tulsa for anything we'd want from a big city. I'll build you the grandest house in town, and we're gonna be so happy.*

"We will be," she whispered, repeating what she had said to him that evening.

Her eyes opened slowly, and she stared up idly, not moving until the phone rang. Rolling over, she reached for the receiver and answered, surprised that it was Steve.

"Hi," he said. "Did I catch you at a bad time?"

"No, I was just . . . going through some old things."

He chuckled softly. "That's what's staring me in the face. I just had a call from the real estate lady in Wisconsin. She sold the house."

"That's great," Sharon said, happy that someone had good news to report.

"Have you had dinner yet?"

"I was just about to fix something," she said, then immediately decided it had been a mistake to tell him that.

"We could both avoid doing dishes if we ate out . . . together."

Her memory flashed her a replay of their last conversation, and she felt as if she were getting ready to take another ride on the Nordstrom roller coaster. Sitting up she said, "I'm really not very hungry, Steve."

"We could just pig out on desserts," he suggested lightly.

That brought a faint smile to her lips. "Sounds like a grand idea, but not a nutritionally sound one."

"You chart the course and I'll follow willingly."

The figurative roller coaster car started up the incline, with her in it. "Dinner," she said softly. "My treat this time."

"Great. How about I pick you up in half an hour?"

"I'll pick you up," she said, her fingers toying nervously with the phone cord. "The place I have in mind isn't far from you. Dress casually."

THE "PLACE" WAS a modest neighborhood shorefront restaurant on Madeira Beach, nothing fancy, and for that reason it didn't draw a mob of tourists. Sharon liked it because they also served in an open-air section at the rear that overlooked the Gulf.

"This was a great idea," Steve said, pouring them both beer from a pitcher.

"Wait until you taste the broiled shrimp."

Raising his glass and mimicking Humphrey Bogart, Steve toasted, "Here's looking at you, kid." As she clinked her glass to his, he glanced at the words on her turquoise T-shirt: Hug a Nurse Today.

After they both had a swallow of beer, he said, "I like your shirt."

"A gift from the owner, the lady behind the bar who whistled at you. I'm on the hospitality committee at work, and we have beach parties here a few times a year. I usually wear this shirt. It tickles her."

Steve almost said it tickled the hell out of him, too. It was loose-fitting, but not so much as to hide the tantalizing peaks of her small breasts. This evening was also the first time he'd seen Sharon in shorts. He decided she should have her long, slender legs insured. But then, he reminded himself, he'd have to think hard to find something he didn't like about her.

Also, there was nothing to dislike about her choice of restaurants, he discovered when the owner's son placed a metal tray stacked high with steaming broiled shrimp on their round concrete table. The teenager added a large wooden bowl filled with a freshly tossed salad and set empty plates in front of them. Using the wooden spoon and fork, Sharon served salad for both of them, and they helped themselves to the luscious-looking shrimp.

"Umm," Steve commented, chewing on one. "Delicious."

"I could eat shrimp seven days a week," Sharon admitted as she dipped one into the bowl of hot lemon-butter sauce.

As they dug into the pile of shrimp, Steve said, "I have to fly back to Wisconsin Thursday."

"Your office will be in safe hands...hopefully."

"That's what I want to talk to you about."

Cocking her head, she asked, "You're not going to give me a pink slip already, are you?"

"No way. I'd like you to come with me."

"To Wisconsin?"

"Uh-huh."

"Why?"

"Why not?"

"Answering a question with a question isn't very satisfying, Steve."

"We'd be back Sunday," he said, refilling her beer glass and his. "Willie can handle the phone calls when he's there, and when he's not, the answering machine is reliable."

The phone calls weren't exactly what concerned Sharon. She realized that going off with Steve for several days—and nights—was tantamount to agreeing to share a bed with him.

"I'd like you to see the house before I sell it," he said, anxiously awaiting a positive response from her.

Undecided, she asked, "Don't you have any pictures of it?"

"Not the same thing. Besides, you're a fairly good conversationalist and I'd enjoy your company."

Spearing a shrimp with her fork, she asked offhandedly, "Aren't you afraid of what Detective Werner will think?"

"Are you?"

She looked up at him. "Yes. He's already convinced I'm a pretty shady character."

"You're pretty, but there's nothing shady about you."

"Or your invitation?"

"You'd be just as safe from me in Wisconsin as you are here. I think it'd be good for you to get away for a few days."

"That's tempting," she said honestly, conceding silently that her major worry was his being safe from her.

"As far as Werner is concerned, he's going to think whatever he wants regardless of where we are or what we do. It's the nature of his job to imagine the worst, I guess. So how about it? Will you come with me?"

"A change of scenery would be good," she said, still uncertain. "What about your parents? What would they think about my traipsing along with you?"

"Sharon," he said, leaning forward, "you worry a great deal about what other people are going to think of us. Werner has his life to take care of, and my parents have theirs. I'm a big boy now, and I have my own life to lead. If my parents are happy with what I do, that's wonderful. If they're not, that's too bad." As she mulled that over, he asked, "Do you feel the need to phone your parents and ask their permission to go away with me for a few days?"

"It would worry them if I did," she said, smiling at the idea. "I've always been rather independent."

"Then be independent now. We need some time away from all the confusion here, some quiet time so we can get our bearings."

She realized he wasn't talking about the problems connected to the investigation, and she admitted to herself that she too would like them to get their bearings.

"You'll come with me?" he asked, tilting his head a little.

"What's the weather like up there now?"

"Chilly," he said, grinning and taking her question to be a positive response.

Changing the subject, she said, "I stopped by Dr. Wilson's home today. He has a new theory that's kind of far out. He thinks some psychotic may have given Richie the overdose."

"A mercy killing?" Steve asked, finding it as hard to accept as he guessed Sharon did.

"It's happened before, here in Florida and in other hospitals across the country."

"At this point I'm ready to believe anything, but one possibility seems as difficult to buy as the next. Did Wilson say if he'd told Werner that?"

"I doubt he did. He just thought of it today."

"Then I'll pass it on to Werner. The more information he has, the better."

"He's going to wonder why you're being so protective of me, Steve."

"We weren't going to care what he wonders or thinks. Remember?"

Easier said than done, she thought as they continued to eat.

After dinner, his arm over her shoulders, they walked down the beach along the water's edge. The sea breeze was balmy, the night sky a black velvet backdrop for a full moon and scintillating stars.

"It's lovely tonight," Sharon commented softly.

As if by agreement, they stopped and sat down on the white sand, facing the moonlight-sprinkled water and listening to the soothing, rhythmic sound of the surf rolling in. Drawing her knees up, she hugged them, and he stretched his jean-clad legs out and rested back on his bare arms, content with the comfortable silence between them.

Sharon sensed the serenity also, a feeling that had been all too rare of late. She was well aware that it wasn't due just to the peaceful ambience; she had sat on the beach at night many times, but never had she felt such a sense of tranquillity. She knew that being with Steve had much to do with it.

As usual she felt the inner stirring that his nearness caused. The feeling was very pleasant, exciting, erotic. Lulled by the sea breeze wafting over her face, she tilted her head back slightly and closed her eyes, wondering what it would be like to be held in his arms, to be caressed intimately, lovingly, passionately.

If she'd had her eyes open, she would have seen Steve gazing up at her as his thoughts traveled a similar but more familiar path. She had awakened his long-repressed desire, and he craved wildly to possess her in every way possible—physically, emotionally, spiritually. She had re-created a yearning in him to love and be loved that was so strong that he thought he would die if she failed to love him back.

But would she? he wondered, scooping up a handful of soft sand and letting it slip slowly between his fingers. She might, he told himself, *if* they had met under different circumstances. There was hope, though, he thought, reminding himself that she was going to Wisconsin with him. They would spend three days at the house—and three nights. Quiet time, he had told her. What he had meant was time for them to get in touch with their true feelings for each other. He did believe she felt something for him. Just what and how deeply, he didn't know. Lying back, he cupped his hands behind his head and gazed up at the stars, hope swelling in his chest.

Drawn by his movement, Sharon smiled down at him. "Settling in for the night?"

"Should we?" he asked, returning her lovely smile and taking hold of her hand. "I'm game if you are."

She sighed when she felt the warmth of his strong hand penetrating hers. It sent a shock wave shooting up her arm and curling into her breasts. She leaned down and crossed her arms over his chest.

"Spending the night on the beach is probably against some law," she said, trying to sound casual, but feeling her entire body respond to the hard, comforting heat of his.

Steve's response to the lovely weight against his chest was equally intense. The tingling started somewhere in his heart and sped to his brain, which sent readying signals scurrying throughout his body, all of the urgent messages winding up with exquisite vibrancy in his groin.

He wrapped his arms around her and eased his hands over her back, luxuriating in the exciting warmth of her body and her feminine softness.

Without thought, as though it were the most natural thing to do, she guided her fingers through his thick hair, feeling her breath coming deeper and deeper. Or was it the more noticeable rise and fall of his chest against her breasts? She wasn't sure. All she was certain of was that her face was getting closer to his, closer and closer.

"Sharon," he whispered just before she touched her lips to his, silencing them in a long, tender kiss.

When she finally lifted her head, she felt as if she had been drugged. Steve's eyes were closed, he was breathing hard and his hands were gently squeezing her backside.

Rolling off him, she sat up quickly and glanced around at the almost deserted beach. Her eyes darted back to Steve, who was still lying there, smiling now, his arms outstretched, his palms flattened on the sand.

"You pick great places for dinner," he said, his words coming with difficulty. "Let's do this again, real soon."

"Uh . . . we'd better go now before we're arrested."

He grinned up at her. "They don't arrest people for kissing." Pushing himself up, he sat cross-legged and shook the sand from the back of his hair as he studied her flushed face. "Anyone ever mention that you have some pretty winsome ways?"

"Blame it on the beer and the moonlight," she said, attempting a nonchalance she didn't at all feel.

Standing, Steve extended a hand and pulled her up. "I was hoping you kissed me because you wanted to."

"That was part of it," she admitted, brushing the sand from her legs.

"That's the important part." Placing his hand lightly on her shoulder, he guided her back toward the restaurant parking lot.

Automatically, too automatically for comfort, Sharon moved her arm around his waist. "You might as well know now, Steve. Moonlight does funny things to me."

"Miss McClure, you're a romantic at heart. I like that, and I like you . . . an awful lot."

Her heart still pitter-pattering, she said, almost to herself, "Obviously I like you, too."

"What do you think we should do about it?"

"We should be sensible and not rush into anything heavy."

"Why not?"

"Because I'm not ready for it."

As they continued walking in the sand, he briefly glanced up at the starry sky. "That's the second time you've pointed that out. Is it something about me, or are you saving yourself for someone else?"

"There's no one else, and there's not a thing wrong with you. Just the reverse."

"If you're afraid of dealing with perfection, don't be. I do have some faults. I'm cranky before I have morning coffee, I hate doing laundry and I don't want anyone talking to me during the last innings of World Series games."

Giving his side a squeeze, she chuckled softly. "With a record like that I'd no doubt find your picture with the most wanted on post office bulletin boards."

They reached Sharon's car, and after she unlocked it, he opened the door for her, then hopped in on the passenger side, asking, "Your place or mine?"

She eyed him sideways. "I brought you here and I'll take you home—your home."

They rode the ten-minute drive in silence, Steve's arm extended over the back of the car seat, his fingertips resting on her shoulder, his thumb stroking it slowly every now and then. When she pulled into his driveway, he saw that she didn't remove her safety belt.

"Coming in?" he asked.

"Not tonight."

"Still a little uncertain?"

"It's not that."

"What then?"

She thought desperately, trying to make sense of the confusion she felt, trying to organize her chaotic thinking as far as Steve was concerned. After the scene on the beach, he had every right to expect that she would spend the night with him. She wanted to so very badly, but some inexplicable force was pulling her back from him, ordering her to retreat to safety, as if a destructive storm loomed ahead of her. How could she tell him something sensible, she wondered, when she couldn't make sense of it herself?

Seeing the tension in her expression, Steve leaned over and kissed her cheek. "No problem," he said with as much conviction as he could muster. "Will I see you tomorrow?"

"No, not tomorrow. I've already made plans." She hated herself for lying, but the dark force that clouded her thinking had become too strong to fight.

"You'll be in the office Monday morning, won't you?"

"Of course. Eight o'clock sharp."

He breathed a little easier, then hopped out of the car and closed the door. Giving her a goodbye wave, he watched her drive off.

"Well," he said, eyeing the man in the moon, "guess it's time to jump into the damn pool again."

CHAPTER THIRTEEN

"How's the job going?" Sharon asked Anna on Monday evening as Debbie carried a plate of snacks from her kitchen.

"Dave's ready for a vacation. They brought in three drug overdoses within a half hour last night. That raised our patient count to eleven. He said to tell you to get your tail back there fast."

"I will as soon as Dr. Benning lifts my suspension. Supposedly Dr. Wilson and Louella are going to talk to him about it."

"That Dr. Wilson sure is nice, isn't he?"

"I like him," Sharon agreed wholeheartedly.

Carrying a can of beer wrapped in a napkin, Marge plopped herself down on the sofa between the two women. "That's enough shoptalk." She slapped Anna on her knee. "How're you doin', girl?"

"Great. After a night on ICU, I crawl into bed and sleep like a baby."

Debbie pulled a dining room chair closer to the sofa. "How do we get Julia to sound as cheerful?"

"Where is she?" Sharon asked.

"She won't be here tonight, claims the kids are down with the flu."

Concerned, Marge asked, "Did she sound all right?"

"Not to me. Her voice was really weak."

"I wish I'd stopped by to see her yesterday," Sharon said. "All I did was catch up on letters and lounge around the apartment."

"Maybe we should call her now," Anna suggested.

Marge shook her head. "Might wake the kids. I'll go by after work tomorrow and see how things are with her. It's about time someone talked turkey to Carlos."

"The way you talked turkey to the bird colonel who was your last husband, or the way you sweet-talk Ted, future husband number four?" Debbie asked, grinning.

"Ooh, the sting of your wit! Listen, girl, if you'd do some marryin', it would cut down the number of available men for me to take in hand. That is Tony's robe hangin' behind your bathroom door, I hope."

"Nosy."

"Nosy? It flapped when I closed the door. Scared the hell out of me." She turned to Anna. "Ted's weird for horror movies. We watched *Dracula* last night. Talk about nightmares! The poor man was bruised this mornin', and he'll probably walk funny for a week."

"Oh?" Sharon remarked. "Did you maim him in your bed or his?"

"In his and, remember, my dear, we are engaged."

"This one's going to last?" Debbie asked, a dubious lilt in her question.

Marge lifted a graceful hand, palm upward. "I *thought* they all would, but they say practice makes perfect and this one's goin' to be perfect." Turning to Anna, she explained, "My last husband and I rarely spent any time alone together. Lookin' back, I don't know why not. Maybe we just didn't have much to say to each other."

"Maybe you didn't want to get really close to any of your ex-husbands," Sharon suggested.

"Close? Honey, I'm a cuddler."

"I don't mean physically. I mean emotionally."

"Unless I've missed an entire breed of man, the ones I've gotten close to are satisfied emotionally if their meals are on time and they can reach for a pair of socks that match. The drivin' forces in their lives seem to be bitchin' about the mortgage and wonderin' what to watch on TV."

Debbie turned from Marge to Sharon. "The men in Nam weren't like that. They were different."

"How?" Anna asked.

After thinking, Debbie said, "The guys didn't have time to worry about things like meals being on time or socks matching, not when they were doing their jobs. Everything was important then, really important."

Sharon nodded. "That was true of the doctors, and especially the male nurses and medics. When they played, they played hard, and when they worked, they worked doubly hard because the stakes were so high."

Leaning back against the sofa, Marge said, "Workin' over there sure was a lot different from what I've been doin' since I got back. There I was able to give top nursing care without all the dumb paperwork I have to do now. I was given so much more responsibility and I always felt really needed and important, especially when I was in OR durin' my first tour. There was such a backup that sometimes the surgeon would work on one half of a guy and I'd work on the other, making incisions and cutting away dead muscle and dead tissue. I was as good at tying off blood vessels and suturing up as most of the docs were. Oh, I know I do a good job now and I'm necessary, but there's not that feeling of urgency, of having to do every bit as much as I'm capable of doing." She turned to Debbie. "You're right. Every working second was terribly important there, and it's different now."

Thoughtfully Anna said, "I felt really needed there, too, particularly when Josh and I made our visits to the leper colony near Qui Nhon. Those nuns who ran it were saints, but those kids—oh, they'd break your heart."

"How come you and Josh never had children of your own?" Marge asked.

The question seemed to startle Anna, so much so that she wasn't able to disguise the regret that momentarily dulled her usually shining eyes. "I don't really know," she answered vaguely.

Debbie cocked her head. "That's wild, coming from a nurse. You do know how babies are made, don't you?"

"Yes," Anna said pensively, as though she were trying to figure out for the first time why she and her husband hadn't had children. "Josh and I went to Vietnam soon after we were married. I guess we were just too busy to plan for a family of our own." She faced Sharon. "There were so many desperate people there who needed our help. When we returned to Buffalo, he took a job at a clinic for the indigent, and I worked at All Children's. My hours were normal, but he put in a lot of extra time. Occasionally we talked about starting a family, but we just never got around to it."

"So," Marge asked, "how come you're not workin' with kids now?"

Anna sighed audibly. "After Josh died, the children I was caring for made me think more and more of the ones we left back in Vietnam. I found myself spending more and more time wondering how they'd grown up... and if they had. I even started to dream about them, and I'd wake up so damn angry with God. I don't know why I started feeling that way after all these years."

Softly Sharon said, "Anger has a funny way of biding its time."

"I'm not angry with anyone!" Marge insisted.

"You just admitted you don't have the job satisfaction you did in Nam," Debbie reminded her. "For a woman whose career is her life that could sow seeds of discontent, to say the least."

"And affect your personal life," Sharon added. "All of your husbands were highly successful in their work and acknowledged for being so. It's reasonable that you'd feel a little jealousy and a little anger."

"What does Ted do?" Anna asked Marge.

"He's a marine engineer consultant."

"Another highly successful man," Debbie noted.

Marge frowned. "Are you ladies suggestin' that my marriage to Ted is doomed to failure even before it begins?"

"No," Sharon said, "but you might want to come to grips with your present job dissatisfaction and face the reality that in Nam we women did a lot more than we're given the chance to do here at home. As you said, we were *really* needed over there."

A brief silence prevailed as the women thought about that. Then Debbie said, "Yeah, it's the having been appreciated that I miss, too. Working in a lounge is okay, but half the time customers aren't listening. It sure was different when I entertained on the wards. Those guys were the greatest. I knew I was needed every second I spent with them, and that made me feel good about myself.''

"Tony needs you," Marge said.

"He needs to be saddled with a lush like he needs a hole in the head."

Sharon smacked her lips in annoyance. "You're using booze as a crutch and you know it."

"A crutch comes in handy when a person is stumbling."

"Every time he gets too close emotionally you make sure he sees you guzzling the stuff," Sharon pointed out. "Don't you see that you're trying to chase him away? You're terrified to let a man get too close to you because you're afraid you're going to lose him just like you lost so many friends in Nam."

Debbie flushed. "That's a riot coming from you. You and Sam didn't last too long. He loved you, he didn't cheat on you and he was working his tail off as an intern. So what was his big crime?"

"I never said the divorce was his fault." Sharon lowered her voice. "We just happened to be together at the wrong time in our lives."

Quietly Anna asked, "What about Steve? Is this the right time for you and him?"

Marge giggled wickedly. "If she's runnin' off to Wisconsin with the man, I'd say it is."

"Don't be so sure," Debbie said. "She'll find some excuse to keep him at an emotional distance. Let's face it. We're all a bunch of screwups as far as relationships go."

"That's certainly not true in my case," Anna said. "Josh and I were very happy together for twenty-two years. We never even had a really serious argument."

Marge frowned. "From what you told us the two of you were so busy takin' care of other people, when would you have had time to argue? Maybe you've been dwellin' on the kids again because you're angry at him for leavin' you alone, with no children of your own. I mean, face it, Anna, if the guy was the saint you're tellin' us he was, you'd have a hard time admittin' you're as mad as hell at him."

"Food for thought, Anna," Sharon said.

Becoming more upset with the direct probings, Debbie said curtly, "Excuse my observation, but I think you nurses have had too many psychology courses. On the other hand, Sharon, how come you and Marge came home so screwed up and so many nurses like Anna and Clara came back and picked up the pieces of their lives without problems?"

"It's a matter of degree," Sharon said, wondering if Debbie was working up to one of her anxiety attacks.

She snickered. "Degree? You'd rather talk up a Freudian storm instead of admitting that some of us are just losers."

"Speak for yourself, honey!" Marge insisted.

Rising, Debbie went to the bar cart and refilled her drink. "I'm the only one here who'll admit to it. Look at you, Marge. You're in love with the wedding march, not the guys you marry. And you, Anna. On your tombstone it's going to read, 'She gave and gave and gave until there was no more to give.'" Debbie's eyes flashed to Sharon. "And you. You just think you're in dandy shape now, but if I'm pushing Tony away, you'll do the same damn thing to Steve. You may finally wind up in bed with him in Wisconsin, but ten to one you won't be able to handle a lasting relationship any more than Marge or I can."

"That's the Scotch talking," Sharon said, her voice barely controlled.

Debbie chuckled and shook her head. "Your trouble, my friend, is that you can be so damn objective about our problems with this PTSD crap, but you can't even see that it's still running your life."

Anna jumped up, grabbed the plate of cheese and crackers and held it toward Marge. "Snack break?"

Smiling, Marge took two. "For me it's always time for a snack break."

Sharon stared at Debbie, her insides churning with hurt and anger. The conversations the women had had in past get-togethers sometimes brought tensions to the surface, but that was why she had started the small group—to give the women a chance to vent their frustrations and to support one another on some very confusing issues. But this time, Sharon decided, Debbie had gone too far.

Desperately Sharon held to her belief that she had conquered her problems with posttraumatic stress. She could see clearly that her hesitancy to let herself become emotionally involved with Steve had nothing to do with her past relationships. He still wasn't convinced of her innocence regarding his brother's death, and she believed he had unresolved feelings about having lost his wife. Two good reasons for her to be cautious.

"Have something," Anna said, holding the plate in front of Sharon.

She waved it away, saying, "No thanks," then she stood. "It's time for me to leave. I have to work in the morning."

"Sharon," Debbie said, standing at the bar cart, her voice more restrained, "you've got to learn to take friendly criticism as well as you give it."

"When it's offered in friendship, I will."

Turning to Marge and Anna, she smiled halfheartedly, then picked up her purse and left the apartment,
her mood as dark as the cloud-covered night sky.

ON WEDNESDAY AFTERNOON Steve glanced over at
Sharon, who was busy at the computer in his office.
Ever since she had come to work Monday morning,
he'd had to tread carefully, and she had seemed even
more preoccupied yesterday. She worked as though
driven, hardly taking time to nibble at the lunch trays
he had brought her.

Over and over again he reviewed the evening they had
spent together on Madeira Beach, and for the life of
him he couldn't see that he had done anything to warrant the cool treatment she was giving him. Nor could
he understand her hasty departures after work every
day.

Not certain what her reaction would be, he said, "I'll
pick you up around 9:00 a.m. to go to the airport. Don't
forget to pack some warm clothes."

"I will," she said, little enthusiasm in her response.

His confusion melding with relief, he rested on the
edge of the table by the computer. "Tell me if I'm
imagining it, but are you upset about something?"

She glared up at him. "Upset? Why should I be upset? Yesterday Werner notified me the case was sched-
uled to go before a grand jury. Only a miracle will save
me from losing my nursing license, and I may go to jail
for something I didn't do. If your father changes his
mind, he could sue me, and when I get out of prison, I'll
be working two jobs for the rest of my life to pay off
what he wins in court, that's *if* I can find a job." She

narrowed her eyes and chuckled bitterly. "So why should I be upset?"

"Werner's passing the results of his investigation to a grand jury doesn't mean the case will definitely go to trial. As far as my father's concerned, he changes his mind daily. Your nursing license is intact now, and I'm not going to let you go to jail. If there is a trial, I'll get you the best defense attorney money will buy."

"Wonderful," she said with a touch of sarcasm. "That means I don't have a thing to worry about, and I can enjoy this mini-vacation you're offering me."

"You don't sound as if you're going to enjoy it."

"Just wait," she said, shoving another disk into the computer. "As soon as I shake the Florida sand from my shoes, I'll be a new person."

What Sharon didn't tell Steve was that she was going with him because she was determined to prove Debbie wrong. She had to, just as surely as if her life depended on it.

Ever since Debbie had lashed out at her Monday evening, Sharon had convinced herself that if she chose to, she could certainly maintain a relationship with Steve or any other man for that matter. In a saner, calmer atmosphere away from Florida she would be able to see things in a normal light. Even Steve had said as much. They both did need some quiet time to sense where their relationship was heading. But if it headed nowhere, it wouldn't be for the reason Debbie had stated. It would be because... well, whatever the reason, that was what she was going to find out.

AFTER THEIR JET LANDED at Green Bay, Wisconsin, the following day, Steve rented a car and they headed east onto Door Peninsula, a narrow, ninety-mile-long finger of limestone and sand that jutted between Green Bay and Lake Michigan.

As they drove northward, Sharon concentrated on the scenery, trying to clear her mind of the problems left behind in Florida. Silently they traveled through the orange gold of the early November landscape: the rolling hills, the bluffs and woods, the dunes, the beaches and the small villages with their white houses nestled in peaceful hollows. Little by little Sharon began to relax.

Steve pulled up in front of a grocery store to pick up a few things. Then they were driving again. Not long after he turned off the highway and followed a gravel road that wound snakelike between centuries-old cedars and withered pines. "There's the house up ahead."

Surprised at its size, she said, "It looks more like a chalet lodge."

"It's got personality."

Sharon scanned the light gray split-level house that fitted comfortably into the heavily wooded site, its deeply ridged roof forming an angled gable at the entrance. Steve parked, then retrieved the two suitcases from the trunk of the car. Sharon removed her garment bag and smaller suitcase from the back seat before following Steve up the wide wooden steps to the front door that was actually on the second level.

Inside the house the furnishings were modern, done in warm earth colors. A sprawling modular seating unit faced the floor-to-ceiling stone fireplace.

"The bedrooms are downstairs," Steve said, leading the way. After leaving his suitcase just inside one of the three bedrooms, he carried Sharon's across the carpeted hallway. "This is your room," he said, placing her suitcase on the upholstered bench at the bottom of the queen-size bed.

She glanced around and decided the room could be photographed for *House Beautiful.* After hanging her garment bag in the closet, she remarked, "For a house that hasn't been lived in, everything certainly is in tip-top shape."

"The real estate lady had a cleaning firm take care of it. I'll bring in the groceries while you unpack. Then I'd better take care of business at the real estate office."

"Want me to go with you?"

"You're on vacation, remember? You make yourself comfortable here. I won't be long."

As she transferred lingerie from her suitcase to a dresser drawer, Sharon heard the front door close and then Steve's bouncing steps on the wooden stairway. Going to the bedroom window, she drew back the green drapery panels and watched as he got into the car. When he drove off, she felt somewhat odd at being alone in his house—and Laura's.

Dismissing the feeling, she returned to the job at hand and took her overnight case into the bathroom, where she arranged her toiletries on the marble-topped vanity next to the green enamel washbasin. Briefly she stared at the birth control pills she'd purchased before leaving Florida. Then she returned to the bedroom and placed the opened package in the drawer with her lingerie.

After a troublesome deep breath, she sank onto the bench at the foot of the bed, trying to make sense of what she was doing. *Going to bed with a man because you love him is one thing,* she lectured herself, *but doing it to prove a point is something else.*

Did she love Steve? Or were her strong feelings for him only a powerful physical attraction? If that was all it was, why was she so hesitant to engage in a romantic involvement with him? In the fifteen years since her divorce from Sam Bruner she'd had a few brief affairs and had lived with Joe for six months while she had worked for the insurance company. None of her attempts at an enduring relationship had lasted very long. Each had started with a bang, then dissolved quickly and painfully for everyone concerned. Five years ago she had stopped trying and had devoted herself solely to her work. Then Steve had popped into her life unexpectedly, upsetting her well-ordered existence. *And here you are,* Sharon chided herself, *acting like a bride on your wedding day.*

Slowly she rose and finished unpacking, unable to will Steve from her thoughts, wondering when the "quiet time" part of the trip was going to start.

She busied herself by changing into tan slacks and a yellow knit sweater, then went upstairs and located the wide kitchen on the other side of the dining room. She decided that the soft drinks Steve had put in the refrigerator were chilled enough, so she took one, wiped the rim with a paper towel and snapped open the top.

In the living room she kicked off her shoes and drew her legs up onto the sofa, staring into the unlit fireplace as Debbie's hurtful words echoed in her thoughts: *If I'm pushing Tony away, you're doing the same damn thing to Steve. You may finally wind up in bed with him in Wisconsin, but ten to one you won't be able to handle a lasting relationship any more than Marge or I can.*

What if Debbie was right? Sharon wondered, experiencing a sinking feeling in the pit of her stomach. She knew that her problems with PTSD had caused the breakup between her and Sam. And the others? They had all accused her of holding back emotionally. Would it be any different with Steve?

"It has to be!" she ordered, jumping up and looking around the room. She saw the radio, rushed to it and turned it to a station playing country music. She increased the volume until the walls vibrated, trying desperately to silence her worrisome thoughts.

The afternoon sun had given way to a gray light by the time Steve returned, carrying two grocery bags.

"I'm sorry," he apologized. "It took longer to close the deal than I thought it would and I stopped at a store."

"What did you do, buy it out?" she asked, taking one of the bags.

"I picked up a few more things I thought we might want."

As she started for the kitchen, she asked lightly, "We are leaving Sunday morning, right?"

"Yeah, but they're forecasting snow tonight. These roads are tricky to navigate until they're cleared. Besides, I want everything to be perfect for your vacation." He removed a white-wrapped package from one of the bags. "Center cut pork chops," he said, smacking his lips. "Even got us some after-dinner mints."

"You're determined that I'm going to gain weight, aren't you?"

"Not to worry. I plan to work it off you."

"Oh?"

From the refrigerator he gave her a boyish smile. "I'm devious. I brought you up here to help me pack. I'm going to send some things to my folks, others I'll ship to Florida."

"Let's make a deal, Steve."

"You're not going to get a negative answer from me during the next three days. Shoot."

"While we're here let's not mention Florida."

"You got it," he said, heading toward the kitchen door. "I've some more stuff in the car."

"Need any help?"

"No. It's just empty boxes and wrapping tape I got at the store."

Soon he was back in the kitchen, slipping off his car coat. Crossing his arms, he brushed his hands over his white cable-knit sweater. "Is it me, or is it chilly in here?" He checked the thermostat and saw that it registered sixty degrees. So he turned it up, then reached for a bottle from the wine rack fixed to the kitchen wall. As he opened it, he nodded to the china cabinet on the other side of the room. "Grab two of those glasses, would you?"

When she did, Steve took hold of her free hand and pulled her along into the living room. "If you'll pour the wine, I'll start a fire."

Minutes later they sat comfortably on the sofa, side by side, sipping a smooth Bordeaux, their legs resting on a square section of the modular sofa that he had repositioned.

"This is nice," he said as he slipped his left arm over her shoulder. "Glad you came?"

"So far so good," she answered, gazing at the yellow gold flames that curled up over the logs.

Steve chuckled. "You say that as if you're anticipating an earthquake."

"Are we fixing those pork chops for dinner tonight?" she asked, attempting to channel her thoughts to something other than his warm hand.

"No. Tonight you get chicken amandine and potatoes lyonnaise. And *we're* not fixing dinner. I am."

Tilting her head toward his, she lifted her eyebrows. "I'm impressed."

"Not warranted. It'll all be cooked in the microwave, except for dessert. I'm going to satisfy that sweet tooth of yours with chocolate key lime pie."

"Chocolate?"

"It was a favorite of Laura's. She showed me how to make it from scratch."

"Oh," Sharon remarked, the upbeat mood she had begun to feel suddenly dimming. But, she reminded herself, Steve's being in the house that he had shared with his wife for so many years was bound to bring back memories. Without thinking she heard herself say, "Laura must have been a good cook."

"She—" he almost said *is* "—was good. France, Italy, China—you name the country and there's a cookbook in the kitchen from there. By rights I should weigh a ton, but it must be something in the Nordstrom genes. I weigh about the same as I did when we got married." He became pensive and his eyes clouded over. "I wish you could have known Laura then. You'd have liked her. Everyone did. She won the congeniality award in the Miss America pageant the year before I met her at the University of Wisconsin. I literally bumped into her as I was carrying an armload of books from behind one of the library stacks. She helped me pick up the books, then smiled at me, and that was it." He shook his head almost imperceptibly. "I couldn't believe she'd be interested in me, never mind marry me."

"You're being modest," Sharon said, her spirits sinking more and more as Steve spoke lovingly of his wife.

"No, realistic. At the time Laura's father was being considered as a presidential candidate. Mine had a florist shop. At school she drove a Mercedes. I had a Chevy with eighty thousand miles on it.''

"Apparently," Sharon said quietly, "family background and finances didn't bother Laura as much as they bothered you."

"You're right, but I didn't realize it then." He faced Sharon and smiled. "For someone who said he didn't believe in dredging up the past, I'm doing a pretty job of doing it, aren't I?"

"The past is always with us," she said pensively, "for better or for worse."

"Let's talk about you," he suggested. "What do you like to do on Sundays?"

"If I haven't worked Saturday nights, I enjoy a leisurely breakfast, lounging around and reading the paper. If I'm really ambitious, I take an early-morning walk on the beach before it gets too crowded."

"So do I," he said enthusiastically. "I didn't know you enjoyed it, too."

"There's a lot you don't know about me, Steve," she said as she rose from the sofa. Looking down at him, her expression turned solemn. "And there's a lot that I don't know about you."

The tension in her eyes brought on a heaviness in his heart. "That's why I really wanted you to come here with me. Now we have a chance to get to know each other, to really discover what we're like together."

"You might be disappointed," she said, moving to the table where she had left the wine bottle.

He set his wineglass down, then leaned back, crossed his arms and inspected her intently. "I hadn't planned on using a scorecard, if that's what you mean."

She pulled her eyes from his and half filled her wineglass. Softly she said, "It's been a while since I've been with a man."

"Compared to me, you've probably been promiscuous." When she turned, he saw the unsettled look on her face. "I didn't mean that the way it sounded. It's just that…well, I've had sex once in the past four years. If either of us has a right to worry about being disappointed, it might turn out to be you."

He reached for his glass and emptied it, then met her steadfast gaze. "Inside I feel like an overwound spring that's ready to snap and head for the moon. If you and I do make love, I'm saying *if,* it might be all over for me when you touch me. That's what I call disappointing for you." After a lingering silence, he held his glass up. "I'm cooking. Mind pouring?"

"We're going to be a great pair," she said uneasily as she took his wineglass. "It's been five years for me."

Steve smiled, more than pleased to hear what she had just admitted. "If we're not a great pair," he said, laughing softly, "we should be damn interesting."

Although unnerved, Sharon found his smile contagious. As she poured his wine, she said, "I can't believe we're being this analytical. We sound as if we're getting ready to pick up again on an old exercise program."

After handing him his glass, she sat on the modular section they'd been using as a footstool, facing the fireplace, her back to him. Steve lowered himself to the carpet and rested his arm alongside her thigh.

For a while they listened to the crackling and snapping of the wooden logs. Then he said softly, "I don't want to scare the hell out of you, Sharon, but I think I'm falling in love with you."

CHAPTER FOURTEEN

SHARON FELT her heart lurch as she gazed down at Steve, who was staring into the fire. The flickering flames cast a burnished gold glow over his face and white sweater. She hadn't expected to hear him say he was falling in love with her. Now that he had she wasn't sure how to cope with it. Once again Debbie's words tortured her: *You won't be able to handle a lasting relationship any more than Marge or I can.*

Steve waited and waited, then said huskily, "Don't hold back. If you feel like laughing, go right ahead."

"I don't feel like laughing," she replied, her voice unsteady. "But maybe it's the wine talking, not you," she said, unable to look him in the eye when his gaze shifted to her.

"Good try, but I think the same thing when I drink a cola or coffee." Matter-of-factly, he added, "It's been that way for a while now."

Again he waited anxiously for some indication of how she felt about him. But he waited in vain. Feeling as though exposing his vulnerability had left him stark naked, he wanted to scream at her to say something— anything! Instead, he remarked calmly, "It would really help my masculine ego if you at least said you admired my courage for setting myself up like this."

Placing her wineglass down on the stone hearth, she eased herself next to him, the firelight glistening in her moist eyes. When he was about to say something else, she placed unsteady fingertips over his lips. "You're not setting yourself up for anything, Steve, but one of us has to be realistic. We've both been under a terrible strain for weeks now, and we both need someone to hold on to, someone to hold us."

As though her hand were a heavy weight, her fingers slipped across his cheek and onto his shoulder. "But we shouldn't attach a label to what we might feel for each other right now. When all of the problems back home are cleared away, we can't be sure how we'll feel then."

"You said you didn't want us to mention Florida while we're here," he reminded her. When she nodded slowly, he said, "All right, we don't give whatever's going on between us a name, but we can't just pretend it's not there."

Her eyes were closed, and her hand was resting limply on his thigh, but her mere light touch created havoc in his groin. His heart thumping wildly in his chest, he took hold of her hand and pressed it against his burgeoning erection that strained his corduroy trousers. "There's no way we can pretend that you don't make me half crazy just by being in the same room with me. And trust me, it's you. It has been ever since that afternoon I brought you the orchid plant. You came into my life and you conquered, lady. Did you ever!"

Slowly Sharon lifted her eyelids, trembling although the fire warmed her skin and the feel of his pulsating desire burned her palm. Meeting his resolute gaze, she slipped her hand from under his and said quietly, "I'm not made of iron, Steve, but I'm ... afraid."

"Afraid?" he asked, taking hold of her shoulders. "What is there to be afraid of? I love you, so that's my problem. All you have to do is like me a little."

"A little?" Guiding her arms around his neck, she slumped against him and buried her face in the curve of his shoulder. "I've been going half out of my mind thinking about you, wanting you."

Inhaling deeply, Steve let out a long, soul-relieving sigh. "That's all we need to know, love," he said, grasping her shoulders and holding her at arm's length, surprised when he saw her face was tear-stained. Gently he brushed away the moisture with a finger. "I guess I've been out of circulation too long," he said, forcing a slight smile, "but as I remember, times like this are supposed to make people happy. Why the tears?"

"I don't know," she answered honestly, interlacing her fingers and staring down at them.

At the moment Steve didn't have conversation on his mind. Each and every nerve end, some more than others, was ready for action. As badly as he craved sensual relief, though, he was determined not to pressure her. He wanted her desperately and right now, but he wanted the need and the relief to be mutual. With her, any other way was unthinkable.

He took hold of her clenched hands, drew them to his lips and kissed her fingers, trying to figure out what could be distressing her so. "You're not afraid of me, are you?" he asked quietly. "I wouldn't do anything to hurt you, not for the world." When she shook her head, he probed further. "Something in the past? A bad experience? Your ex-husband—did he hurt you?"

"No, not physically," she said, her voice as soft as Steve's had been. "Sam was a gentle man." Realizing she had never told Steve about him, she said, "I was twenty-four when I left the army and began working as a surgical nurse at a hospital in San Francisco. Sam was an intern there, and after dating for a few months, we married." She paused to order her thoughts. "Everything was fine for about a year, then suddenly in OR I started having flashbacks about the horribly mutilated patients I'd had in Vietnam. That led to anxiety attacks and periods of depression. At that time no one talked about posttraumatic stress."

With an ineffectual smile she said, "One psychiatrist I went to for help told me I was just another neurotic woman. Now, of course, I know why I was acting the way I did. But at the time I was blaming my problems on everything other than my wartime experience. I even blamed them on Sam, who was too overworked as an intern to be supportive when I needed him. He'd never been in the service, so when I did try to talk to him about what I was going through, he couldn't understand. He reminded me that I was a nurse and that people die in hospitals. Anyway, we divorced soon after that. Then things got worse. Everything connected with the hospital reminded me of what went on in Vietnam, and I had to give up nursing."

"That's when you went to work for the insurance company," Steve said, his heart aching now for her past hurts. He moved next to her, placed an arm around her and drew her close.

"Yes," she said quietly, "and things did get better. No more nightmares, and the anxiety and depression diminished after a while. I began dating, but the few serious relationships I had didn't last long. The strange thing is I just didn't care enough to get deeply involved. So I said, 'Why bother,' and avoided serious entanglements—until I met you, Steve. Now I'm not sure what I should do."

"Not sure what you should do, or not sure what you want to do?"

Grasping his hand that rested on her shoulder, she squeezed it. "I know what I want to do, but I'm afraid to, and I don't understand why."

"You know I'd never hurt you," he said, kissing her silky hair. "If you're afraid you'll hurt me, don't be. I won't ask for any commitments from you. But I'd be lying if I said it doesn't matter if we make love or not. I want us to desperately, but only if you want it also." Tilting her face toward his, he gazed into her shining blue eyes. "Do you?" he asked quietly.

Her heart in her throat, she smiled softly. "Yes, Steve," she whispered, and drew his face closer, confirming her reply with a gentle kiss.

Hand in hand, Steve and Sharon descended the steps to the downstairs level of the house, the green-gold globe of the hallway light illumining their way as they entered her bedroom. Once inside, he folded his arms around her and returned the kiss she had given him upstairs. His was not as gentle, nor was it wildly ravishing. He steeled himself, determined more than ever to make sure he pleased her before giving in to the urgency of his own pent-up needs.

But it wasn't easy for him to hold back. Even through their sweaters he could feel her warmth and the supple lines of her feminine form. He let one hand drift lower down her back to glide over the soft roundness below, the intimate contact sending shock waves tearing throughout his tense body.

He dragged his mouth from hers, drew her sweater up over her head, then removed his own. One by one their garments fell to the carpet before he pulled back the satiny spread, comforter and top sheet. In a graceful but powerful motion he swept her up in his arms. He carefully lowered her onto the bed and sat next to her, smiling down at her.

His chest constricted as he slowly slipped a hand through the silken waves of her hair, its softness caressing his fingers. As though mesmerized, he guided his glistening gaze over the fine arch of her eyebrows, her long lashes, the delicacy of her sculpted nose and alluring, sensual lips. When he noticed the contrast between his tanned arm and the creamy white skin over the swell of her breasts, a lump caught in his throat, and he swallowed hard.

With exquisite tenderness he took one pinkish tip between his fingers, feeling it stiffen under his touch. Then he cupped the breast in his palm, delighting in its warm, supple weight. He eased his hand downward, across her slender side and over the silky curve of her hip. "You're even more beautiful than I imagined you would be," he murmured hoarsely, still sitting beside her, not daring to align their bodies yet.

She, however, yearned for the closeness. She longed to feel his arms around her, his body warmth melding with hers, his lips on hers once again. She wanted to lose herself in him, wanted him to lose himself in her.

Feeling his fingertips graze down her leg, she shivered and placed a hand on his thigh, surprised by the heat of his firm flesh. Emboldened by his quick intake of breath, she eased her fingers onto his manly hardness, its throbbing quickening her heartbeat.

He gasped, pulled her hand away quickly and held her palm to his lips in a long kiss. With closed eyes he struggled to will away the savage sensations that threatened his precarious control. After long, intense moments he rested her hand on his chest and smiled down at her. "Take it easy, love," he pleaded.

She slid over a little and patted the warm sheet where she had been lying. "You can't sit there all night," she advised as calmly as she could.

"I don't intend to," he informed her, and brought his legs up onto the bed.

When he rested on an arm, his eyes steadfast on hers, she placed a hand on the side of his smiling face, feeling the light stubble along his strong jawline. Slowly she trailed her fingertips down the side of his neck and onto his shoulder, then over his arm, testing his hard biceps. Her desire for him increasing by the moment, she guided her hand over his broad lightly haired chest, then trailed a fingertip down over his smooth abdomen before raising herself to a sitting position. "Lie back and get comfortable," she said softly.

Doing so, his eyes narrowed as he grinned. "What's on that mind of yours?"

As soon as his head was on the pillow, she slipped next to him and crossed her arms over his muscular chest, teasing one stiff nipple with a fingertip. "We're going to take things slowly, just as you want."

"That remains to be seen," he said as he eased his right arm under her and wrapped it around her waist. "Just remember there's no pool here, and I'm not about to jump into Green Bay."

"I don't want you to move . . . not just yet, anyway."

"Before we get to the 'yet' I've got to make a quick trip to my bedroom."

Guessing he meant for protection, she tangled her fingers in his hair. "I've taken care of that," she said, appreciating his thoughtfulness.

Again he smiled, hoping that she now wanted him almost as much as he had wanted her for so long. Reaching down, he drew her right leg over his, moaning with pleasure when he felt its weight mold onto his thickening erection.

Sharon felt the rock-hard maleness embedded in her soft inner thigh. It had indeed been a long time since she had been with a man, but as she gazed at the loving smile on Steve's face, she felt as if she had never been with anyone before.

As Sharon touched her fingertips to his lips, Steve was hardly able to believe his fantasies were actually happening. Slowly he guided his free hand down over the back of her velvety smooth thigh. Then he grinned and murmured, "You feel so damn good. I think I'm getting the hang of this again."

"The hang of what?" she teased. "You're just lying there."

"This is part of making love, too... the nice, comfy part," he said, arching slightly and rubbing her thigh with his hot, twitching flesh. "So is this," he added, rolling her onto her back and nuzzling the valley between her breasts. "Umm, you smell so damn good, too." Dotting kisses over the swell of one breast, he took her nipple in his mouth and suckled slowly, gently. And effectively.

Sharon writhed under his hand that was now rhythmically massaging the silky triangle of hair that shielded her moist, tingling femininity.

"Do you like that?" he whispered, glancing up at her with warm, smoky eyes.

"Oh, yes," she murmured, then felt his agile lips minister to her other breast as his hand continued his slow, tantalizing caresses.

She sighed openly when his probing finger entered her, began to search and then discovered that particularly sensitive spot. Catching her breath, she thrust one hand into the hair at his nape and rubbed her other up and down over his muscular back, digging her nails into his hot flesh when she began to tingle all over.

"Steve," she murmured, barely able to speak, "you said we were going to... take things easy."

He reared his head up and smiled. "With you this is wonderfully easy."

"I'm beginning to feel a little... tense," she admitted, closing her eyes.

"That makes two of us," he said huskily, then raised himself, positioned his body between her legs and flattened his palms on either side of her. "What should we do about it?" he asked, his skin rippling when the sensitive tip of his swollen flesh grazed her silk-soft hair.

"This," she suggested, her palm and fingers warming when she grasped his hot thickness and stroked him slowly before guiding him into her. "Ahh," she sighed, knowing she would be tight.

He felt her tender resistance and, although his heart was pounding like a jackhammer, he immediately curbed his desire to thrust wildly. Instead he remained stone-still, restraining every tortured muscle in his body. When he felt her hands grasp his thighs and saw her arch upward, he dared to breathe again and began to sink down and into her.

A glorious surge of ecstasy spiraled through him as he felt her caress him, take possession of him, curl about him intimately. His face close to hers, he arched his head back slightly and closed his eyes, savoring the unique, exquisite sensations that threatened his consciousness. "Oh, God," he moaned with sheer delight, "this is what skydiving must feel like. Don't even move, love... or I've had it."

She was sorely tempted to. For all his size his weight felt wonderful, as did the little twitches his body was making deep inside her. When she felt his arms embrace her, his mouth on the side of her neck and then his moist, warm tongue tracing the inner curves of her ear, she dragged her hands down over his back and dug her fingers into his firm buttocks, then began undulating under him.

"Sweet Jesus!" he groaned, arching back as his entire body shuddered again and again and again.

Basking in his unrestrained exultation, Sharon gasped as she quickly joined him, feeling her own release with the same intensity, the same electrifying sensations, the same joy. At long last she thought she was spent, but when Steve took her lips in a frenzied kiss, she found herself repeating the dizzying climactic spasm.

A world later he rolled onto his back, taking Sharon with him in his firm embrace. With his head sunk into the pillow, he rested hers over his frantically beating heart and stared up at the light fixture, luxuriating in the wondrous dream state that came to a man in the sweet afterglow of ardent lovemaking. The feeling was so awesome, though, that he realized he had never felt quite the same way before, not even in the early years of his marriage. He couldn't comprehend it, but intermingled with his feelings of intense excitement and manly pride was an immense sense of peace and an urgent desire to care for and protect the woman in his arms. Inhaling the sweet scent of her, he closed his eyes and smiled softly. Between jagged, dragged-in breaths he mumbled, "I told you . . . not to . . . move."

"I couldn't help myself," she confessed, smiling against his chest as she smoothed a hand over the fine hairs of his firm, warm thigh. "You got me all funny."

"Funny?" His eyes snapped open and he tilted up her chin. "I'll show you funny." This time his kiss was long but agonizingly gentle. Gazing at her, he said, "You're a nurse. What's good for bedsores?"

Her eyes widened. "You have bedsores?"

"Not yet, but we're both going to by Sunday."

"You talk big, Mr. Nordstrom," she said, slapping his chest, "but I get hungry three times a day."

"Ah! Now that you've had your way with me, all you can think about is food."

"Man does not live by sex alone."

"This man would die trying to if it could be with you." He gave her a loving grin that made her heart dance. "Before, when I said I loved you, I didn't realize how much I do. Now I know."

Sharon sensed an inexplicable shadow settle between her and Steve, some vague, dark barrier that dragged her down from the heights of happiness she had been experiencing. Willing it away, she lowered her eyes and said quietly, "No labels, remember? We agreed." She rose from the bed and began gathering their clothes. "Now, about this chicken amandine you promised me."

Steve also sensed that some barrier had suddenly loomed up between them, and it confused and hurt him. In his heart he had thought that once he and Sharon had shared the ultimate intimacy, surely she would feel the same way he did. But she didn't, he realized. He had to face that, he told himself, recalling that he had promised he wouldn't ask for any commitments from her. If that was the only way he could be with her—and love her—he would have to accept it. For now, anyway.

Silently he watched Sharon lay their garments over the back of a chair, then he followed her with his eyes as she took her blue robe from the closet and slipped into it. When she turned toward him, he forced a smile. "The belief that the way to a man's heart is through his stomach is highly overrated."

"It's not *your* stomach I'm thinking about. Move it."

With a flourish he tossed back the covers and bounded from the bed. "You sound like the drill sergeant I had in basic training."

"I was a first lieutenant."

"Then you should know how to put another log on the fire while I hunt down my bathrobe." Heading for his bedroom across the hall, he swatted her on the behind.

In the living room Sharon was reaching for a log when she heard the front door being opened and a man's voice call, "Steven!"

Standing erect, her surprised eyes clashed with those of a tall, robust-looking gray-haired man who held an overnight bag in one hand, a key in the other.

At that moment Steve entered, barefoot, wearing a short yellow terry robe. "Dad?" he exclaimed, his smile giving way to a shocked expression.

CHAPTER FIFTEEN

DAD! Sharon felt as if some monstrous hand were squeezing her insides. Even under the best of circumstances she had no desire to meet Steve's father. And she was in her robe, yet. If only the floor would open up so that she could vanish!

At first Steve's father seemed similarly ill at ease, but then his craggy face broke into a half smile and his blue gray eyes, duplicates of his son's, twinkled. "I came at a bad time, didn't I? This young lady must be that someone special you mentioned."

Still startled, Steve asked, "What are you doing here?"

Dropping his overnight bag onto one of the easy chairs, the older man said, "Your mother nagged me into driving up here to give you a hand packing." He faced Sharon and smiled openly. "We didn't know you already had a helper, a mighty pretty one, too, I'd say. Aren't you going to introduce me?"

Steve hesitated as he ran a hand over the back of his neck. Then he said to Sharon, who stood rigid. "My father, Carl Nordstrom. Dad, this is ... Sharon McClure."

The gray-haired man's smile froze and his eyes turned dark as they narrowed. Disbelief twisting his features, he jerked his head toward his son. "Sharon McClure," he asked, as if the name were bitter on his lips, "the nurse who . . . killed your brother?"

His accusation cut into Sharon's heart like a surgeon's scalpel, the pain sharp and debilitating. Her legs weakened, and she thought she would fall, but Steve's supporting arm was suddenly holding her.

"Sharon didn't kill Richie!" he said with conviction.

"Then who did?" his father demanded.

"That's what the police will find out."

Carl Nordstrom's eyes settled on Sharon's bare feet, then drifted up to the pained expression on her face. Without looking at his son he said, "Meanwhile she's helping you go through Laura's personal things, huh?" His reproachful eyes darted back to Steve. "What the hell's warped your thinking? Don't you have a shred of decency left in you?"

His face reddening, Steve's voice turned hard. "You don't know what you're saying."

"I know my son's dead."

"Sharon had nothing to do with that."

"And Laura, your wife for fifteen years, was like a daughter to your mother and me. How could you forget her so quickly? What has this woman done to you, Steven?"

Sharon swallowed hard, trying to rid herself of the terrible tightness in her throat so that she could excuse herself from the room, but she couldn't even get one word out.

When she started to turn, Steve gripped her shoulder securely. "No, don't leave," he ordered. "You were invited here. My father wasn't."

Raggedly she pleaded, "Please, Steve. Let me go."

The key Carl Nordstrom had been holding clinked when he threw it onto the table next to the chair. "Since when did I have to be invited into your home?" he asked, profound hurt apparent in his voice.

"Since when have you appointed yourself judge and jury over what happened to Richie?" Easing Sharon down on the chair by the fireplace, he went to his father and took hold of his shoulders. Softening his tone, he said, "I know the loss and pain you're feeling, and the bitterness. I'm going through all that myself. I loved Richie, too, and I wanted to strike out in anger, but until we know what really happened, there's no justice in hurting innocent people."

"And she's innocent?" the older man asked, his accusing gaze sliding toward Sharon.

"I believe she is," Steve said evenly.

As he defended her, Sharon cringed, feeling as though she were already on a witness stand. How long would he have to go on defending her? she wondered. How long would she have to live a marked woman in the eyes of so many people? Would their doubt ever end? Would Steve's? Oh, why hadn't she remained in Florida! Coming with him, she now knew, had been a disastrous mistake.

With a jerky movement Carl Nordstrom shrugged off his son's grasp and picked up his overnight bag. "Phone your mother and tell her I'm on my way back."

"That's crazy, Dad. It's a four-hour drive. Spend the night here, and—"

"And what? Sleep soundly, knowing that—" he nodded curtly toward Sharon "—she's taking Laura's place in your bed."

"Laura's dead!" Steve blurted out.

"So is your brother!" Turning quickly, Carl Nord-strom rushed from the house.

The instant the door slammed shut Steve whirled around. "Sharon, I'm so sorry. He was the last person in the world I expected to see tonight. He had no right to—"

"Your father had every right to say what he did and to think whatever he was imagining. Look at us!" Her arms flew out sideways. "What else could he think?"

As she started to pace, Steve said, "He's not usually like that. He's upset now."

"Why shouldn't he be? He found you shacking up with the woman he thinks killed his son!"

Calmly Steve said, "We weren't shacking up."

"What would you call it?" she asked, her eyes flaring, her pulse pounding.

"We were loving each other. Is that a crime?"

"Try asking your parents that."

"I told you once that I have my life and they have theirs."

Her head splitting, Sharon looked directly at him. "And I have mine. What's left of it." That said, she spun around and charged into her bedroom and shut the door.

Leaning against the closed door, she let her tears flow and hugged herself, overwhelmed by the awesome emptiness and loneliness she felt. She was emotionally exhausted by the ups and downs she had been through the past few hours. She had been swept to the height of happiness with Steve, then to the depth of despair as he had argued with his father. Closing her eyes, she realized how wrong she had been in reaching out to Steve, in letting herself get too close to him, in lowering the protective barrier she had set into place so many years ago in Vietnam.

"Sharon," Steve called softly, knocking on her bedroom door. "We need to talk."

She covered her mouth to silence any response she might be tempted to make.

"Don't shut me out like this. Please don't," he begged, flattening his palms against the door.

Her silence ripped through him, shredding the memory of the joy and contentment they had shared earlier. Stepping back slowly, he returned to the living room, lowered himself onto the chair by the fireplace and fixed his dull gaze on the dying embers.

"MORNING," Steve said matter-of-factly, attempting to disguise his dark mood. He smoothed the tape over the box he'd packed with china, then looked up at Sharon again. "Sleep well?"

"Yes," she lied, scanning the wrapped and addressed boxes strewn throughout the kitchen. "Apparently you stayed up all night."

Disregarding her comment, he nodded toward the counter. "Just made a fresh pot of coffee."

"Thanks," she said, her voice a dull monotone.

"You're welcome."

She checked his cup and saw that it was half-full. "Want yours heated up?"

"No. I'm already on a caffeine high now."

As she poured her coffee, she asked, "Have you had breakfast yet?"

"No, I'm still stuffed from the dinner we *didn't* have last night."

His cutting remark didn't hurt Sharon as badly as it could have. During the long, miserable night, she had tossed and turned and then disciplined her emotions, steeled herself into believing that nothing would ever hurt her again.

"Fix something for yourself," he suggested, assessing the controlled look on her face. "They say breakfast is the most important meal of the day."

"They know what they're talking about."

"I'm glad someone does," he muttered as he ripped the final length of tape and rubbed it down over the cardboard box.

Sharon felt Steve's hostility, but wasn't sure if it was directed at her or the damnable situation they found themselves in. What was supposed to have been a "quiet time" together had turned out to be depressing and solemn. Long before the sun rose she had decided that the sooner they got back to Florida, the better for everyone concerned.

"Tell me what to do," she said, "and I'll help."

He glanced at her with tired eyes. "I'm just about finished. It'll take two trips to the parcel express office to ship this stuff. I can do that while you enjoy breakfast."

"Then we can leave?" Sharon asked hopefully.

His hands thrust on his hips, Steve eyed her sharply. "Are you *that* anxious to get back to Florida?"

"Aren't you?"

"No, I'm not. I've got this sudden craving to sit on my ass and do nothing." He raised a hand and held his thumb close to his index finger. "I'm this far from being clinically depressed."

"Exercise should help."

"What do you think I've been doing half the night?" he asked curtly as he slipped into his car coat.

When he grabbed a box and exited via the kitchen door, Sharon slumped back against the counter, debating whether or not to pack, call a cab and head for the airport while he was gone. No, she told herself. Steve deserved better than her walking out on him. This entire business was more her fault than his. He had been hurting more than she had realized ever since Laura's death. Who would blame him for latching on to the first woman who showed him sympathy and...and what? Loving kindness? Nurturing? Willingness to go to bed with him? Her eyes swept to the door when Steve trudged back in.

"Forgot the damn car keys," he mumbled, then scooped them up from the kitchen table and carted out another box.

Put on a happy face, Sharon, she ordered herself. *You did it often enough in Nam when you felt like screaming.*

She glanced out the kitchen window and saw Steve plodding toward the car in three inches of snow that had fallen overnight. Turning, she spotted a smaller box across the room, went to it and picked it up, which wasn't all that easy; it was heavier than she thought it would be. She had barely lifted it when Steve returned.

"What are you trying for—a hernia?" He jerked the box from her and huffed off with it.

As he came and went, he listened to the clanging and banging of frying pans and the refrigerator door being opened and slammed shut. By the time he had finished loading the car for the first trip, tempting aromas of sausage, frying eggs and toasted English muffins filled the kitchen.

His stomach growling, he asked, "Are you hungry, or are you cooking for two?"

"Yes and yes," she tossed back at him. "You can try working off your depression by setting the table."

Cocking his head, he smirked. "I planned to."

"Then plan on eating silently."

"A comment on my table manners?"

"On your mood. You lack joie de vivre this morning."

"I wonder why," he remarked gruffly, reaching into a cabinet for plates.

Sharon gritted her teeth as she flipped the sausage patties, but she tempered her tone. "Last night was as difficult for me as it was for you."

"The early part or the latter?"

Her eyes flicked to his. "After the company arrived." She focused on the eggs in the other frying pan. "Sunny-side up?"

"Over light," he mumbled. "Why did you give me the silent treatment? I hate that, damn it, just hate it! I don't know how to handle it."

Concentrating on her cooking, she said, "We both needed some thinking time."

"And you came up with?"

"What happened last night, the early part, was just something we had to get out of our systems. We did and that's that. Let's not make a big deal out of it."

"Jeez," he said between clenched teeth. "You go to bed with a woman and you think you know her." Jerking two linen napkins from a drawer in the sideboard, he plopped them on the table. "I don't want you to get a swelled head, lady, but to me it was a big deal!"

Not looking at him, she said, "Give me your plate."

He did, staring at her as she placed two eggs and several sausage patties on it, along with a buttered English muffin. "Start in before it gets cold," she advised.

"Cold?" He took the plate and headed to the table. "It's cold enough in here to hang a side of beef."

Sharon knew he wasn't talking about the temperature in the warm kitchen. Sitting across from him, she poured them both coffee. "I didn't put salt on anything."

"Concerned for my health?" When she didn't respond, he leaned back in the wooden chair and studied her bland expression. "Considering that last night wasn't a big deal for you, how was I . . . on a scale, say, of one to ten?"

Her eyes glued to her breakfast, her heart and head pounding, she said stoically, "Your eggs are getting cold."

With one wild swoop of his hand Steve sent his plate, coffee cup and utensils flying across the room and splattering against the refrigerator door.

Once again Sharon drew upon the little trick she had learned so many years ago in a country far away. Removing the napkin from her lap, she folded it carefully and calmly placed it on the table. Silently she rose and went into the living room.

In seconds Steve was standing behind her, his fingers digging into her shoulders. "I'm sorry," he apologized candidly. "That was a stupid thing to do."

He didn't know what else to say to her. Telling her that she had hurt him more than he had ever been hurt in his entire life would be equally stupid. And what difference would it make? Somewhere along the line he had totally misread her feelings for him because, as she had warned him, he had wanted to so badly.

"Look," he said quietly, "I'll clean up the mess and take the boxes down to UPS. When I get back, let's drive somewhere and have breakfast."

She stood stone-still and silent, so he removed his hands from her shoulders and headed back to the kitchen.

A half hour later he returned from his quick trip to find her in the bedroom, packing.

"What are you doing?" he asked, knowing what she would say.

"I'm going home," she answered as she gathered her lingerie from a dresser drawer.

Steve squeezed the wooden post at the bottom of the bed with an iron grip. "Our reservations aren't until the day after tomorrow."

"You can cash my ticket in. I have a credit card."

When she snapped the suitcase shut, it sounded like thunder to him. "I said I was sorry."

"I believed you," she said coolly.

"Just how guilty do you want me to feel?"

"Steve," she said calmly, "I don't want you to feel anything as far as I'm concerned."

"That's a neat trick, the way you turn it on and turn it off."

"Turn what on and off?"

Slumping onto the bed, he raked his fingers through his hair. "Either I'm losing my grip on reality, or you gave a hell of an impression of liking me last evening."

"I do like you. I just don't want to be with you."

"That clears up everything nicely...for you maybe."

But it wasn't all that clear for Sharon. She was acting instinctively, maneuvering for self-preservation. Having let Steve get close to her, she was positive she was bound to lose him. There had been too much against them to begin with: his brother's mysterious death, Detective Werner's foregone conclusion that she had been responsible, Steve's basic doubts about her and his unresolved feelings for Laura, and then his father's bitter accusations. That had been the final straw, and Sharon had withdrawn into the protective shell that had served her so well in the past.

After taking a deep breath, she faced him and said softly, "The only thing that's really clear to me is that we're making each other miserable."

"Miserable," he repeated spiritlessly, his head lowered. "That's when time goes by slowly." His heart wilting, he looked up at her with soulful eyes. "Why do you have to leave right now? Would one more day with me be so difficult to take?"

"What would we talk about, Steve—the weather? And how long would it be before you threw something else into space? Neither of us needs that."

"What if I promise to behave?"

His dismal tone and forlorn expression captured Sharon's heart, and she sank down onto the bed next to him. Clasping her hands tensely, she said, "You must have friends up here. Throw a party. Do something wild."

He eyed her sideways. "I have friends, but I don't want to be with them. I want to be with you, and I'm not in the mood for a party or anything wild. I came up here for some quiet time, remember?"

She remembered all right, and she'd looked forward to the quiet time, during which they were both going to figure out where they stood with each other. But she had found out, although the time hadn't exactly been quiet.

"Please stay... just until tomorrow. I'll check with the airline and see if we can leave in the morning instead of Sunday."

Weary, she had to force her words out. "Be honest with yourself, Steve. If I stay, we both know what will happen, and then you'll feel guilty again. The funny thing is, I'm not sure if it will be because of Richie or Laura.''

"The guilt that I live with," he said quietly, "is because of myself and no one else."

Sharon examined his downcast expression, wondering what he meant. "Certainly," she said, trying to understand his enigmatic words, "you don't feel guilty because Laura died."

"No, but often I think of her. I try to remember the early years, yet I keep recalling the last one."

"Advanced stages of rheumatoid arthritis can be very difficult to live with. I'm sure you did everything to make her as comfortable as possible."

"I could have done more for her."

"Steve, you're blaming yourself needlessly, but I know what you mean. I felt that way in Vietnam. Even though I worked sixteen hours a day and longer sometimes, I always thought I should have been able to do more. It left me with a feeling of guilt, and knowing it was unwarranted didn't always help." She rose from the bed. "It's something I had to deal with, and you'll have to do the same about any unwarranted guilt you may feel about Laura."

He hadn't intended to say more about the guilt that had been gnawing at him for almost a year. It was something he knew he had to live with in silence, because he believed it was too horrendous a secret to share with anyone. Perhaps it was his keyed-up emotional state that had come to a head last night and again this morning at breakfast. He didn't know, but something deep within compelled him to share his burden finally.

"The guilt I feel," he admitted darkly, "isn't unwarranted. When I said I didn't believe in dredging up the past and ruminating over it, I was really speaking about one particular incident in my life." He glanced at Sharon's attentive expression, then he asked, "Remember when I said I'd had sex only once in the past four years?"

"I remember." Her eyes lingered on his troubled ones.

"That one time wasn't with Laura." He took a long, tortured breath before continuing. "Four months before her death she insisted I make the trip to Sarapiqui Canyon in Costa Rica. That's when I found the blue cattleya orchid. Blue," he explained in a hollow voice, "is an extremely rare color for an orchid. To me it was like an archaeologist opening an ancient tomb and finding that it hadn't been desecrated." He chuckled painfully as he shook his head. "So I celebrated...too much. There was this friendly lady in the cantina, and she helped me celebrate. I've regretted it ever since, and I will for the rest of my life."

Sharon heard the misery in his voice, and although she now realized his guilt wasn't unwarranted, she did believe he was torturing himself unduly. "Steve," she said softly, sitting next to him again and touching his arm, "considering the circumstances, my guess is that you've paid enough for that one indiscretion in fifteen years of faithfulness. You can't go on beating yourself for the rest of your life. I know what guilt can do to a person. There are things I've done that I'm not proud of." She thought for a second, then asked, "You didn't tell Laura, did you?"

Again he shook his head slowly. "But after I returned from Costa Rica, she said I seemed depressed. She was always worried that she wasn't being fair to me or to our marriage."

"She must have loved you very much."

"Too much. It wasn't until after she died that I realized she thought *she* had been the cause of my depression."

"Oh, Steve," Sharon whispered, then tightened her fingers on his arm. "And now you blame yourself for what she might have thought, don't you?"

"Shouldn't I . . . after what I'd done?"

"Can you possibly believe that Laura would have wanted you to blame yourself like this?"

"No, she was too forgiving and loving a person."

"Why, then, are you making yourself so miserable?"

"I wouldn't be, not if you'd stay just until tomorrow."

Feeling she was being boxed in again, Sharon wanted to run away, but she also wanted to comfort him. Uneasily she said, "I don't know, Steve."

"Please," he said, holding her hand between his. "I feel such peace and contentment when I'm with you. I won't do anything to upset you. There's a little inn a few miles down the road. We can have a quiet dinner there, then get a good night's sleep and leave in the morning."

She hesitated for long moments, then, against her better judgment, she nodded.

Before Sharon could change her mind Steve rose, reached for her red trench coat, which was draped over the foot of the bed, and held it open for her. "Let's take a little walk."

"In the snow?"

"There's a pair of galoshes in the hall closet that you can wear. It's a gorgeous day and the cool air will do us both good."

Minutes later they were walking along the high, snow-covered bluffs that surged up from the blue gray water of Green Bay. Stopping at the edge of the limestone cliff, Steve's hand in hers, Sharon glanced down, listening to the sound of the breakers pounding against the cliff wall. Her gaze drifted up to the dark-winged birds sweeping across the immense cloudless blue sky, then over the marble-white ground to the nearby leafless snow-trimmed birch trees.

"I wish I had brought a camera," she said, scanning the wintry landscape.

"When I take the rest of the boxes in, I could pick up one at the store."

"No. I'll remember all of this. The setting reminds me of a Christmas card."

His gaze slanted back toward the house. "Christmas used to be a happy time up here. I had the house built as a first anniversary present for Laura. She loved it."

"I can see why. It's roomy but cozy. You're going to miss the house, aren't you?"

"In some ways, but if I held on to it, it would be too much of a reminder of the past." He bent down, scooped up a handful of snow and made a ball with it. He tossed it over the edge of the bluff and watched as it arced and fell into the water. Moving to a nearby tree, he leaned against it and shoved his hands into the side pockets of his tan car coat. "What you said inside made a lot of sense. I don't want to be a slave to the past any longer. I want to focus on the future. You should also."

Sharon chuckled softly and glanced out at the sun-dappled water in the distance. "I'm not sure what the future holds for me. So much depends on what Werner finds out. Until now nursing has been almost my whole life. I'm not sure how much enthusiasm I can work up for anything else.''

"The future has a way of surprising us. It looked pretty grim to me before I met you.''

Her gaze returned to Steve's. "And now you see the future as being rosy?''

"It could be, for both of us, nursing or no nursing.''

Smiling, she asked, "Are you offering me a permanent job in your office?''

"No. I'm offering to love you for the rest of my life, if you'll marry me.'' He saw the smile on her face evaporate. "It wouldn't be a bad life,'' he promised. "We could travel to the four corners of the earth on orchid-buying sprees. And it's not too late for us to start a family.''

When she abruptly started back toward the house, he caught up with her and matched her stride. "Is the idea so crazy?''

As she trudged through the snow, she said, "I'm beginning to think you are.''

"Because I love you?''

"Because you're conveniently forgetting a few major points.''

"Such as?''

"Your father, for one. He wouldn't exactly be thrilled with the idea.''

"You'd be marrying me, not him.''

"And how would it look to Detective Werner? Brother of deceased gets nurse to do away with him to collect his insurance money, then brother and nurse take off into the sunset to live happily ever after.''

He stopped, took hold of her arm and spun her around. "There's one more major point you haven't mentioned. Do you want to marry me?''

Sharon felt a sudden chill, but it wasn't because of the cold wind sweeping across the water onto the high bluff. The frigid feeling came from deep inside as she wrestled with Steve's question. She wanted to answer yes. Desperately. But something warned her she shouldn't. That "something" was nebulous, yet it was too powerful to disregard.

"Do you?" Steve asked again, his words softer now.

"Right now I can't even think straight," she answered, lowering her eyes.

Feeling as if she'd doused his face with ice water, Steve broke the hold he had on her arm. "Here I am taking too much for granted again." After a brief pause, he said, "But I'm not going to apologize this time."

"There's nothing to apologize for," she said, her voice as faint as his.

Quietly they made their way to the house, and once inside, Steve said, "I'll take the rest of the boxes to UPS. Then I'll change our reservations to tomorrow."

Sharon nodded absently. "While you're gone I'll fix us some lunch to keep us going until dinner."

"I promise to watch my table manners," he said, managing an awkward smile before he went into the kitchen to cart the boxes to the car.

The afternoon dragged along for both of them, but their spirits lifted a little during dinner at the charming country inn. Their conversation was overpolite, their forced smiles and brief spurts of laughter unreal, but it did lessen the inner tension that each felt.

When they returned to the house, each went to their separate bedrooms. In his heart Steve was certain that, regardless of Sharon's understanding words, she did blame him deeply for what she had kindly called his "one indiscretion." He even blamed himself because he hadn't told her how cheated he had felt during the long years of abstinence. Try as he might he was never able to completely suppress the physical cravings that had tortured his very normal masculine body. And he always thought that, for love of Laura, he should have been able to.

For her part Sharon was sure she was mentally unstable. She had treated Steve's offer of marriage as if he had tendered her a proposition. Yet they *were* compatible, to say the least, and there was every chance that they could be happy together.

Why not? she wondered as she slipped into her nightgown. She had to believe that Detective Werner would eventually uncover the truth about what had happened to Richie, and Steve would finally put his nagging doubts about her innocence to rest. Carl Nordstrom's attitude toward her would surely change. She would have her job back at the hospital, and she would be free to plan for a future, just as Steve wanted them to do now. Why was she being so negative? Her life with Steve could be wonderful.

She thought of the quiet and sad way Steve had said good-night before she'd closed her bedroom door. More disturbing was the aching yearning she felt to be with him now. Being apart seemed so senseless. It was almost as if she were punishing herself and him for something she couldn't explain.

For being happy? she wondered, feeling worse by the second.

Her eyes drifted to the bedroom door, her loneliness and need for Steve heightened by the stony silence surrounding her.

"No," she whispered. "Being apart doesn't make any sense."

Seconds later she eased the door to his room open, and the soft light from the hallway rayed across his face. He was lying in bed, bare-chested, his hands clasped behind his head.

Immediately he raised himself onto his arms and gazed at her silhouetted figure standing in the doorway. "Sharon," he murmured, her name spoken on a surprised breath.

"I knew I wouldn't be able to sleep...not alone."

He drew back the covers, inviting her into his bed. "I wouldn't have been able to sleep, either."

She eased herself down next to him and sank into his embrace, feeling so very content and wonderfully relaxed as his arms and his warm body curled around her.

"This is where you belong," he whispered, kissing her silky hair. "This is where we both belong... always."

Slipping her arm around his waist, she emitted a soft sigh and nuzzled his warm neck, wanting to believe him with all her heart and wishing they could remain just as they were for eternity, but she knew she was wishing for something that could never be. In the morning they would return to Florida, and she would have to face life's hard realities once again. She had tonight to be close to Steve, though, and that would have to suffice. Slowly her eyelids closed and she drifted off to a peaceful sleep, secure in his arms.

CHAPTER SIXTEEN

ONCE BACK IN FLORIDA, the reality that Sharon had dreaded brightened soon after Steve had dropped her off at her apartment. Louella phoned, saying that she and Dr. Wilson had convinced the chief of staff to lift her suspension.

"Can you report to work on Monday night?" Louella asked.

Hardly able to believe it, Sharon smiled into the receiver. "Of course!"

"Good. Estelle starts her vacation Monday, but Anna said she'd stay on for a while longer. If you can, try to talk her into taking a permanent slot on ICU."

"I'd love to have her on the unit, but if she decides to take a permanent position, I think it would be on a children's ward."

"That would help, too, but staffing ICU is the problem at the present."

Sharon didn't have to guess why, not considering the way the hierarchy had turned on her after Richard Nordstrom's death. She could understand why every nurse on the unit probably felt vulnerable working there now.

"Okay, then," Louella said, "I'll mark you in your old schedule starting Monday."

"I'm looking forward to working on the unit again."

"Yes, I'm sure. But just how long you'll be back will depend on what the grand jury decides on the Nordstrom case."

"Have you heard anything from Detective Werner in the past few days?" Sharon asked quickly.

"Well, probably I shouldn't be passing this on, but he came by my office yesterday. He was very curious about your personal life. Naturally I was reluctant to discuss it, but I felt I had to cooperate with the authorities."

"And?"

"I told him I didn't know of any man you were seeing regularly. He thought that strange because you are...somewhat attractive. I knew exactly what he was thinking, so I pointed out that just because you didn't flaunt a man, that didn't mean you hadn't been seeing one. I certainly didn't mention Steven Nordstrom's name, though."

Feeling as though her face had been instantly sunburned, Sharon stiffened and fought hard to control her voice. "To be honest, Louella, I had hoped Werner was doing more than inquiring into my sex life. As far as Steve Nordstrom is concerned, I never laid eyes on him before his brother died."

"But you must realize that the police have to cover every possibility, that is if Richard Nordstrom wasn't given an overdose of morphine accidentally. If he had been, it would certainly simplify our problems here at the hospital. The chief of staff's office has been bombarded with phone calls from reporters who aren't content with being told the matter is being investigated."

"I sympathize with Dr. Benning's problems, but my life is in a shambles."

"Oh, yes, of course. I'm not diminishing that aspect at all, but I know for a fact that Dr. Benning would stand by you firmly if you did admit that Nordstrom's death could have been an accident."

On the verge of yelling at the woman, Sharon wrestled with the anger she felt. "I'll be on duty Monday night, Louella. Thank you for calling." She hung up, too upset even to move.

Fantasizing the worst scenario, she again visualized herself on a witness stand, trying to convince a jury that she hadn't known Steve before his brother's death. And what if she had? That wouldn't prove they had dreamed up a scheme to kill Richie to get his insurance money.

But, she thought, sinking onto the sofa, what if some low-minded prosecuting attorney questioned her and Steve about their relationship after his brother's death and asked if they had spent any time together. Where? Doing what? Under oath neither of them would lie about what had happened at his home on Door Peninsula. And Carl Nordstrom's testimony certainly wouldn't help.

"You're flaking out!" she warned herself, jumping up. Quickly she returned to the bedroom to finish unpacking, unable to think about anything other than the precarious situation in which she and Steve might soon find themselves.

Should she phone him and tell him what Louella had said? No, she decided. It would just upset him, as well. The better course might be for them not to see each other until Richie's case was closed.

She slammed her suitcase shut and placed it back in the closet, then went into the living room, where she stared at the phone. She had agreed to have dinner with Steve tomorrow night. Now that didn't seem like such a good idea. Then she remembered that Debbie and Tony were driving to Tarpon Springs for dinner. Maybe she should go with them. No. Steve had been invited, too.

What to do? she wondered. Coming up with nothing, she decided to call Debbie and tell her the good news, that her suspension had been lifted, and also explain that she couldn't meet with the women at her condo Monday night.

DEBBIE DIDN'T HEAR the phone ringing in her apartment, since she was lying on the beach behind her condominium, soaking up the late-afternoon sun with Tony.

"Wonder how Sharon's enjoying the snow in Wisconsin," Tony said as he applied sunscreen on Debbie's back.

Lying on her stomach, her face resting on her overlapped hands, Debbie answered languidly, "It's probably reminding her of Vietnam. When I got to Pleiku, it was freezing."

Tony flipped down the cap on the plastic container and dropped it into Debbie's straw beach bag. Moving onto his side, he dug an elbow into the sand and rested his jaw in his palm as he studied her, thinking how lovely she was.

Her eyelids opened to mere slits, and she smiled at him. "You'd better put on some of that lotion yourself."

"Naw. I was born with a natural tan."

"On you it looks great." When he flashed her one of his wide-mouthed grins, it exaggerated the dimples at the corner of his lips. "When you're promoted to lab chief, the girls at the hospital aren't going to give you any rest.''

"It's not definite yet, just rumors on the grapevine.''

"You'll get it. They'd be crazy not to put you in charge. You're one in a million.''

"That great, huh?" he asked, cocking his head playfully.

"Don't get all puffed up, but everything about you is great.''

Gently he pushed back stray tendrils of golden blond hair that curled over her face. "So," he asked, "how come you don't find me irresistible?''

"The good news is that I do.''

"And the bad?''

"I'm fighting it.''

"Why?''

"Because I like you," she answered, sitting and drawing her knees up.

He watched silently as she reached into her beach bag and withdrew a green silk scarf. She formed it into a triangle, draped it over her head and tied it under the back of her hair. When she crossed her arms over her knees and gazed out at the calm water, he said, "Instead of liking me, I hoped to hear you say you loved me. I love you.''

"One should profit from one's mistakes... so they say.''

"Forget whoever they are. Why don't you listen to what I say?''

Debbie glanced his way, her long eyelashes shading her hazel eyes. "I'm curious, Tony. What does a man really feel when he says he loves a woman?''

"That depends on how he thinks she feels about him. If he believes she feels the same way, those three little words just tumble out joyfully. If he's not sure how she feels, he's taking a hell of a chance and has to force them out."

"Yes," she said quietly, "being in love has its risks."

"Living without love has its risks, too."

Stretching her legs out, she leaned back on her hands and turned her head to watch some children playing down by the water's edge.

"Debbie, is my—"

"Let's change the subject, Tony, please."

"No. Is my wanting to be the most important person in the world to you asking so much?"

"Maybe not now, but someday you'll thank me for not tying you down."

Running the back of his fingers up her arm, he said, "I want to be lassoed and branded by the sheep lady from Texas."

She tilted her head back and laughed softly. "You don't lasso sheep. You herd them." Eyeing Tony teasingly, she asked, "But what should I expect from a city slicker like you?"

"For starters," he said, twisting his body around and resting the back of his head in her lap, "love, loyalty and—" he grinned up at her "—great sex, not to mention a horde of Italian relatives who are dying to meet you."

"You were doing pretty good up until the relatives," she advised him with mock cheerfulness.

"You anti-Italian or something?"

"What do you think?" she asked, easing a finger over his lips.

He moved her hand to his chest and covered it with both of his. "I think you should come home with me over the Christmas holidays and meet them."

"If I go to Orlando, I'd rather visit Disney World. Besides, my Texas drawl would probably make your relatives hysterical."

"Are you kidding? You'd charm the socks off them. Course you'd have to eat a lot of Italian food in the family restaurant. Christmas Day we'd have a turkey, though, and for New Year's, Mamma always cooks a—"

"Tony," Debbie interrupted, "the lounge is incredibly busy during the holiday season."

"Christmas is a time for families, too, even in Texas, I'd guess."

"I suppose."

Stroking her hand slowly, he asked, "Aren't you ever going to see your parents again?"

"Don't start with me, Tony," she warned.

He lifted himself to a sitting position and looped his arms around his raised knees. "I'm not starting anything. I'm just asking a simple question."

"There's no simple answer."

"Then give me the complicated one."

She faced him, her eyes now a cool stare. "The daughter my parents saw off to Vietnam never came back."

"Debbie Weston did."

"They wouldn't recognize her, nor would they want to."

"I can't believe that."

Her lips curved into a wry smirk. "Then believe this. When I worked in New Orleans, I was known as the Texas Twister, and it had nothing to do with the way I danced."

"Stop it!" he said sharply, grabbing hold of her arm. "You started this chitchat about family."

"I'm talking about you now and this habit of putting yourself down and trying to shock me. It won't work. Like it or not, lady, I'm sticking with you for the long haul. I'm going to be your conscience and make your life miserable until you realize what a good thing we have going for us."

Lowering her eyes, Debbie said softly, "There's an old saying about a leopard and its spots. You might want to look it up."

He lifted her chin and gazed into her moist eyes. "I don't have time for research right now. I'm too busy being in love."

Debbie moved her head sideways, then gathered her things and stood up. "Being in love is a luxury I can't afford right now."

As she strode over the sand toward the condominium, Tony called her name, but she didn't stop.

ON SUNDAY MORNING, after a restless night, Sharon pulled into the parking area by Steve's greenhouses, telling herself again that she was right in finally having decided to inform him about Louella's talk with Werner. Finding Steve in the office, she did so.

"Your friend Louella," he said stiffly, "has a lurid imagination."

"She's my boss, not my friend." Sitting on the chair by the computer, Sharon asked, "Do you think Werner could seriously believe we planned Richie's death?"

"I don't know, but I imagine he comes across a lot of coldhearted people in his work. I'll go to his office in the morning and thrash this business out with him."

"I'll go with you."

"No. I might come up with some words no lady should hear, and now that you'll be working nights again, you'd better get back into the routine of sleeping during the day." After a long pause, he admitted, "I'm going to miss you around here." His eyes swept over the order she had brought to the office. "Things have never been this organized before. Having all the records computerized is going to be a big help."

She wanted to say she would miss being with him, too. However she held back the words. "I haven't completely finished, but it'll just take about a half hour," she said, then switched on the computer.

Working on his records was the last thing he wanted her to do right now, but he didn't want her to leave, either. "Okay," he said, nodding. "I'll check the messages on the answering machine." His eyes lingered on her for several moments, then he went to the opposite side of the office.

Sharon took one of the disks that Steve had said could be erased and inserted it into the computer. She was surprised to find it contained notes that had nothing to do with the orchid business. "Steve," she called after scanning the information on the screen, "did you want to keep this?"

"What?" he asked, starting back across the room.

She read a little more, and her voice took on a quizzical tone. "I'm not sure what it is—something about medical insurance."

He leaned down and peered at the screen. "Where the hell did that come from?"

Intently they both read the notes that indicated that area doctors might be fraudulently billing insurance companies for patient treatment not given or for treatment in which the charges were grossly inflated.

Finally Steve said, "This must be what Richie was working on the day he was hit by someone's car. His computer was in the shop, so he used this one."

"This is a story he was working on?" Sharon asked, scrolling to the last page of the notes.

"Not according to his boss at the newspaper, but it could be something he was researching to see if there was a story in it."

"Look at the last line, Steve." She read it out loud. "Check out Dr. Shaw."

"Do you know him?"

"There are half a dozen Dr. Shaws in the area. The only one I know is Franklin Shaw. He and Dr. Wilson used to be partners in a private practice, but Dr. Wilson would never have been involved in insurance fraud. Whoever Richie meant, it's got to be one of the other Shaws."

Steve reread the final notes his brother had made. "I wish he had said why he wanted to check on Dr. Shaw."

Thinking back, Sharon said, "When I worked for the insurance company in California, we were involved in several cases of fraud. A few unscrupulous doctors billed private insurance companies and Medicare for testing and follow-up procedures they never did. One doctor submitted 522 false claims, totaling nearly two hundred thousand dollars. A psychologist actually billed and received payment from Blue Cross for more than half a million dollars for sessions with people he'd never even met."

"Richie must have thought this Dr. Shaw was doing something like that."

"It can't be Franklin Shaw," Sharon insisted. "He's a very respected man and a dedicated doctor. When he has a patient on ICU, he'll come by to check on them in the middle of the night sometimes. Not all doctors—"

She stopped in midsentence, then stood slowly and took a few steps as her thoughts raced back to the morning Steve's brother died.

"What's the matter?" Steve asked.

Her fingers grazing her throat, she said, "I just remembered something. Dr. Shaw was on ICU the morning Richie went into cardiac arrest. He had a terminal patient there." Quickly she added, "But that doesn't mean he's the Shaw Richie was referring to."

"It doesn't mean he's not, either. Let's get a copy of these notes for Werner." Steve sat in the chair Sharon had vacated and instructed the computer to print the information on the disk.

As they waited, Sharon said, "If Dr. Shaw is involved in anything illegal, Dr. Wilson could be hurt professionally because of their past association."

"Maybe, and maybe not."

"Steve, even a rumor of wrongdoing could hurt his professional reputation, just as suspicions could still destroy mine."

Gathering up the printouts, he said, "We can't overlook the possibility that both Wilson and Shaw might have been bilking insurance companies."

"I can't believe that! I was there when Dr. Wilson worked desperately to save Richie's life, and you heard how he defended me at the inquiry. I'm positive he was responsible for getting my suspension lifted. The least we can do is alert him that Werner may be checking up on him."

"If we did, it would give him time to get rid of any evidence that he was involved in something crooked, something that might have driven him to kill Richie."

"That's ridiculous!"

"Is it? Wilson was on ICU the entire night. No one would have thought twice about his going into the isolation room whenever he wanted to. What if he somehow knew Richie was working on the insurance fraud story? Shaw or Wilson could have been behind the wheel when Richie was run down, and either one of them could have finished the job in the hospital."

She stared at him icily. "Now you're the one with a lurid imagination. You don't know Dr. Wilson the way I do."

"And you don't seem to understand that if I'm right, my theory could prove your innocence once and for all."

Sharon shuddered, feeling shocked and hurt as she realized that the doubt in Steve's mind that she had thought he had long put to rest had resurfaced. "My innocence," she echoed grimly. "In the eyes of the public I might be innocent, but what about you, Steve? Would I ever really be innocent?"

"You're overreacting, Sharon."

"Am I?" Her rapid breathing felt like sharp pins stabbing her chest. "I've cared for hundreds of patients on ICU during the past four years. They were all strangers and still they trusted me. Do you have any idea how much it hurts when the person you love *doesn't* trust you? No, of course you don't."

"Sharon," he said, his words measured, "I don't understand why, but you're shoving that barrier between us again. It's getting to be like clockwork with you. Every time we get really close, you find some reason to back away. It's as if you're afraid to let yourself get too close to me."

Sharon tensed, her backbone stiffened by confusion and opposing emotions: anger, love, fear, helplessness.

Then, for no explainable reason, she imagined that she was back in Pleiku, exhausted as she passed on scalpels, clamps and sponges to the surgeon operating. She ran the back of her rubber-gloved hand over her perspiring forehead, then continued to hand the doctor forceps and retractors, all in stony silence. Her inner ear reheard the anesthetist say, "He's gone," and her mind's eye saw the surgeon toss the retractor onto the tray as he ordered, "Get the next one in here!"

Her swirling thoughts rushed back to the present, and she focused her stinging eyes on Steve. She needed to get away; she had to!

When she turned abruptly, he took hold of her shoulder. "Can't we talk this out?" he asked, his voice taut.

"Talk what out, Steve?" Her voice was equally strained. "You're so very sure you already have all the answers."

In seconds she was in her car, tearing away from the house.

"Sharon!" he yelled over the sound of screeching tires, but she didn't stop.

As she headed up Gulf Boulevard, she wiped away the tears that burned her eyes. The flashbacks that she'd thought were a thing of the past were returning. God, she couldn't cope with that, not again!

It's the tension, she told herself, the stress of recent weeks. Everything had been going so well before she'd met Steve. Was it something about him, or was she, as he'd accused her, deliberately forming barriers between them? Of course not. Why would she? He was the one who wasn't thinking clearly. Yes, it was his grief over his brother's death that was making him lash out at everyone, including Dr. Wilson.

She knew Steve was right in turning over Richie's notes to Detective Werner immediately, but she felt obligated to warn Dr. Wilson. She had gone through enough shocks to want to spare him being interrogated suddenly by the police without having had a chance to prepare his defense. She wished she'd had just such a chance before Werner had hit her with that anonymous phone message during the inquiry.

Arriving at Dr. Wilson's home on Belleair Beach, she parked in the driveway and rushed up the front steps. He answered the door, saw her tense expression and invited her in, aghast when she explained why she was there.

"So you're bound to be questioned," Sharon explained.

"Insurance fraud? That's crazy. I've even treated patients who couldn't afford my usual fees. So did Franklin."

"I told Steve that the Dr. Shaw in his brother's notes had to be someone other than your ex-partner, but the police will no doubt question every Dr. Shaw in this area. I thought you should know, Dr. Wilson."

"Uh . . . yes, Sharon. I really appreciate the warning."

"Please, though, don't mention what I've said to Dr. Shaw yet?"

"Why not, for heaven's sake?"

Clasping her hands nervously, she explained, "Even though it's not likely, what if he was billing insurance companies illegally? He could have done so without your knowing it."

"Anything's possible," he allowed, "but Franklin—?"

"Dr. Wilson, so many unlikely things have been happening lately that nothing would surprise me anymore. Besides, we're talking about a police investigation, and I know that neither of us wants to be accused of interfering with it. If Detective Werner learns I told you and you told Dr. Shaw...well, it could look as if we're all trying to cover up something."

Wilson thought about that. "You're right, but there's nothing the police can find that will prove Franklin was a crook!"

"Then he has nothing to worry about."

"Yes, you're right. Again, thank you for telling me, Sharon."

"I had to. You've been very good to me."

Both their heads turned toward the front door when it opened.

Seeing Sharon, Louella commented, "Another social call?"

Quickly Wilson said, "Sharon just stopped by to thank us for talking to Benning on her behalf."

Louella set her handbag down on a table in the living room. "As I remember, Sharon, you already thanked me. Regardless, Clara will be back tomorrow, so you and I will be working together again. I hope the night shift isn't going to interfere too much with your private life."

"It won't," Sharon assured her, then made her goodbyes hastily and left.

The minute she did Louella asked Wilson, "What did she really want?"

"There's big trouble," he muttered, going behind the mahogany bar at the side of the room. He poured a straight shot of bourbon and swallowed it in one gulp.

"What kind of trouble?" Louella asked as she perched on one of the leather-topped bar stools.

"Nordstrom's brother found some notes that the damn reporter had made. They mentioned Franklin's name. Well," he corrected himself, "just *a* Dr. Shaw, but now the police will scrutinize the insurance claims of every Dr. Shaw."

"Oh, God!" Louella moaned. "They'll find out."

Wilson poured another drink, then plunked the bottle down hard. "I told Franklin he was crazy to think he could get away with it!"

"Jimmy, you should have gotten out of the partnership sooner."

He leaned his elbows on the bar and covered his face with his hands. "Why, why did I let him talk me into it? We were doing great financially. Why did he have to be so goddamn greedy?" After another swallow of bourbon, he chuckled bitterly. "I'm a fine one to talk, considering I accepted a good twenty thousand on fraudulent billings."

"You gave ten times that amount in care to people who couldn't afford it."

"I doubt if a jury will think of me as a humanitarian if they ever find out I was in the car when Franklin ran Nordstrom down. I couldn't believe he did that! He said he was just going to talk to the man again. God, I can still see Nordstrom's shocked expression when he stared into the headlights."

"No one's going to find out!" Louella insisted.

"You'd better hope not. It was damn stupid of you to give him that morphine."

Louella blanched. "What did you expect me to do— let him walk out of the hospital and go to the police? Franklin didn't have a chance to get into the isolation room. Dave Schaeffer stuck to him every second he was on the unit."

"Christ, Lou, being guilty of insurance fraud is one thing, but murder is another!"

Her voice ragged, Louella said quietly, "I'd do it again, Jimmy, if it meant keeping you from going to prison."

He reached over the bar and grasped her hand. "How the hell did we get into a situation like this? We can't blame everything on Franklin."

"Why not? It was all his fault."

"If only you hadn't killed Nordstrom. I could go to the police now and tell them what Franklin and I did."

"Don't be stupid. He'd say that you were driving the car. It would be your word against his."

"They'll probably find out, anyway, once Nordstrom's brother gives them the notes."

"We can't panic. We've got to think." She got up from the bar stool and began pacing nervously. "What did Sharon say about Franklin being mentioned?"

Wilson prodded his memory. "Something like 'check on Dr. Shaw.'"

Biting down on her lower lip, she thought some more. "And the clerk at the insurance company alerted you that Nordstrom wanted to see the past claims Franklin had submitted . . . not yours."

"Right. What are you getting at?"

"The only one who can tie you into the hit-and-run incident is Shaw. The police know he was on ICU about a half hour before I gave Nordstrom the injection. What's to stop them from believing he did it?"

"He would have to have given it to him no more than five minutes before he arrested. You used enough morphine to do away with all the patients on the unit."

"It had to be enough to act quickly, or Sharon would have seen he was having respiratory problems." She pondered the situation some more, then said, "Dave can't swear that Franklin didn't get into the isolation room unnoticed. It was hectic and Dave was as busy as the other nurses."

Massaging his forehead, Wilson said, "I doubt if Franklin will volunteer to be the scapegoat."

"He wouldn't stop defrauding the insurance companies when you asked him to, would he?"

"No, but—"

"And he tried to kill Nordstrom with his car."

"Lou, having tried to isn't the same as having done it."

"He was going to. He gave me the morphine syringe, didn't he? And it's his fault we're in this mess now."

Wilson peered at the icy glare in her eyes. "What are you thinking?"

"Franklin should pay, not us. Jimmy...you've got to silence him."

"What?"

"He's the only one who can implicate us. You'd lose your license to practice and be imprisoned, and I could wind up in the electric chair."

"Don't say that!"

Her voice became soft, pleading. "I love you, Jimmy, and if you love me half as much, we don't have a choice. Franklin's as guilty as sin. Instead of the state of Florida, you'd be his executioner. We could forget about the past and get on with helping the sick. Daily we'd be doing our own penance, but in a meaningful way. What good would we be doing anyone in prison? And think what the publicity would do to your children."

Squinting, Wilson chugalugged another drink. "What are you suggesting we do?"

Louella sat down again and cupped her hands around his. Her voice conspiratorial, she outlined her plan. "After Sharon told you about Nordstrom's notes, you confronted Franklin. He admitted defrauding insurance companies, running Nordstrom down and injecting him with the overdose on ICU. He was repentant and said he would turn himself in. Then you came home and we spent the evening together."

Caught up in the scenario, Wilson asked quietly, "What really happens?"

"You said he keeps a loaded gun in his desk drawer at home."

"He got it after his house was broken into."

"His wife's away now. You get his gun and use it at close range, then wipe off your fingerprints and place it in his hand. The man couldn't bear the guilt and the shame he felt."

"No suicide note?"

"Women are prone to leave notes, not men."

"When do we do it?" Wilson asked huskily.

"You do it, the sooner the better... this evening."

"There's no other way?"

"No, Jimmy, there isn't."

CHAPTER SEVENTEEN

SHARON LISTENED to the phone ringing for the third time in half an hour, sure that it was Steve. Grabbing her purse, she rushed from her apartment, got into her car and drove off, not sure where she was heading.

She knew Debbie would be working, and one by one she thought of reasons not to drop in on her other friends. Soon she found herself pulling into the parking lot next to the shorefront restaurant on Madeira Beach where she and Steve had dined.

For long minutes she sat in her car, staring blankly through the windshield, oblivious to the evening stars twinkling against the night sky. Then her mind's eye began playing tricks with her again, and she visualized herself and Steve lying on the sand by the water's edge. Her arms were propped on his chest. He was smiling up at her. The memory was so vivid that she could now feel his arms around her.

Leaning forward, she rested her hands on the steering wheel and laid her forehead on them. Her eyes closed, and suddenly she was back in Cu Chi. Incoming mortar shells pounded fiercely outside the hospital, competing with the high-pitched orders of harried doctors and nurses all around her as she furiously cut away partially burned battle fatigues.

In her tormenting vision Sharon saw herself glancing down at the face of the soldier lying on the table, knowing it would be Doug's. But this time it wasn't; it was Steve's face she saw.

"No!" she screamed, and pounded her fists on the steering wheel, oblivious to the shrill staccato sound of the horn.

Her head jerked to the left when she heard a sharp knocking on her closed car window.

"You all right?" a wide-eyed man asked.

"Uh...yes," she responded, her heart pounding as she raked her fingers through the side of her hair. "I'm okay."

"If you say so," he said doubtfully, then took his lady friend's arm and led her toward the restaurant entrance.

Get a grip, Sharon ordered herself as she rolled down the windows to let the cool night air flow through the car. *You're not hallucinating. You're just confusing memories.* But why Steve? He'd never been anywhere near Vietnam.

Her darkest memories activated, she realized she was shaking and knew she had to talk to someone who would understand. Quickly she searched her purse for her address book, then hopped out of her car and hurried to the outdoor telephone box.

When Anna answered her phone, Sharon's words rushed out. "I'm sorry for calling. I know you're working later tonight. Were you asleep?"

"No. I'm just sitting here watching TV. What's wrong? You sound upset."

"Could I come by just for a few minutes, Anna. I need to talk to you."

"Sure, but you didn't have to phone. I'll have fresh coffee ready by the time you get here."

"Thanks. I'll be there in a few minutes."

Fifteen minutes later, when Anna opened her apartment door, she examined Sharon's tense expression. "C'mon in," she said, closing the door after Sharon entered. "You look as if you've seen a ghost."

"There are a few of them following me around. That's what I wanted to talk to you about."

Really concerned now, Anna said, "Make yourself comfortable. I'll get the coffee."

After sinking onto the sofa, Sharon let her eyes roam around the small but cozy living room. On one shelf of the wall unit she saw a photograph of Anna and a smiling bearded man. Joshua, Sharon guessed. Next to it was a group picture of Anna and several young Vietnamese women, all in white nursing uniforms. Beside it, another of Anna with bandaged children.

Sharon lowered her eyes to her entwined fingers, then looked up when Anna returned with their coffee. "Thanks. I like your apartment." She glanced at the framed prints on the wall. "Manet, aren't they?"

"Yes, and the candy dish is silver plate," Anna said, smiling as she sat next to her. "Now what do you really want to talk about?"

Placing her untouched coffee down, Sharon folded her hands and squeezed them. "I think I'm losing it again, Anna, just the way I did when I first got back from Nam. I thought that stuff was over and done with."

"For some people it never is, but I got the impression you were doing pretty good."

"I have been...for years, but recently I'm having these flashbacks again."

Anna picked up Sharon's coffee cup and handed it to her. "When I was working with children in Vietnam, I saw the effects of posttraumatic stress again and again, even in the little ones who weren't physically hurt. They'd go through a nervous anxiety first. Then they'd become deeply depressed. Fortunately most of the children's problems diminished with time.''

Annoyed with her sudden feeling of helplessness, Sharon moaned, ''I know all about the symptoms of PTSD.''

''Then you should know that everyone doesn't respond to excessive stress in the same way, and that having insight into the problem doesn't always stop the flashbacks or the nightmares of what happened. Look at Debbie. She's trying to numb the memories with alcohol. Marge is denying them, and Julia is about ready to turn off reality to avoid thinking about them.''

''Marge phoned me,'' Sharon said quietly. ''She took Julia to the Veterans Administration Medical Center. She's beginning outpatient treatment.''

''Good. Julia needs all the support she can get right now. But back to you. You're going through a lot of stress, and it's no wonder your nerves are frazzled.''

Leaning back against the sofa, Sharon said, ''I've felt worse, but I was really shook up just before I phoned you. I was sitting in my car, and suddenly I was back in Cu Chi. One night I looked down and saw a friend of mine on the table, but this evening it wasn't Doug. It was Steve's face staring up at me.''

''How good a friend was Doug?''

''We were going to be married, but he died that night.''

''It doesn't take a genius to see that now you're terrified you're going to lose Steve, too.''

''You can't lose what you never had,'' Sharon said morosely.

"It'd be risky to accept what he's offering, wouldn't it?"

"You're getting Freudian on me now."

"The good doctor had a lot to say about love and how important it is in people's lives. Has Steve told you he loves you?"

"He says he does."

"Do you love him?"

"He's still not sure if I accidentally killed his brother or not, but his father's convinced I did. He may bring criminal charges against me. Also, I'm not certain that Steve's come to terms with his wife's death."

"None of that answers my question. Do you love him?"

Jumping up from the sofa, Sharon paced the length of the room. "I went to bed with him in Wisconsin."

"That's sex. I'm still trying to find out if you love him."

She spun around. "Yes, I love him!"

Anna smiled. "Was it as difficult to admit that as it sounded?"

Yes, it had been extremely difficult. Not only was her heart thumping wildly, she also had a dark premonition of disaster, the same dreaded feeling she had experienced several times when she'd been with Steve. She sat down slowly and took a sip of coffee, then cradled the warm cup in her hands. "Steve claims I put barriers between us."

"For good reason probably. You don't think you can survive being hurt again. I knew nurses in Vietnam who had to shut off their emotions to function. Most were able to turn them back on when their feet hit home soil, but some still haven't."

"I know the feeling," Sharon said pensively, realizing Anna was describing her, at least about having had to steel herself to be able to do her job in Vietnam. But she hadn't considered herself emotionless during the past twenty years, only a woman who hadn't yet met the right man for her.

"In the best of times we women feel extremely vulnerable when we fall in love," Anna observed. "Because of what you've been through, you think you risk a lot more. What you have to decide is if Steve means enough to you to take that risk."

"I remember telling Debbie much the same thing about Tony."

"Then I suggest you listen to some of your own good advice."

Half smiling at Anna, Sharon asked, "How did you get so smart?"

"It came with age and a lot of help from a man I loved very much." She thought for a moment, then said, "When Josh died, I didn't just grieve for him. I was terrified to be without him, and that fear hasn't gone away completely yet. But since meeting you and your friends and seeing what they're still going through, I think I'm starting to get things in perspective."

She rested an arm on the back of the sofa and slipped her fingers through the side of her silvery white hair. "I used to blame my fears on things like having to take care of the things Josh usually did, having to pay all the bills and all that mundane stuff. That's not what really frightened me, though. I'm healthy, educated and I have sufficient financial security. My guess now is that at some time during those five years in Vietnam, the horrors didn't cause me to turn my emotions off, but I used Josh as a buffer against the horrible insanity over there. Then, when I found myself without him, I had to face not only the future alone, but the past also. Knowing that almost totally immobilized me.''

She reached over and took hold of Sharon's hand. ''But you and your friends made me realize I'm stronger than I think.'' She smiled warmly. ''I hadn't really made up my mind, but now I have. I'm going to apply for permanent duty on the children's ward at the hospital.''

''Oh, Anna, that's wonderful. It'll be a blessing for them and so good for you.''

''And what about you and Steve, Sharon, and those barriers? If you do love him and can't come up with logical reasons for backing away from him, perhaps you need to do some hard thinking about why.''

''I may just do that, and thanks for letting me bend your ear.'' Giving Anna's hand a quick shake, she rose from the sofa. ''I'd better leave and let you get ready for work.''

On their way to the door Anna smiled. ''We're all looking forward to seeing you on ICU tomorrow night—'' she laughed softly ''—especially Dave.''

''No more than I am. Being busy will give me less time to think about a lot of things.'' Holding one of Anna's hands, Sharon kissed her on the cheek. ''Good night, and thanks again for being a good friend.''

Driving home, Sharon felt better somehow. None of the problems that stared her in the face had evaporated, but she felt the stirrings of an inner strength that made her believe she could possibly cope with them. Most important, her confusion about her feelings for Steve began to lessen. She mulled over what Anna had said about other nurses who had to turn off their emotions to function in Vietnam and that not all had been able to switch them back on when they returned home. For the first time Sharon fully realized she had done just that. And, as Anna had also suggested, she was going to have to decide what part she wanted Steve to play in her life.

She did love him with all her heart, and she believed that he loved her just as deeply. But although she regretted the hurtful words she had said to him, she couldn't rush back and throw herself into his arms, not yet. When she went to him, and she would, she needed to go as a vindicated woman. His doubts about her innocence was one barrier, she knew for certain, that was not of her making.

STEVE RAPPED his knuckles on Detective Werner's paper-strewn kitchen table. "This is it, I'm telling you," he said adamantly. "You've been looking under every rock for a motive. Now you've got one."

"*If* these notes were made by your brother."

"Come off it, Aloysius."

"Al," the detective reminded Steve, then took another swig from his bottle of beer.

"Aloysius, Al, whatever. Do you think I'd actually dream up this stuff and try to pass it off as Richie's? What the hell do I know about insurance fraud?"

"Miss McClure worked for an insurance company for several years," Werner said dryly. Trained to be observant, he took note of Steve's face reddening and his hands balling into fists.

Werner pushed himself up from the chair, went to the refrigerator and took out another bottle of beer for his guest. Opening it, he thrust it at him. "Take a swallow of this and cool down." As Steve did, the detective remarked, "All I'm saying is what a good prosecuting lawyer would lay out before a jury. Anyone could have come up with these speculations. There's no proof in any of this stuff that any doctors are ripping off insurance companies. The name Shaw could have come from a phone book."

"What do you need before you check it out—a signed confession by one of the Shaws in the directory?"

"I'm gonna check it out."

Steve glared at him. "Why the hell didn't you tell me that to begin with?"

"I don't like to drink alone," Werner said with a mock grin. "Only lushes do." The sound of raucous laughter came from the living room, and he tilted his head toward the kitchen door. "You kids turn that TV down! We're trying to talk in here!" Facing Steve again, he lowered his voice. "Look, try to see how this case stacks up from the department's view. Your brother makes you the beneficiary of his insurance policy. The nurse you're having an affair with gives him an overdose of—"

"Don't start that crap again, Al."

"I'm not saying I believe it anymore, but waving these papers under my boss's nose isn't going to convince him to pull the case from the grand jury. We're up to our keisters investigating solid murder cases."

"My brother's dead. That's pretty solid, isn't it?"

"Solid enough for a suit against the hospital for wrongful death."

"Bull! You try looking at it from my point of view. One—" he held a rigid finger up "—Richie's researching a medical insurance scam. Two, someone runs him down in a car. Three, that doesn't kill him, so the someone who ran him down or somebody else who's medically savvy finishes the job while Richie's helpless in his hospital bed."

"This Dr. Shaw maybe," Werner said, glancing at the notes again.

"The same one who was on ICU the morning Richie died. He used to be partners with Dr. Wilson, who certified my brother's death as cardiac arrest. If you don't follow up on this, I'll—"

"You'll do zip," Werner said gruffly. "Ever hear of harassment? This is a police matter and we'll handle it as such."

"Just as long as you handle it and don't put those papers in a pending file somewhere."

Werner chuckled. "I thought all you florists were docile guys."

"I thought all you cops were guardians of justice."

"You'll get justice. It might take a little while, though, time to check on the insurance claims all our Dr. Shaws have submitted in the past few years. I'll start with Franklin Shaw first thing in the morning. That satisfy you?"

Taking a last swallow of beer, Steve stood. "Al, you renew my faith in the war against crime."

After leaving Werner's house, Steve drove by Sharon's apartment building and glanced up at her dark windows, guessing she wasn't at home or that she had gone to bed early. He was anxious to tell her about the conversation he'd just had with the detective, but he knew how upset she had been when she left his office earlier.

As he headed home, he wondered if he should phone her in the morning. No, he decided, time apart was what they both needed right now. He'd wait a day or two and then find out if there was any way to salvage what they had shared together.

"CAN YOU BELIEVE IT?" Dave asked Sharon as they walked from the elevator toward the nurses' station on Monday night. "His wife found him at home a few hours ago when she got back from Miami."

Sharon was still stunned, having just learned that Dr. Franklin Shaw had committed suicide. "Does anyone know why he did it?" she asked, tossing her tote bag onto the desk in the station.

"Not a hint so far. Wilson might have a clue, but he's off tonight."

Just then Anna stuck her head in the doorway. "Welcome back," she said cheerfully. Then she asked Dave, "Would you give me a hand with Mrs. Tucciarelli? She keeps pulling her catheter out." Anna looked back at Sharon and arched her eyebrows. "Dave's the only one she wants near her."

"The curse of having these magic fingers," he quipped, wiggling them as he followed Anna into the ward.

Sharon shook her head and began reviewing patient charts and the doctors' orders, but her thoughts drifted back to Dr. Shaw's sudden death. Something was wrong, very wrong. Had Dr. Wilson told him of her visit?

Her unsettling ponderings were interrupted when Dr. Rosenthal entered and they began the night's work.

Three hours later, as Sharon and Dave took time for a quick coffee break, she told him about the notes Richie had left in Steve's office.

"That doesn't mean it was our Dr. Shaw," Dave pointed out.

"It's a little too coincidental that he just put a bullet in his head, and remember, he was here on the unit the morning Richard Nordstrom arrested. Dr. Shaw could have given him the injection of morphine."

"But he didn't. The two patients I had were in the beds right next to the door to the isolation room. One of the patients was Dr. Shaw's. I was with him the entire time he was here."

"Couldn't he have come back and slipped in without your seeing him?"

"I was busy, but not blind."

"Are you that sure?"

"Sure I'm sure."

"No orderlies or other staff people went into the isolation room for just a second or two?"

"No. The only people who went in there were you, Louella and Dr. Wilson."

One of the other nurses tapped on the window and beckoned to Dave. Putting his coffee down, he muttered, "Someday I'm going to get to finish a whole cup."

Alone in the nurses' station, Sharon tried to put the pieces together. If Dr. Shaw hadn't given Richie the overdose, and she hadn't, the only other possibilities were Louella and Dr. Wilson.

A sickening feeling settled in the pit of her stomach as she realized that Steve could have been right. Dr. Wilson might have been involved with his partner in insurance fraud. If Richie had been able to point the finger at Dr. Shaw, Dr. Wilson must have realized that he would be exposed also. But how could she prove any of this?

Her eyes strayed to the phone, and she quickly dialed Steve's number.

When he answered groggily, she said, "Steve, it's Sharon. I'm sorry to wake you in the middle of the night, but I thought you'd want to know that Dr. Shaw shot himself."

"What!"

"His wife didn't find him until late last evening."

"Damn," Steve muttered. "Werner was going to check out Richie's notes and start with Shaw."

Lowering her voice, she said, "Yesterday I told Dr. Wilson about the notes. He promised he wouldn't tell Dr. Shaw, but now . . . well, what if he did?"

"And then Shaw killed himself," Steve added, "rather than be arrested for fraud and murder."

"It's the murder business I'm not too sure about. I'm almost certain that only Louella and Dr. Wilson went into the isolation room the morning Richie died. It's possible that Dr. Wilson did have a part in the insurance scam, and he could have given Richie—"

From the corner of her eye she saw Louella standing at the doorway. "I'll call you back in a few minutes," she said abruptly, and replaced the receiver.

Smiling, Louella asked, "How's it going up here?"

"Busy as usual," Sharon said matter-of-factly. "Already I feel as if I haven't been gone."

"ER's sending up a burglary victim. Do you need any more help on the unit?"

"No, we're in pretty good shape tonight," Sharon said, wishing Louella would leave so she could call Steve back.

"Good. Let Dave handle the new admission. I need your advice on a disciplinary action being brought against a nurse in CCU."

"*My* advice?"

"I want a more objective opinion than I'm getting from her head nurse."

"What's the problem?"

"The file's downstairs in my office. It'll only take you a minute to review it."

After Sharon told Dave about the new admission and that she was going to Louella's office, the two women took the elevator to the first floor, then walked through the near-deserted corridors to the west wing of the hospital, which was used mainly for daytime physical therapy.

Closing her office door behind them, Louella took a file from her desk drawer and opened it. "This nurse has admitted using narcotics she got from the unit, and she's agreed to go into a drug-treatment program, but she wants us to let her continue working while undergoing treatment. Her head nurse wants her on duty, but I'm afraid the temptation might be too great for her. You know the nurse in question, what do you think?"

"I hate these drug cases," Sharon said frankly, then took the file, sat down on the chair next to the desk and perused the papers, her back to Louella.

"Would you like a cup of herbal tea?" Louella asked.

"Thanks, no. I've got to get back upstairs."

As Sharon concentrated on the reports, Louella opened the wall cabinet silently, took out a gauze pad and doused it with ether.

Instantly Sharon's nostrils twitched at the pungent odor. She lifted her head and gasped when Louella thrust the ether pad onto her face. The file flew up and papers scattered as she struggled fiercely to pull the woman's hands away from her face. But with each jerking movement Sharon inhaled more of the potent anesthetic.

Shocked more than terrified, she tried to fight the creeping paralysis that began to numb her brain. In seconds her fingers loosened the desperate grip she had on Louella's arms, and her body went limp.

Panting, the night supervisor withdrew the ether pad from Sharon's face and let her slump backward against the wooden chair. For a horrified moment Louella stood motionless, her panicky thoughts racing as she tried to decide what to do next.

She dropped the gauze pad into the metal receptacle next to the cabinet, then went to the office door and peered out. It was deathly quiet in the dimly lighted corridor, as she expected it would be at this time of night.

Quickly she went into the room across the hall and returned with a wheelchair. Struggling, she manipulated Sharon's limber body into the chair and pushed it close to the door. Again she checked the corridor, then wheeled Sharon down the hall and into the now semi-dark room used for hydrotherapy. Perspiring and still not sure what to do next, Louella nervously pushed back locks of hair that had been tousled in the struggle.

Wide-eyed, she glanced around the long room, then went to the nearest step-down square tub and took hold of the handle on the water faucet. "No," she mumbled, jerking her hand back. "Why would she drown herself down here?" Her trembling fingers flitting over her lips, she thought some more, then wheeled Sharon to the far corner of the room and covered her with a white sheet before scurrying back to her office.

Grabbing the phone, she dialed quickly and tapped the receiver impatiently as she waited for James Wilson to answer. When he did, she ordered huskily, "Get down here right away!"

"What? Lou, it's almost four o'clock."

"Shut up and listen! Sharon knows everything. We've got to get her and her car away from the hospital now. She's in the hydrotherapy room unconscious."

"What the hell did you do?"

"Jimmy, there's no time for explanations now!"

"How are you going to explain her just walking off the job?"

"I'll get her things from ICU and tell Dave she feels sick and wants to go home. You've got to do something with her, a car accident or anything. I have to get back on my rounds or people will become suspicious. Just get here fast and wait for me in the parking lot!" She slammed the receiver down and covered her eyes with a trembling hand.

HIS FACE FLUSHED, Steve charged toward the nurses' station on ICU. When Sharon hadn't called him back, he had phoned her and had been told she had left the unit with the night nursing supervisor, Louella Frawley. Fearful that the woman had overheard Sharon's conversation with him, he'd rushed to the hospital.

"Where's Sharon?" Steve asked the man in whites in the nurses' station who was preparing medications.

Dave spun around. "She went home ill. Can I help you?"

"How long ago did she leave?"

"About fifteen minutes." His memory of the inquiry flashed him a name. "You're Steven Nordstrom, aren't you?"

Not answering, Steve tore back to the elevator, sure that he had seen Sharon's car in the parking lot.

Just as he came out of the side exit of the hospital, he saw a nurse, who was carrying a familiar-looking plaid tote bag, run toward Dr. Wilson. He was getting out of the car parked next to Sharon's. Steve stepped behind a tall bush, watching as the nurse unlocked Sharon's car, tossed the tote bag inside and handed Wilson the keys. She said something, then grabbed his arm and they rushed toward a door to the west wing.

Silently Steve followed. Inside the building the nurse entered an elevator and Wilson hurried down the corridor. Steve decided to follow him, but at a cautious distance.

Hugging the wall in the semidark corridor, he trailed the doctor around one corner and then another, seeing him enter a room on the right side of the hall.

Seconds later Steve was inside also, every muscle in his body tensing when he saw Wilson pull the sheet from Sharon's slumped body.

"You son of a bitch!" Steve growled, and charged at the man.

Wilson barely had time to straighten and half turn before Steve's fist struck him full force, sending him crashing against the tile wall.

"Don't!" Wilson wailed, crossing his arms in front of his face.

Steve lunged at him again, his arm drawn back ready to strike. Sharon's low moan stopped his fist in midair, and his head jerked toward her. Wilson darted toward the door, but Steve was faster. Grabbing hold of the man's jacket, he whirled him around. With one powerful blow he sent Wilson sprawling across the floor unconscious.

In a flash Steve was at Sharon's side, shaking her gently. "Are you all right? What did they do to you?"

Dizzy and sick in her stomach, Sharon moaned weakly, "Ether."

Steve's eyes shot around the area. At the far end of the long room he saw a glass-enclosed office and rushed to the door, but it was locked. He took a step back, rammed it with his shoulder and it flew open. Quickly he dialed the operator to get help for Sharon and to alert security.

CHAPTER EIGHTEEN

DAWN BRIGHTENED the gray sky over Steve's house as he exited the bedroom and returned downstairs where an anxious Debbie and Tony waited.

"How is she?" Debbie asked softly.

"Asleep," Steve said with what he hoped would pass for an assuring smile.

Tony slumped onto the chair by the fireplace, his expression somber. "Louella and Dr. Wilson? I still can't believe it."

"Believe it," Steve said, lowering himself onto the sofa. "Wilson couldn't talk fast enough to blow the whistle on Shaw and Louella Frawley. Werner told me the good doctor was in the car when Shaw ran my brother down. Then Louella finished Richie off on ICU to keep Wilson from going to jail."

"God," Tony said, "never in a million years would I have thought Wilson could have killed Shaw and was about to do the same to Sharon."

"Thank goodness she phoned you, Steve," Debbie said, resting on the upholstered arm of Tony's chair. "If she hadn't—" She shook her head. "I don't even want to think what could have happened."

"Let's not," Steve suggested. Then he asked, "Would you two like some breakfast?"

"I'll fix it," Debbie offered. "You stay here in case Sharon wakes up. Just head me toward the kitchen."

NIGHTSHADES AND ORCHIDS 291

"Thanks. It's through there," he said, nodding to his right.

"I'll give you a hand," Tony said, jumping up to follow Debbie from the room.

Inside the kitchen, as he readied the electric coffee maker, he glanced over at her. "When things like this happen, it makes you realize how precious time is."

"I know," Debbie agreed as she removed a carton of eggs and a package of bacon from the refrigerator, still deeply unnerved by Sharon's brush with disaster. "I feel like a sad excuse for a friend. The last time I saw Sharon I said some pretty stupid things. I wouldn't be surprised if she never wanted to speak to me again."

Tony took the eggs and bacon from her and placed them on the kitchen counter. "The Sharon we both know isn't going to hold a grudge against you no matter what you said."

"It was the way I said it. She accused me of pushing you away, and I told her she couldn't handle a relationship with Steve. God, I've got a big mouth when I drink. The words don't seem to pass through my brain before they spill out."

"So you tell her you're sorry, you kiss and make up and you learn from the experience, just as we both should learn from this one." He paused, then grasped her shoulders gently. "Debbie, I meant it when I said that time is precious. It's not right for us to just let it slip by. What almost happened to Sharon should prove that to us."

Sighing deeply because she knew he was right, Debbie eased her arms around his waist. "You're right, Tony. Time is precious, and so are you."

"Then marry me."

Pulling back from him, she held him briefly with her eyes, then reached for the stainless-steel bowl lying on the counter and began cracking eggs into it. Quietly she said, "I can't change overnight, Tony."

"I don't want you to. It's women who marry men hoping they'll change. Men marry women hoping they won't change, not a lot, anyway."

She smiled softly. "You'd nag me to death about the drinking."

"We both know why you drink so much. You could get the kind of help you said Julia's getting."

"I can't go to the VA. I'm not considered a veteran."

"There are other organizations." He examined her downcast expression, then said, "As far as our work hours go, I've decided to switch to night duty."

Debbie shot him a determined sideways glance. "You're not going to give up the promotion."

"If I have to make a choice between it and our spending more time together, I am. No job is as important to me as you are."

Debbie felt profoundly touched by the sacrifice he was willing to make for her, and some of the hopelessness that was her constant companion began to slip away, leaving her with a dim, optimistic feeling she wasn't used to. But in her heart she feared that if she grasped at the happiness Tony offered her, he would ultimately be the one who would regret it.

"And," he added, "it's my way of reminding you that I love you."

As she searched the cabinets for a frying pan, she said, "That's how you feel now, but you're young. You'll get over it."

"You're wrong, Debbie, dead wrong." Taking a little blue velvet pouch from the inside pocket of his jacket, he said, "I've been carting this around for months now—" he withdrew a ring "—waiting until the right time to ask you to wear it. Will you?"

"It's beautiful," she murmured, gazing down at the diamond ring, then she looked up at him with glistening eyes, "but I can't let you sidetrack your career by turning down the promotion. You've worked so hard."

"For us," he said, pausing to search her anxious eyes. "Oh, Debbie, we could be so happy together."

A stronger wave of hope overshadowed her fear, and her face brightened even more. "You're so very sure of that, aren't you?"

"As sure as I am that I'd be miserable without you. You don't want that, do you?"

"No," she whispered, brushing away the tear that rolled down her cheek.

"Honey, things don't get much better than they are between you and me. I know you worry about a lot of things and have doubts about our future together, but trust me, they're unwarranted. We can't change the past, but we can shape our future. The most important thing is the way we honestly feel about each other. Do you love me?"

"Yes," she replied in a wisp of voice, feeling as though Tony's loving words were tearing away the remnants of the protective shell she had taken refuge in so long ago in order to survive.

"Then," he said, tilting her chin up, "let me do the worrying for both of us right now. Wear this ring and say you'll marry me."

Her heart racing, she said, "On one condition."

"Anything!"

"You forget about the night work—" she saw his enthusiasm fade "—and I'll get a daytime job with the Red Cross . . . after our honeymoon."

Grinning from ear to ear, he slipped the ring on her left hand. "Now you're stuck with me for life."

She smiled in earnest, but then looked uncertain. "I hope your parents are as understanding as you say."

"They'll adore you, and my mother will have the time of her life organizing our Christmas wedding."

Debbie thought of her own mother, and Tony's remark about how precious time was suddenly made her realize she had squandered it without meaning to. "Will you come by the condo after work?"

"Come by? I'm moving in this evening."

"Good," she said, nodding. "I want you to hold my hand when I phone my parents."

His arms flew around her. "I was hoping you would. Do you think they'd be shocked if I suggested we descend on them for Thanksgiving? It'd give them a chance to look me over."

Her head resting on his shoulder, she inhaled a deep breath. "I don't know what to expect, Tony. They haven't heard from me in a long time."

"I have a feeling you're going to be pleasantly surprised," he said, then kissed her lovingly, and Debbie felt a joyful lightness in her heart, a warm and safe feeling that she hadn't experienced for so many years.

In the living room Steve's thoughts were in turmoil. In a matter of hours so many things had changed. The why and how of Richie's death was no longer a mystery, and Sharon no longer had to live under the shadow of suspicion. She and he were now free to— To what? he wondered.

Dark events had brought them together, intimately so, but was the bond that connected them strong enough to hold them together? Would she still blame him for the nagging doubt he'd had that she could have accidentally killed Richie? Had he been so wrong in believing that possible before all the facts had come to light? Should he have believed in her more? Perhaps.

Now, he realized, she was free either to accept his love or to reject it. He had to admit that since meeting Sharon, their emotions had been constantly jarred by so many things: the investigation, his dealing with the guilt of his one mistake during his marriage and Sharon's coping with terrible memories of her courageous service in Vietnam. Could they now set the past aside and plan for a future together? He knew he could. How Sharon would feel was something else altogether.

His thoughts a jumble of confusion, he climbed the carpeted stairway and stepped silently to the open door of the bedroom where she lay sleeping. He leaned a shoulder against the door frame and gazed at her.

What could he say to her that would express the deep love he felt for her? He wanted to protect her and keep her safe from any future danger that might threaten her. He wanted her life to be happy and fulfilled always, even if she chose to live it without him. His heart ached at that possibility.

When Sharon stirred, he rushed to the bed, sat beside her and gently stroked her hair. "It's all right, love," he said comfortingly. "You're safe now."

Slowly her eyes opened and she murmured, "Steve?"

"I'm right here."

She raised her hands and gripped his arms. "Louella, she—"

"I know. It's okay. She and Dr. Wilson are in custody." He drew her up, enfolded her in his arms and rested her head on his shoulder. "No one's ever going to hurt you again. What happened is in the past and we have our future ahead of us...if that's what you want."

Tilting her head up, Sharon gazed at him silently, thinking that she wanted her future to be with him more than anything in the world. Whatever had happened during the past hours, she felt positive that she had finally been vindicated in Steve's eyes. And that, she had thought, had been the only thing keeping her from running to him. But why did she sense a dark premonition of disaster?

Quietly Steve asked, "Do we have a future together?"

"Be honest," she said softly, lowering her eyes. "If I hadn't accidentally found Richie's notes, wouldn't you still be wondering if I had been responsible for his death?"

"Sharon," he demanded, taking hold of her shoulders and giving her a little shake, "why are you always testing me? Why are you always trying to find a reason to keep me at a distance?"

The tension in his voice and the desperate look in his eyes caused her to throw her arms around his neck. Her forehead tucked in the crook of his shoulder, she tried to formulate an answer, to break through her inexplicable fear of reaching out to him emotionally.

"Why, Sharon?" Steve asked again, tightening his hold on her.

Without thought she suddenly blurted out, "Because I'm afraid I'll lose you!"

Her tears trickled from her eyes, and as her spontaneous words echoed in her ears, Sharon realized she had

finally admitted the truth to herself. She didn't understand why the admission had come so suddenly. Had it
been her conversation with Anna or what Debbie had
said in anger? Had it been the terrifying experience she
had just been through? Sharon didn't know, but she was
so very sure that her fear of loving Steve and losing him
was terribly real.

"You're not going to lose me," he insisted, rocking
her in his arms and stroking her back soothingly, "and
I'm not going to lose you, not ever. We have too wonderful a future ahead of us, and our children will keep
us too busy to dwell on the past."

"I wish I could feel as certain, Steve," Sharon whispered. "Julia's children haven't kept her safe from the
pain of her memories. What if my memories come back
with a vengeance?"

"I'll be by your side, and together we'll deal with
them."

"Yes," she said. "If my memories come back again,
I truly believe that together we'll be able to deal with
them. But you know, I have a feeling I may be truly free
of them at last."

Tenderly he lifted her in his arms and carried her to
the French doors. With one hand he pulled them open,
and the morning sun streamed over them.

"See, love," he said smiling. "It's a beautiful new
day for us."

Her arms around his neck, Sharon gazed out as the
sun's rays shone over the multicolored flowers and
sparkled in the pool. Resting her head against his, she
asked, "How many children, Steve?"

"Enough to keep you off the night shift for a long
time," he answered, grinning. Then he lowered her feet

to the carpet. "We'll have better things to do with our nights."

Hand in hand, Sharon and Steve walked out onto the balcony, the warm sun on her face feeling as comforting as the warmth of his hand holding hers and the exquisite glow she felt in her heart.

Harlequin Superromance®

COMING NEXT MONTH